Malaren

In his third novel, N.E.David continues his expl... ...e lives of individuals under stress in ... larity of Nick's writing makes his n...  best yet. Well crafted and totally con... ing the reader involved in this type ... ...ls it off with aplomb.

Alan Gillott, writer and broadcaster

A tale of loss, friendship, dark secrets and human vulnerability expertly weaved by the very talented N.E.David. The stupendous setting of Lake Malaren in Sweden makes this story even more enthralling. A must-read.

Daniela Norris, author of *Recognitions*

Nick David writes with compassion and wit. He weaves strong characterisation with superb imagery throughout the novel. The reader feels empathy for the protagonist, Alan Harrison, as he struggles to come to terms with the tragic death of his wife. The novel sizzles with unexpected events, including an epiphany that provokes the next step on Alan's life journey.

Cathie Devitt, author of *Don't Drink and Fly*

Reading a novel by N.E.David is like receiving an invitation to dinner with new friends. His ease of writing is no accident as he skillfully draws us in to a gripping story enhanced by the tragedy and beauty of the Swedish landscape. An unforgettable read.

Steve Norris, Chair of York Writers Group

A moving and absorbing story of a man coming to terms with his grief.

Pamela Hartshorne, author of *Time's Echo* and *House of Shadows*

Malaren

A Swedish Affair

Malaren

A Swedish Affair

N.E. David

Winchester, UK
Washington, USA

First published by Roundfire Books, 2016
Roundfire Books is an imprint of John Hunt Publishing Ltd., Laurel House, Station Approach,
Alresford, Hants, SO24 9JH, UK
office1@jhpbooks.net
www.johnhuntpublishing.com
www.roundfire-books.com

For distributor details and how to order please visit the 'Ordering' section on our website.

Text copyright: N.E. David 2015

ISBN: 978 1 78535 531 8
978 1 78535 532 5 (ebook)
Library of Congress Control Number: 2016941206

A CIP catalogue record for this book is available from the British Library.

Author's Note
The characters in this book are entirely fictional and are not intended to be a representation of
any real person, alive or dead.

Design: Stuart Davies

Printed in the USA by Edwards Brothers Malloy

We operate a distinctive and ethical publishing philosophy in all
areas of our business, from our global network of authors to
production and worldwide distribution.

Part One

Loss

One

I was not in the habit of attending funerals – trust me, it's not something you'd want to make into a hobby. I was in my early fifties, so in that respect I suppose we were betwixt and between (I say 'we' as if Susan were still here – sometimes I have trouble with the idea that she's not). Our children were both in education and healthy: Jonathon on the point of graduating, Philippa preparing for her 'A's, and although we'd heard of people who'd died young (48 or 49 in one case, cancer of the liver or so we were told) these were things we mostly read about in our Sunday papers rather than anything that touched our immediate circle of friends.

Thankfully, both sets of parents were still intact, although mine were older and more fragile. They were also three-hundred miles away and had professed themselves happy to make the journey. *Your father won't drive but we can always get the train.* In the end it was deemed too much for them. One death in the family was more than enough – I'd no intention of precipitating another. *D'you think you'll be able to manage?* my mother had asked, fervently hoping that I'd tell her I could. I'd mumbled something to the effect that I'd cope, but I said it more to relieve them of the responsibility than out of any feeling of confidence. In the event, things proved far more difficult than I could ever have imagined.

Ironically, Susan's parents were still very much alive – and in the case of Vivienne, my mother-in-law, almost unbearably hearty. So much so that she'd not even bothered to consult me as to whether I could manage but had automatically assumed that I could not and had accordingly 'taken over'. She and Bernard had arrived almost immediately after Susan had fallen ill, although to begin with they'd had the grace to realise it wasn't appropriate to intrude on a household already under pressure and had booked into a local hotel. Ever solicitous as to the health of their daughter, they'd come to the hospital each day armed with the prescribed amount of fruit and flowers and had been every bit as attentive as I was. When Susan had finally slipped away, rather than give up their hotel room and go home, they'd elected to turn up on my doorstep, announcing that they'd come to help me with 'the arrangements'. Answering the door to their knock, I'd been confronted by the determined figure of Vivienne, towing not just her husband in her wake but also a wheeled suitcase. And at what was a particularly low moment, and lacking both the spirit and the energy to resist, I foolishly let them in.

Vivienne immediately made herself at home and set about 'the arrangements' as if it were a military operation, commandeering the spare bedroom as her headquarters and setting up base camp in the kitchen. Whatever I might have said to the contrary (which, I freely admit, was not much at the time) I was not to be allowed to 'do' anything; it was all to be left up to her. I don't believe for one moment that she'd taken pity on me and wanted to be of help. Her motive, I'm sure, was that I wasn't to be trusted to do the job properly and she'd prefer to do it herself. I'd always had the impression that she'd never thought me good enough for her daughter in life, never mind death, and there was even a lingering suspicion that I was somehow to blame for Susan's illness. The suggestion that I hadn't done enough, if ever voiced, was one I'd have fought to the last as I'd been as assiduous in Susan's care as it was possible to be. I had nothing to reproach myself for. But, once she'd gone there didn't seem any point in fighting it and I was happy to let things go. If Vivienne had something to prove, well fine, let her prove it. I did not. In fact, nothing seemed to matter any more.

And so the tiresome but necessary business of making the arrangements passed me by. To tell the truth, I had no interest in what flowers we should order, whether the casket should be in oak or in teak, where we should hold the reception or how many people we should invite – to me these were irrelevancies now. To give my mother-in-law credit, she was probably right and these were duties I was not fit to undertake because ever since Susan had passed away, I'd been in a world of my own. And while Vivienne had dominion over my affairs, busying herself on the telephone or down at the shops, I would invariably find myself slumped on the sofa in the sitting room, lost in my own thoughts and what I believed to be grief. It wasn't of course, that was to come later, but for the time being I thought myself terribly hard done by.

Occasionally I would look up and there would be Bernard, my long-suffering father-in-law, sitting in the armchair he always repaired to, half hidden behind his copy of the *Daily Telegraph*. From time to time our eyes would meet and he would give me that weak-as-water smile of sympathy he so often used, as if to say he understood my predicament and that this was something we shared. Then he would retreat behind his paper and I would be left thinking how much like Harold Wilson he looked and how at any moment he would take his pipe from out of his pocket and light it with a match from a box of Swan Vestas which he would use to tamp down the bowl. Calm and collected, he'd learnt to keep out of the way while his wife got on with affairs.

Vivienne, meanwhile, would be clattering about in the kitchen, slamming cupboard doors and rattling pots and pans. For all that she accomplished (which, to be fair, was a great deal) Susan could have done the same but with half the fuss. She'd acquired her mother's energy and skills but thankfully she'd not acquired her temperament. So Bernard and I were left in communal commiseration – he with me for the loss of my partner, I with him for the loss of his daughter and the behaviour of his wife. To be honest, I was grateful to be left alone. It gave me the time to do something that Vivienne could not – I had to learn how to mourn properly and I had the well-being of my children to think of.

I think it was my desire to absorb their grief which initially prevented me from expressing my own. I wanted to take away their pain, to shield them from the world and above all, hold them back from sliding into the same pit I sensed was looming in front of me. They had futures, bright futures, and I was determined they would not be compromised purely by the loss of their mother. We'd reached a crossroads and if I could guide them safely beyond it, their paths lay upward. To lighten their journey, I was prepared to relieve them of whatever load I could carry – but as to the direction I would take myself, post-mortem, I had no idea.

Up until the point of Vivienne's arrival and the imposition of martial law, we'd been too busy looking after ourselves to dwell on things. In the three weeks that Susan had been in hospital, we'd learnt how to fend for ourselves (or at least, Philippa and I had – Jonathon at that point was still at college) and we were totally taken up with the practicalities of daily living. I still went to work, Philippa to school and at the end of each day before we set off to visit the patient, we met as a culinary committee round the kitchen table and debated what we should eat for tea. I could boil an egg (but not much more) and Philippa knew how to prepare a salad, but these basic skills would not suffice for long and we soon entered the world of ready-made meals, chicken dippers and takeaways. When Jonathon came home for the Easter break, our pool of gastronomic knowledge increased but little and we went on much as before, although the need for us to congregate at the same time and in the same place each day to eat at least had the effect of drawing us together as a unit.

Then, just as we'd become close, suddenly it was all over and our tea-time debates were replaced by meetings of an altogether different ilk. We no longer argued about who was going to cook what but contemplated how we were going to survive at all in the aftermath of our loss. Apart from that, we'd completely lost our appetites and thereafter mealtimes were something of a sham, conducted more often than not in an unbearable silence until someone (usually Philippa) would push their plate away, stand up from the table and announce that they were going to their room. That usually meant tears, and within minutes of her departure Jonathon and I would hear her sobbing, her cries echoing through the paper-thin walls of our house. For a few moments my son and I would sit in a form of quiet respect, then he too would abandon me – *I think I'll go upstairs, Dad* – and I would be left to contemplate their half-eaten meals and the debris left behind. These were times when I was grateful for the need for washing-up, forgoing the convenience of the dishwasher and resorting to the use of the sink as a means of employing my hands. As I scraped the remains of our dinner into the bin, it was not just our efforts at self-sufficiency that seemed fruitless.

Later on, once I'd tidied up and with an empty evening in front of me (there were no more visits to the hospital now) I'd creep along the landing to stand silently outside their doors, hoping for a signal to enter. I desperately wanted to knock and be asked in to give whatever comfort I could – but they were entitled to their solitude and reflection as much as I was doomed to mine. My hand would be poised above their door, knuckle ready to strike, but then I'd think the better of it and withdraw to my own room with as much grace as I could muster. God knows how I whiled away my time. Eventually I'd drift off to sleep and the prospect of another gloomy day.

Now I come to think of it, Vivienne's intervention was perhaps not as helpful as it might have first appeared. We'd at least begun the dreadful process of grieving and however awful it might seem, there were signs that we might get through it. But now there were strangers in our house, we felt invaded and unable to express ourselves as we would wish. True, we no longer had to worry about cleanliness and catering (Vivienne did it all) but these were tasks that had given us structure in the early days and once deprived of them, it served only to add to our general sense of uselessness. We were banned from the kitchen and with our regular meeting place denied us, we were forced to inhabit the sitting room with Bernard. He wouldn't have said 'boo' to a goose, never mind his wife, but we still felt unavoidably constrained and we'd sit about in long morose silences looking down at our hands rather than at each other. The only place we could find relief was in the solitude upstairs.

One night after dinner, a day or so before the funeral, I left Vivienne to do the clearing away and retreated to the privacy of my room where I sat on the edge of the bed and stared mindlessly out of the window. Before long there was a knock at the door and Philippa came in. Red-eyed and speechless, she plonked herself down next to me. Then her arms were about my neck, her head was on my shoulder, and she burst into tears. I drew her close but we didn't speak as for once in her short-lived teenage life I had no need to ask what the matter was. It was the first time she'd come to me, but it was not the first time she'd come to the room under similar circumstances. In the past it had been Susan that she'd clung to and confided in when she needed comforting – the loving side of that testy Jekyll and Hyde relationship which existed between mother and daughter. The other, which included shouting and the slamming of doors, I had yet to experience – but I knew it would always be followed by reconciliation.

Jonathon must have heard us talking or perhaps he'd caught Philippa padding across the landing because he soon joined us and we sat, all three, perched on the end of the bed, gazing out of the window just as I had done a few moments before. I seem to recall a street light and a line of a neighbour's washing – but whatever we were looking at, it didn't seem to matter. We were together, we'd escaped the tyranny that stalked the rooms below and at last we had a chance to be alone.

After we'd dried our eyes (we were all crying, even Jonathon), we breathed deeply in an attempt to compose ourselves. We didn't need to speak, but when we did it was in a low whisper as if we feared being overheard. It was Philippa who started things off. Being the youngest, I suppose she had the most to lose.

"Dad? What's going to happen to us?"

This, together with a thousand more like it, was a question to which I did not yet have an answer.

"We'll manage, sweetheart," I said, falling back on the same response I'd given my mother. Although in Philippa's case, there was a specific supplementary.

"I mean, Grandma's not going to stay forever, is she?"

"No, luv, she's not." I'd already made my mind up on that, whatever else.

"So it'll just be the three of us from now on?"

"I guess so."

For a few moments this seemed to satisfy her – but there were other burning issues boiling up beneath that fragile teenage skin.

"Dad?"

"Yes, sweetheart."

"I don't want to go back to school."

Perhaps I should have seen it coming, but collateral damage of any kind is hard to predict. At another time my stock response would have been *Why not?* but this was not the moment for standard parental logic. What was needed now was sympathy rather than argument. Later on, the line *It's what Mum would have wanted* would come to hand – and be used a dozen times – but it was still too early for that. There could be no place for reason in a world that wasn't making sense.

"I understand," I said. "It must be difficult."

"There just doesn't seem any point."

"I know, I know." I turned toward Jonathon, sitting on my left and looking steadfastly down at the floor. "What about you?"

We were just at the start of the Easter holiday, a period he'd set aside for study with his finals due in May. But if Philippa could at least articulate her fears, he could not, and he resorted to shaking his head.

"Ok," I said, not wanting to push it. "Well, we don't need to decide on these things now. Let's just try and take it day by day."

There didn't seem much else I could say – although I did have an ulterior motive. A certain ceremony was looming on the horizon and until we'd cleared that hurdle there could be no discernible future.

Outside the window, the street lamp shone a sickly orange, coating the line of washing with a pale and ghostly glow. I searched for my children's hands along the bed-spread and clasped them tight as if our lives depended on it. They might not know it, but at that moment I needed them every bit as much as they needed me.

Two

I have two abiding memories of the day in question. First, that it was unseasonably cold – even for March – and I can remember thinking that I'd worn the wrong clothes. Second, the dreadful sound of great clods of earth thundering onto the lid of Susan's coffin. As for the rest, it was mostly a blur.

I've come to the view that funerals are designed for the specific purpose of fostering grief. Some would say they're designed to relieve it, but I beg to differ. Whether you like it or not, everything about them brings out that tremendous feeling of sadness which is so hard to dispel. The ubiquitous colour of black, the pungent smell of the flowers, the dour and dismal expressions on the faces of everyone concerned – they all conspire to produce an overwhelming sense of depression. Even the words of the service encourage it (*Blessed are they that mourn, for they shall be comforted*) and from the moment you open your wardrobe door and decide what clothes you're going to wear, your head is already telling you this is not going to be a happy occasion.

Now, I'm just as emotional as the next man. You could argue that doesn't say much and to judge my sex by our outward appearance, you'd probably be right. But deep inside we hurt every bit as much as do women – it's just that it takes a lot more to fetch it to the surface. And in my case, the natural instinct to suppress my feelings is allied with a streak of insubordination. I was being told to do something with which I felt inwardly uncomfortable and I rebelled against it. Yes, I was numbed by the loss of my wife, but I was equally determined that I was not going to break down in public. And besides, the day was not about me and I had no desire to be the centre of attention. We were there to honour Susan and my duty was to her and to looking after our kids.

The cars arrived promptly at nine-forty-five. I'd no need to look at my watch. They weren't going to be late, and the time of their arrival was imprinted as indelibly on my mind as it was on the schedule Vivienne had pinned to the notice board next to the fridge. She could not have been more precise – service at ten-thirty, reception at the oh-so-aptly-named Memorial Hall at twelve noon. Woe betide anyone who fell behind and spoilt her carefully planned day. Although, of course, it was a day when woe betided us all.

I was just about to open the wardrobe when the cars drew up and on the point of making that fateful decision as to clothing. I suppose I must have given it *some* thought in as much as I knew it would be black, but the detail of it escaped me as I feared holding things up and incurring the wrath of the she-dragon. Either that or I was blinded by my desire to remain composed. I'd already put on a white shirt and I automatically selected my darkest suit and the black tie, but even as I began to do it up there was a knock on the bedroom door and Jonathon was calling.

"Dad? You'd better come down. Grandma's asking where you've got to."

And in my haste to comply, I neglected to take any form of coat.

We assembled in the hallway. Vivienne was pulling on a pair of black leather gloves that matched her hat and handbag while Jonathon, unused to the imposition of a shirt and tie, arched his neck uncomfortably. Philippa stood beside him in what was effectively her school uniform, her pockets stuffed with tissues in readiness. Bernard had finally been persuaded to leave the comfort of his armchair and looked almost unrecognisable in a long, dark overcoat and muffler – so much so that for a moment I took him for a member of staff from the funeral directors. But they had remained a respectful distance outside and their presence was a pleasure we had yet to endure.

Vivienne glanced briefly at each of us in turn as if she were inspecting troops, brushing the flecks from Bernard's lapels. But if she noticed I lacked outer clothing she did not think to tell me and I remained physically, as well as mentally, unprepared. I took a deep breath, opened the front door and with our hearts in our mouths we stepped out from the privacy of our home and into the spotlight of public attention.

It was actually snowing. Not hard, I'll admit, just a few spits and spots drifting down out of what looked like a clear blue sky. They hardly amounted to flakes but there were enough of them to form a thin white powder that swirled around like dust in the occasional gust of icy wind. I'd thought neither to look at the forecast nor out of my window that morning and even now I did not see the significance of it as my attention was taken up by the sight that confronted me immediately outside our house.

Drawn up at the pavement beyond the front garden was the grim outline of a hearse. I suppose I should have expected that too, but as I say, I was unprepared and it caught me quite off guard. A hearse, I told myself, i.e. a vehicle, such as a car or a carriage, used to carry a coffin to the grave. Its appearance was every bit as forbidding as its definition suggested and there, true to its purpose, behind a snow-stained window and lying beneath a covering of flowers was the wooden box which contained what I assumed was the body of my recently departed wife. I'd hoped to steel myself and I was happy to attribute the shudder that descended my spine to the weather.

It was the first time I'd seen the coffin, although there'd been an opportunity before. We'd been offered the chance to pay our last respects at the undertakers prior to the lid being closed and it being sealed up. But we'd declined. It was another ordeal that neither I nor the children wanted to subject ourselves to. More grief, if you like, that we didn't need. And anyway, it was not how I wanted to remember her, a pale and ghostly form couched on a bed of white satin. My recollections had far more colour to them (her cheeks would have reddened in the icy wind) and I wanted to keep it that way. It hadn't seemed right to spoil things for the sake of one last look.

Meanwhile, a queue had formed behind me and Jonathon was pulling at my sleeve. "Dad? This is our car over here."

Behind the hearse was an ordinary black saloon. An attendant, stiff with cold despite his overcoat, was holding open the door. He ushered me and the children in but before we could move off, there was Vivienne rapping at the window. I wound it down enough to let her post the sheet of paper she was proffering through the gap.

"Here – you'll need this. Bernard and I are in the car behind with Don and Katerina. We'll see you at the church."

Then, thankfully, she was gone and I was left clutching my copy of the schedule she'd taken down from the notice board. It may have seemed cruel but for a moment I thought what it must have been like to have had Margaret Thatcher as a mother-in-law.

We eventually set off, but only at walking pace. When we'd clearly failed to pick up speed, I leant forward to look further down the road to see what was holding us up. Twenty yards in front of the hearse, one of the attendants was leading us down the street at dead-beat pace. As part of our 'arrangements' we were being paraded in front of our neighbours. If I'd ever failed to extol my wife's virtues in life (and to be fair, I might admit to that), Vivienne was determined to make up for it in death.

"What's going on, Dad?" Now Philippa was leaning forward too.

"We're in a procession," I said. "Just until we get to the end of the street."

"Oh my God! That's awful. How embarrassing."

She cowered down below the level of the window and assumed the same position as she had that night in my room, her head against my shoulder.

"I'm not sure I can do this."

I sensed her tears were already forming.

"Yes you can," I said. "You have to, sweetheart." I took her hand and squeezed it hard. "We all have to."

It's what your mother would have wanted.

We drove on to the T-junction where the hearse halted, a door opened and the attendant got in. Mercifully, we were not kept waiting long as there was a space in the traffic and we pulled out onto the main road and away.

It was a quarter of an hour to the church, but it felt like an eternity. Long enough, you would have thought, for us to compose ourselves and prepare for what was to come – although, on reflection, no amount of time could ever have sufficed. Philippa had already dissolved, I was on the brink and as Jonathon sat silent beside me, I guessed that the lump in his throat was probably the size of the one in mine.

We drew up at the lych-gate and got out. I still had hold of Philippa's hand and now I took Jonathon's too and we clung together as we waited for the coffin to be unloaded. The rear door of the hearse swung open and the acrid smell of the flowers rushed out at us. I desperately tried to think of cat pee and wet washing and other ordinary things while the coffin was brought out and hoisted onto the shoulders of its six attendants. This was another task I had declined. The duties of a pallbearer involved a weight I was ill-equipped to bear. There was a difficulty at the lych-gate but it was soon resolved and we followed the casket and its train toward the main building.

The minister stood waiting by the entrance. There were flecks of snow on the black of his robes and I heard him say *God bless you, my son* or *God be with you* as I passed and I remember thinking how I was not his son and neither did I want the presence of God but how I would have much preferred that of my wife. She, however, was imprisoned in the box which had already preceded us and was now sitting squarely on a bier at the centre of the crossing.

We took our seats in the pew at the front. Someone was playing the organ, although no one had yet started singing. Soon, the music stopped and the minister arrived. I wondered whether we were supposed to stand up and with nobody in front of us to give us a lead, I started out of my seat but caught the slight movement of his hand as he motioned me back down. Then he started speaking – *We meet in the name of Jesus Christ* – and I knew the service had begun.

I remember little of what came next. There were hymns, that I do recall, and I may even have tried to join in the singing as I remember glancing round at Philippa to share her hymn sheet and finding it splashed with the product of her dripping nose. Jonathon was not in a much better state so I resorted to staring resolutely forward at the chancel as part of my fierce determination to stay strong. Somewhere in-between there were probably prayers and readings, but I wasn't really listening and they passed me by.

The one thing I knew I must not do was look round at the coffin. If I were to allow myself that, I knew I would be lost and there could be no recovery. And so I avoided it, but I could still not prevent myself from thinking about Susan, even to the point of wondering why she wasn't there with me. Then I fell in and realised how stupid I was and I thought of what she might say to me – *You numpty* – and how she would hate all the fuss.

Then it was over as quickly as it had begun and we were on our way out, shuffling from our pew to fall in behind the wooden box and follow it on its return journey. The organ started playing again and we walked awkwardly in tune, Philippa clinging to one arm and Jonathon to the other as we tried to avoid contact with the myriad sets of eyes that seemed to mark our progress down the aisle. As we reached the porch, from somewhere close behind came the disconcerting rustle of paper as Vivienne attempted to pull her schedule out of her handbag.

You may have been to a funeral yourself. If so, the chances are it will have been a cremation but few, I suspect, will have been at a burial. It's a chilling experience. And in my case doubly so, as I was not just appalled by what I saw but as soon as we stepped outside I began to suffer for the lack of a coat and immediately started shaking. It had stopped snowing but the wind had got up and in the words of our neighbour, I was 'nithered'. Some may have thought it was fear, others that I was about to break up, but I can assure you it was merely the cold. By then my senses were as numb as my body.

We crossed the churchyard to where the hole had been dug; an ugly gash in the white of the snow-covered ground. The minister was already there, one hand clasping the wrist of the other, a spare finger keeping his place in the Book of Common Prayer. He began to read as they lowered the box gently into the hole.

We have entrusted our sister Susan to God's mercy, and we now commit her body to the ground.

The next part I'd expected, but the words still had an eerie ring.

Earth to earth, ashes to ashes, dust to dust.

This was the point at which I was supposed to begin the ceremony of filling in. I'd thought of gravel, a shower of small stones cascading into the pit but the clods I was given were frozen chunks, solid as rock, and rumbled with a noise fit to wake the dead. And for a moment I wished that they would and that Susan would hear it and would rise up and come back to us. And if ever there were a time when I wanted God to exist, that was it. A light would come down from the sky, a choir would sing and He would perform one last miracle as in sure and certain hope of the resurrection He would transform Susan's frail body and she would appear before us.

But there was no light, no choir and no miracle, and as hard as I prayed, nothing changed. The wooden box remained motionless in the pit and gradually began to disappear as spade by spade, they shovelled in the earth. Even then, when the ground had closed over her and they started to put back the turf, I still couldn't believe that she'd gone.

Three

The Memorial Hall was packed. Most had gone there straight from the church – it was only us few close family members who'd been obliged to stay on and witness the heart-rending ceremony of Susan's interment. We were the chosen ones, remember – *Blessed are they that mourn*. And so by the time the children and I arrived, fresh from the cold and with signs of distress still stamped on our faces, the proceedings were already in full swing.

I say 'proceedings' for the want of a better word. No one, especially Vivienne, would have wanted to call them festivities. I'd already noted the careful use of the term 'reception' on her much-vaunted schedule, my copy of which I'd hurriedly folded in four and shoved in the side pocket of my suit. It was not to be called a wake either, as I suspect that in the case of my mother-in-law it brought to mind the Irish version of such affairs with its joyous music and sense of enforced jollity. As far as Vivienne was concerned, this was not a celebration, this was an occasion for reverence and there was not much jollity to be found in endless rounds of salmon-and-cucumber sandwiches with their crusts cut off.

My immediate concern was to find a means of warming up. I'd gained some respite in the car on the way back from the churchyard, but we'd stopped for a minute outside the hall to compose ourselves and the icy wind had done its work once more. My hands were now red-raw and my body felt chilled to the bone.

In the far corner opposite the door, a welcoming radiator beckoned and I headed in its direction. But the route between me and the relief that it promised was blocked by some thirty to forty people, most of whom I hardly knew, and the prospect of innumerable expressions of sympathy loomed. As much as I might wish to receive them, for Susan's sake if not my own, there was time enough for that later on and to ease my passage, I decided to play the aggrieved widower and set off with my excuses to hand. I was still in control, but only just, and I did not want to risk tipping the balance.

But whatever resolve I set out with was soon undermined as I found myself bogged down in a mire of commiserations. For the most part the crowd was comprised of Susan's coterie of friends and acquaintances. I had little in the way of family (parents distant, a sister somewhere in Canada) and almost no associates, or at least, none that I would want at an occasion such as this. Susan's family wasn't large either, her brother Don, his wife Katerina and an assortment of aunts and uncles, but she possessed the happy knack of befriending almost everyone she met and over the years she had compiled an eclectic mix of adherents. They ranged from the Chair of the local W.I. to the girl who worked in the flower shop round the corner. And while many of these relationships could be counted as casual, they each had a common bond in that they all loved Susan for herself. At their heart was a group she'd formed from her working colleagues in the X-ray department at the hospital. They knew me as Alan, but to most of the people present I was merely Susan's husband, and in some cases, just plain Mr Harrison. They were all eager to tell me how sorry they were.

It must have been a terrible shock...

We couldn't believe how quickly it happened...

I just don't know what to say...

You know our thoughts are with you and the children...

If there's anything I can do to help...

And to tell the truth, these expressions of support were easy to cope with. No one had a bad word to say about Susan, so all I had to do was nod politely and say thank you and tell them how much I appreciated their concern. What I feared were questions which required answers, and in particular – *What are you going to do now?* It was still too early for me to respond and fortunately, still too early for anyone to ask.

Ten minutes later I emerged from the throng, verbally battered and bruised and seeking to claim my place by the radiator. But by then the relentless onslaught of conversation had warmed me through and I had no need of it. Apart from that, it was already occupied and the short, stocky figure of my brother-in-law was toasting his backside against it. Other than in church that morning, I'd not seen Don for a while. Our paths rarely crossed and with the exception of Susan, we seemed to have little in common. My recent ordeal had exhausted me and I didn't know where to begin. Thankfully he found a way.

"Great minds..."

"I beg your pardon?" I'd yet to recover from the press of the crowd and didn't immediately catch on.

"I said, 'great minds'," he repeated.

"Oh," I said, as the penny dropped. "You mean the radiator. Yes, I suppose so. I'm afraid I got rather cold in the churchyard."

"I'm not surprised. I saw you weren't wearing a coat."

"I know. Don't laugh, but I completely forgot to put one on this morning."

"I can understand that. There must be a lot on your mind at the moment."

"There is, Don. More than I'd care to tell you."

"I can imagine..."

And suddenly I realised that I'd put myself in danger of being drawn into just the kind of debilitating conversation I'd been seeking to avoid. But either Don knew that and wanted to avoid it too or, as was more likely, his thoughts were in another place, just as were mine. He let it pass, then nodded meaningfully at the heaving throng.

"This doesn't help. I was watching your progress through the madding crowd. Did they give you a hard time?"

"You mean Susan's army? The monstrous regiment of women?" It was an expression about her friends I'd often used to tease her with. "No, not really. They're only trying to be helpful.

They thought the world of her you know."

"I'm sure they did."

There was a thoughtful silence, then Don said, "I'm really sorry, Alan."

I assumed this was aimed solely at me, but I had no desire to be singled out. Yes, I'd lost a wife, but he'd lost a sister, and there were others who'd suffered too. I sensed that this might be as close as he would get to something personal but just as I declined to be the centre of attention, I didn't want to push him into the spotlight either.

"We all are, Don."

"I just wish I'd come to see her more often. It's not as though it's difficult for Christ's sake – there are flights from Stockholm several times a week. But there's always something…"

He tailed off into what was threatening to become a period of melancholic regret. I knew the signs well enough – I'd been there several times myself in the course of the last few weeks. We were dancing on the edge of a pit of remorse – one false step and we were in.

"You mustn't blame yourself like that, Don. We all do it."

He went quiet for a moment, then suddenly snapped out of it. "I can't imagine you'd be interested but you're welcome to come and stay with us, by the way – any time. If you need a break, we'd be pleased to have you. I promised Katerina I'd tell you."

Don had married a Swedish girl and had emigrated to be with her. It seemed to have worked well and he'd been gone over thirty years. Susan, on the other hand, had never wandered far from home.

"Thanks," I said. "I'll bear it in mind."

There was another short silence, then Don asked, "How are the children taking it?"

"Pretty much as you'd expect," I replied. "Philippa's a bit of a mess at the moment, but funnily enough, I think she'll be alright. It's Jonathon I worry about most. You know what boys are like.

He just sits there, staring into space. There's barely an expression on his face but you get the feeling there's something tremendously important going on underneath. But you can't get to it – well, at least I can't. He's got his finals coming up in a couple of months' time and I simply daren't ask whether he's doing any work towards them or not. Maybe we should ask to put things back a year and wait until everything's settled down. The danger with that is then he'll have nothing to focus on and he'll just drift. God knows how he feels about it all. At least with Philippa I can usually tell what she's thinking – she wears her heart on her sleeve. With Jonathon, I haven't a clue."

"Sure."

It was as long as I'd spoken to anyone in recent weeks about anything of any substance. There was something vaguely cathartic about it, but I was wary. If I pulled the plug out completely there was a chance that the bath of emotion I was wallowing in would all come flooding out and I wasn't ready for that yet. All the same, it couldn't do any harm to let go a little.

"They fought like cat and dog you know – but they loved each other dearly."

"What? Your two? I find that hard to believe."

"No, not the children. I was speaking about Philippa and Susan."

"Oh, you mean that hormonal mother and daughter thing? Tell me about it. It's exactly the same with Katerina and Lisbet. When they get started up I have to go and hide in the woodshed."

I registered the fact that Don had a woodshed. I was immediately envious – there were times with Vivienne when escape to such a place would have been a godsend.

"But you're right," he continued. "Give them twenty-four hours and they're back together as close as… Well, you know what I'm talking about."

"Yup. Women – you can't live with them…"

…and you can't live without them.

I stopped before I could finish my sentence. In trying to make a joke of it, it had awkwardly backfired on me. Strange, that as much as we both wanted to avoid it, all roads seemed to lead to the same place.

We fell silent again, interrupted this time by the arrival of a tray of the salmon-and-cucumber sandwiches. We both declined. I had no appetite for food and not much more for conversation either. Don was not one to object – we were men and preferred our tight-lipped strength. But we still had formalities to get through.

"How's Katerina?" I asked.

"Oh, she's fine. A bit jumpy after the flight, but she'll be ok. She doesn't get on too well with aeroplanes."

His comment rang a bell. Susan had been the same, a fact which helped explain why we'd never been to Sweden.

"When did you come over?"

"Yesterday. We're staying at a hotel near the airport."

"I'm sorry, but nobody told me. I'd have put you up at our house but I have guests already. I expect you've heard."

"Yes." Don smiled. "That was very brave of you."

"I don't think I had any choice to be honest. Your mother—"

"Shush." He put a finger to his lips. "Not a word... Walls have ears."

And I suppose it was the reminder of having to spend the next couple of days in the company of the she-dragon and her mate that prompted me to issue an invitation.

"Why don't the two of you come over for an hour or two? We could have a drink and spend a bit of time together."

Visits from Don and his wife were few and far between. And from a personal point of view, they could help me fill what was becoming a very big hole.

"Hmm, difficult..." He grimaced. "I'd like to, Alan, but we're going back early tomorrow morning. Things to do and all that."

"That's a shame. Well, never mind..." As much as I might

need some company I wasn't going to make an issue out of it. "In which case, I'd better go and say hello to your wife before you disappear altogether. What have you done with her by the way?"

"Vivienne claimed her to help in the kitchen. I gave her permission to go. Not that she needs it, of course," he added hastily. "But anything that keeps my mother occupied and out of my hair is always welcome – not that I've got any these days." He rubbed at the top of his progressively balding pate. By way of compensation, his jawline supported a manicured silver stubble.

I manufactured a grin. "Well, it's good to see you, Don. I'm sorry it had to be under such sad circumstances. Maybe next time it'll be a happier occasion."

"Yes, Alan, let's hope so."

We shook hands. I was about to pull away but he tightened his grip and held on and for the first time since the conversation had begun we were looking each other in the eye.

"I meant it by the way."

"You meant what?"

"About Susan. You see…" He tailed off again and I sensed that the same lump which had invaded Jonathon's throat at the church was now rising in his.

"It's ok, Don, I understand. You don't need to say anything."

"Thanks Alan, I appreciate it."

He clapped me on the shoulder one last time, I recovered my hand from the vice that had been squeezing it and headed off in the direction of the kitchen.

I was supposed to be looking for Katerina. But I'd been unavoidably detained and following my conversation with Don, I'd lost the run of my kids and now I was looking for them too. Fortunately, they were all in the same place. Either Vivienne had pressed them into service or they'd come to the conclusion that working in the kitchen was preferable to having to mingle with the rampant hordes in the hall. Jonathon had taken off his jacket and with his sleeves rolled up above the elbow, had his hands immersed in a sink full of washing-up. I raised an eyebrow. This was a sight we were unlikely to be treated to at home – but these were extenuating circumstances and on this occasion I could forgive him. At a worktop opposite, my daughter was helping Katerina rearrange the plates of salmon-and-cucumber and it looked for all the world as though her aunt had taken Philippa under her wing. As for Vivienne, the she-dragon herself was conspicuous by her absence and I assumed that with everything under control in the catering department, she'd gone out to talk to the masses.

I stood in the doorway, hands in pockets. I wasn't looking for work.

"Hey guys – everything alright? I see Grandma's got you roped in."

"Actually, Dad." Philippa turned to face me. "I hope you don't mind but I think we're better off in here. I couldn't face that lot." She pointed toward the hall where the steady thrum of voices drifted in through the doorway.

"That's ok," I said. "I know exactly what you mean."

"Anyway, where have you been? We were wondering where you'd got to."

"I've been talking to your Uncle Don."

Katerina put down the knife she'd been using and wiped her hands on a tea towel. I'd always found it difficult to think of her as Swedish. The tendency is to imagine Nordic women as tall, leggy blondes but Katerina was none of these. That's not to say she wasn't attractive but the qualities that appealed in her were displayed far more discreetly. She was shorter than Don for a start and had dark brown hair that hung in tight curls about her neck and shoulders. As to her legs, it was difficult to make judgement as they were invariably encased in a pair of faded jeans – even today she'd chosen to wear a trouser suit and flat heels. She could well have passed for an Italian, but to dispel any doubt there was always that trace of a Scandinavian accent.

"Oh dear. Has my husband been pestering you?"

"No, no," I said. "Not at all. In fact we've been having quite a nice chat. Anyway, it's good to see you."

We hugged and kissed cheeks and I wouldn't have known things were any different from normal were it not for the fact that she held on to my hand for a split-second longer than usual. I fervently hoped this was not the prelude to some further expression of grief. If so, I'd have preferred to delay it until later and when we were out of sight of the children. They'd already been exposed to more than enough emotion for one day – as had I. It only wanted one more *I'm sorry* and our whole house of cards might come tumbling down.

But Katerina was a parent too and with her niece and nephew settled and under control, she wouldn't want to rock the boat. Instead of which it was I who transgressed with the use of the 's' word.

"I'm sorry you can't come over to our house. Don says you're travelling back tomorrow."

"Yes. We'd have liked to stay longer but we had to make a decision about flights and we weren't sure whether, under the circumstances..."

"No, of course..."

Once again, we skirted round the elephant that haunted every room.

"You must come and visit us in Sweden. Did Don say anything about it?"

"Yes, he mentioned it."

"Good. I told him to make sure he invited you. What did you say?"

"I told him I'd think about it."

I suddenly felt under more pressure than I needed. It was as if she were being overly nice and trying to make up for something – for Susan, for not coming to see her enough, for not staying over, whatever. And just at that moment I couldn't cope with it.

"To be honest, Katerina, I think it's a little bit early for me to be making any plans."

"Ok..." Then, perhaps because she thought she'd try out on me the same therapeutic ploy she'd used on the children, she said, "Now, why don't you make yourself useful and go and take this tray of sandwiches round for your guests." She picked up the dish that she and Philippa had been preparing and thrust it in my direction.

I looked out into the body of the hall. The madding crowd had not yet abated; Susan's army was still in possession of the field and somewhere in the middle of it all Vivienne was holding court, her matching black handbag and gloves suspended from the same hand that deftly balanced a plate of assorted canapés while she picked at them carefully with the other. The thought of venturing back out from the safety of the kitchen appalled me. If there was one day when I could be excused from such duties, then surely this was it.

"Actually, I think I'd rather not."

Katerina stepped up to volunteer. "That's ok. I perfectly understand. I'll go." She began to remove her apron. "You stay here with these two. You might want a few minutes on your own." She took the dish and went out into the throng, closing the door behind her.

I turned to face the children. We were alone for the first time since leaving the house and I felt a surge of parental protection wash over me.

"Come here, you two."

I extended my arms and bid them join me. Jonathon seemed bashful but still extracted his hands from the sink and dried them off while Philippa had already removed her pinny. We cuddled up in the middle of the room.

"So, how are we doing?" I asked.

"Ok, I guess..." Philippa nestled under my chin. I kissed the top of her head, and I'd have done the same for the boy but he, thank God, was taller and I settled for rubbing the top of his arm.

"D'you know what?" I looked at each of them in turn. "I think we've done our duty for the day and I think we should go home."

My offer was genuine enough, although perhaps a little selfish in as much as I was looking for a way out for myself and I thought I should give them the same opportunity. The sight of those serried ranks packed in the hall had convinced me not to stay any longer.

"It's alright, Dad, you go. We're ok here." Philippa glanced across at her brother, who gave the slightest of nods. "To be honest, I'm enjoying spending time with Auntie Kate. We don't get to see her that often and you know how we get on together."

The thought hadn't occurred to me – that having been deprived of the presence of their mother for the last fortnight, they might value the company of another woman. It was a feeling I had yet to experience.

"Are you sure?"

"Sure."

"Ok. Here's what we'll do then. I'll go and call a taxi. I'm sure somebody will give you a lift home – but if not, here's the fare for one for you."

I took a ten-pound note from my wallet, folded it neatly into four and pushed it into the top pocket of Jonathon's shirt. Beneath his rolled-up cuffs there was still a trace of soapsuds. For a brief but precious moment we hugged again, then I let them go and made my way out to the foyer.

It took less than ten minutes for the taxi to arrive. It was lunchtime on a Thursday, we were in the middle of the Easter break and with the children off school there must have been little in the way of trade. It had stopped snowing and the midday sky glared bright blue but I was still fearful of the wind and crouched inside the doorway in the hope of finding some shelter.

As the car drew up and I hurried towards it, a movement caught my attention. Outside in the cold, Bernard was standing on the gravel. He'd dispensed with his coat but the waistcoat he wore constantly beneath his suit added that extra layer of insulation. The pipe he kept in his pocket was now clamped firmly between his teeth as he did indeed tamp down the glowing bowl with a box of Swan Vestas. A quick puff of smoke whipped away in the wind and as I passed by, we exchanged our customary smiles.

Sitting in the back of the taxi, I could imagine what Vivienne had said to him: *If you insist on continuing with that filthy habit, I shall have to ask you to go outside.* I fervently hoped that somewhere at home, Bernard had a woodshed like Don's – or at least access to something similar where he could escape and indulge himself in peace. For a moment I pitied him and thought that there were times when life seemed particularly cruel and unfair. His wife was alive and hateful whereas mine was dead and yet loved.

The house was deserted but oppressively warm. Vivienne had decreed that the heating should be left on permanently while she and Bernard were in residence, even through the night. It was not something Susan and I had ever done and although we might have had our differences about the temperature, we'd always turned things off before going to bed. On cold mornings it gave us an excuse to snuggle up together.

The thermostat in the hallway had been turned up to 22 degrees and in a calculated act of defiance I returned it to its normal position. I took my jacket off, went through to the kitchen and put the kettle on.

It was like an oven in there, the heat having risen to a level where you could have grown lilies or orchids or whatever flowers you cultivate in hothouses. Steam from the kettle began forming on one of the panes. I undid the catch to open the window and a blast of fresh air gusted in.

Outside in the garden there was still a dusting of snow. The rear of the house faced north and generally got little sun. Next to the fence, a solitary bird feeder hung empty from its hook. Consumed by the events of the past two weeks, I'd neglected to fill it and now I felt a pang of guilt. It had always been my responsibility to keep it topped up – a 'blue job' as Susan had called it. 'Pink jobs' were cooking and shopping, while housework and gardening were shared. That might sound a bit old-fashioned but it was an arrangement that suited us well. So the bird feeder was down to me and every morning before I went to work, come rain or come shine I was sent out to replenish it so we could stand in the kitchen for five minutes before we went to work, drinking our tea together and watching the birds. I think it was her favourite moment of the day.

Then I remembered how much she loved 'big sky', how she never painted her nails, how the skin round the corners of her eyes crinkled when she smiled, how she always spelt 'accommodation' wrong in the emails she sent to guest houses, how she was scared of spiders but would never dust a cobweb because she said it was someone's home, how I could never watch the football when Coronation Street was on, how she was always losing her mobile phone and I was forever having to ring it so she could find it, how precious her kids were and *HOW MUCH I MISSED HER.*

Then I started welling up and I knew it had been a mistake to come home on my own but I just couldn't stand the endless stream of simpering smiles and sympathy any longer. I'd stayed strong and kept it together in the church. I'd survived the burial and the Memorial Hall but now I'd reached the end of my tether and I did what any man with any sense of feeling would have done. I poured the rest of my tea down the sink, put my head on the kitchen table and wept for England and for Susan.

Four

Then it was Good Friday and someone else's turn to die. And didn't we know it. The media, of whatever kind, were full of images of Christ on the cross in all his glory. There seemed to be no escape, and any attempt to let the outside world in and relieve the gloom that weighed on our house was compromised by a constant diet of pious religious sentiment. I turned on the radio and got 'Thought for the Day'. We had a new Pope and there was no end of speculation as to what he would and would not do in the everlasting glory of God and how, through the death of his son Jesus Christ, He would save our souls. Our problem was, it wasn't Christ we were mourning.

My in-laws were still with us, and Vivienne's stifling presence in the kitchen meant I was forced back into aimless occupation of the living room. The children understandably stayed upstairs, so I was obliged to sit on my own with Bernard. By now I'd begun to develop a fondness for the old boy as we seemed to share something in common. He, bless him, went out to buy a paper straight after breakfast, his partial intention disclosed by the bulge in his suit pocket where he kept his pipe and matches. He returned over half an hour later, far longer than it took him to walk to the shop and back, a copy of the *Telegraph* tucked under one arm and bearing the faint smell of tobacco smoke.

The front page of his paper carried similar messages to those I'd heard on the radio. I resorted to turning on the television, but that provided no relief either. The only alternative to pictures of the Pope, of Jesus and of the Cross were innumerable children's cartoons. These proved unbearably jolly, and finding myself caught between the sublime and the ridiculous there was nothing to suit my mood.

In an effort to rouse myself, I thought about doing some gardening. It was the natural occupation for an Easter weekend and would at least get me out of the house. I got no further than the back door. When I opened it there was a blast of the same icy wind that had nithered me the day before. There was still a dusting of snow and the ground looked hard as flint.

I remembered that the bird feeder was empty, and purely out of habit went to fill it. But I could no more return to the kitchen and stand in front of the window, drinking tea and watching the birds than I could forget why. Nothing, it seemed, could take that away. The kitchen belonged to Vivienne and the day belonged to God. If she couldn't save us then He certainly could. He would look after us, and with all the paraphernalia of heaven, the angels, the archangels, Jesus, the Cross, whatever, there would be nothing for us to worry about. One thing was certain – He could definitely do the gardening. And, for all I cared, anything else He chose. I retreated back to the living room and asked if I could share Bernard's paper.

They left early on the Saturday morning. Vivienne professed she had 'things to do at home' but I suspect that by then she believed she'd done enough to justify her departure. Thinking me incapable, she'd come to do justice to her daughter. Susan had been buried with full military honours, her friends had been treated with the respect they deserved and everything had been done in a manner which befitted the heights to which Vivienne had elevated her (a fact, incidentally, which was reflected in the bills which arrived in the following week, and which, although everything else had been 'taken care of', I was left to pay. I consoled myself with the thought of the money from the insurance).

And so the dead had been accounted for and the living were left to fend for themselves. Although not quite, as Vivienne had one last parting shot which she delivered as she got into their car.

"I've left a cottage pie for you in the fridge."

I smiled as graciously as I could. "Thank you so much, Vivienne. I don't know what we'd have done without you."

Bernard, who'd been given permission to drive, must have

caught the irony in my voice as the corners of his mouth turned up just that little bit more than usual.

The children had emerged from their rooms to see their grandparents off and we all stood on the doorstep to wave goodbye. Then they were gone and their car was disappearing round the corner. We trooped back inside, and once the door was closed behind us we felt the weight rise up from our shoulders. We could not yet generate anything like a party atmosphere, but there was at least the hope that things might return to normal. But what 'normal' meant and what 'normal' was in our new and unexplored condition, we had yet to discover.

Our immediate concern was the state of the larder. We decided to retake possession of the kitchen and inspect its contents. Apart from the cottage pie, the fridge was virtually empty – a pint of milk, half a tub of Flora and a small piece of cheese but that was all. It was, however, spotlessly clean and its insides shone with a reflected light that bore testament to Vivienne's standard of housekeeping. *Spoil that if you dare!*

The pie itself was in a large Pyrex dish covered in clingfilm and sat squarely in the centre of the middle shelf. Jonathon eyed it with suspicion.

"What's that?" he asked.

"It's a cottage pie," I said knowledgeably.

"So, what's a cottage pie?"

"Well, it's like a shepherd's pie only different."

Susan had always made shepherd's pie so I thought it was something they could relate to.

"How different?"

I was now getting out of my depth and I looked to Philippa for help. Thankfully she was able to assist, but did so in her bored schoolgirl tone as though Jonathon and I were the only people on the planet unaware of the information she was about to impart.

"Shepherd's pie's made from lamb, cottage pie from beef."

"Beef?"

We looked at each other in horror. We were in the middle of the horsemeat scandal and the word 'beef' had deeply disturbing connotations. Added to which, it had only recently recovered from the taint of CJD.

"Well I don't like the look of it," said Jonathon.

Neither did I, but on this occasion I felt bound to defend my mother-in-law.

"I'm sure Grandma wouldn't have used anything that wasn't suitable."

The children remained sceptical. And even if I'd been able to convince them of the integrity of cottage, or even shepherd's pie, the fact was it was far too practical for our liking. What we needed was comfort food, but having scoured the cupboards we found none. And so we compiled a list, and in the newfound spirit of family co-operation, mounted a shopping expedition and returned from the supermarket laden with bags of crisps and pizza. Vivienne would have been horrified.

That night we feasted in front of the television and watched the first in the new series of *Dr Who*. Afterwards, when we'd discovered there was nothing else to do, we felt full and yet curiously deflated as we realised that our first attempt at normality was over. I don't remember much about the next two days. I must have finally gone out to do some gardening as I do recall that the snow had gone, the weather was bright and sunny and that I was outdoors. Beyond that, it was just another blur.

On the Tuesday I went back to work. I think that was probably a mistake. Things were still too fresh in my mind and I simply wasn't ready. And yet, when could I ever have been ready? Better to face up to it now, I thought, rather than wait. If I were to wait, it might never happen.

The alternative was to sit around the house, mope and feel sorry for myself. Ok, so I *did* feel sorry for myself but I didn't want to admit it – or at least I didn't want to let it show. The best way of doing that, I told myself, was to get straight back down to it before the rot set in. Besides, I needed something positive to do. There are twenty-four hours in every day and that's an awful lot of time to fill when you've no one to share it with. Alright, you can spend eight of them in bed, twelve if you really stretch it out, but then you've the other twelve to take care of and the prospect of daytime TV, endless game shows and the company of Jeremy Kyle is enough to drive anyone back to work.

So I decided to 'buckle up' as Susan would have put it and grasp the nettle. I say I wasn't ready. I thought I was as I'd spent most of the previous evening mentally preparing myself. I was also determined to get a good night's sleep and I'd deliberately avoided drinking coffee after dinner and settled for a cup of herbal tea instead. I was in bed by ten, but still awake at one with everything rattling round in my head, although I must have dropped off soon after as the next thing I knew it was six-thirty and my alarm was jangling. So were my nerves, and suddenly the prospect of returning to my place of work didn't seem so inviting in the cold light of day. I was about to leave the comfort of my trench and go over the top – and just like the soldier this implied, no amount of training could possibly have primed me for the real thing.

My job was as senior actuary for a life-assurance company. When the children were young, I remember them asking their mother, *What does Daddy do?* And she replied, *Well, he's ever so clever. He's a professor of difficult sums* And yes, I did have a doctorate, but it was not of the kind that was of use in a medical emergency, a fact which often puzzled the kids when they were ill. Life companies specialise in risk and reward. I was an expert on risk – but not on reward, which was something Susan always joked about when it came to negotiating salary.

The office block I worked in was located in the centre of town by the river. It was impractical to drive, so in bad weather I took the bus and in good weather I rode a bike. That day the weather was good. The snow had ceased and although it was still cold, it was settled. I was glad of it. The thought of being cooped up on the bus did not appeal, and with the bike I was theoretically in control of my own destiny. Plus the helmet I was obliged to wear provided a degree of anonymity I found useful. Although I couldn't keep it on all day.

My desk was on the seventh floor. The lift was packed to capacity and I cannot begin to tell you how self-conscious I felt. My fellow passengers were, for the most part, strangers, but somehow I felt they all knew. It was as if I had BO or a huge scar on my cheek but nobody wanted to mention it. As we ascended and one by one they got out, I swear they all looked round at me and treated me to another of those simpering smiles. The next day I took to the stairs. I was heavy-legged from the bike ride and puffed my way to the top, stopping on the occasional landing to catch my breath. Anything but the lift.

But even the stairs could provide only a brief respite from scrutiny. The office I inhabited was open-plan with windows on all sides. Being fairly high up, it afforded a panoramic view over the city and was known by the occupants of the lower levels as 'Seventh Heaven' or 'the Goldfish Bowl'. The greater your length of service, the closer to the edge you sat. I'd been there twenty-two years and had gained one of the coveted positions next to the windows. Nevertheless, I was still open to public view. The pressure was almost unbearable.

It soon became clear that no one wanted to take the risk of talking to me. I was damaged goods and had to be treated that way. If they had anything to say they did so by means of the sympathy cards they left in my absence (my in-tray was full of them) but to speak to me directly was dangerous. Those who were brave enough to walk past my desk did so with lowered eyes or at best a polite nod, but no one wanted to engage in conversation. Some, I noticed, would even take a detour rather than their usual route for the purpose of avoiding me, and on my visits to the water cooler I invariably found myself alone.

I began to yearn for someone to say something, even if it was only *Good morning,* or that someone would arrive with a pile of paper – *Here's the print-out you ordered, Mr Harrison* – and add it to the burgeoning contents of my in-tray. Or, that I'd be asked to go to a meeting to discuss the preparation of the figures for the previous quarter (it was the first week in April and they were due). But there was nothing. It was as if I didn't exist. With the best of intentions I was being given my space but to be truthful, I didn't really want it.

I waited until everyone had gone and the office was empty before packing my bag. I say empty but the cleaners were in, two young women chirruping away while they emptied the bins and hoovered. After a while, they switched off their machines and came over.

"We heard about your..." they paused as they thought it through "...news, Mr Harrison. That's a terrible thing to happen. We're ever so sorry."

The 's' word again. But this time I didn't mind it. There was a look of genuine concern on their faces and somehow I knew that these were people who understood loss and at last I could say thank you. I went home with my faith moderately restored.

But if I thought this was a sign that things would improve, I was very much mistaken. Whatever my new life might hold, I was not going to be broken in gently. Every organisation has its rumour mill, and news of my return must have permeated the building as the following day I was aware there were people on my floor I would not expect to be there. Call me paranoid if you like, but I was convinced they'd come to gawp at me as if I were some circus freak and were whispering behind my back.

Look, that's Harrison over there, next to the window, fourth desk down from the front.

Ah yes, I've gotcha. And he's the one whose wife has died?

Yup, that's it.

Hmm... So what's the story? What did she die of?
Well, that's the thing – nobody seems to know.
Really? You don't suppose...?
Not a chance. Forget it. Alan Harrison? He wouldn't harm a fly...

The only place I could find sanctuary from these intrusions was if I took refuge in the gents and locked myself in one of the cubicles. Once inside I could sit on the toilet to my heart's content – but in truth my own company was no more comforting than that of my colleagues. I was too introspective by half and before long I'd find myself staring at the splashes on the stone floor where my tears had plopped out onto the tiles.

I tried desperately to think of something else to do and eventually came up with a plan. I tidied myself up as best I could, went back to my desk and spent the rest of the day calculating the odds of a woman born on the 5th August 1960 (Susan was a Leo and it showed) dying on the 19th March 2013. Using a combination of the raw data we kept on computer and the application of our standard mortality tables I came up with an answer of 527,136 to 1. Then I remembered that I should have allowed for the fact that Susan wasn't a smoker and the odds went out to 763,877.

Why I should want these figures and what I thought I could do with them, I had no idea. After all, what did they actually mean? That there were 527,136 other women that I could have married and who wouldn't have died? (763,877 if you only counted non-smokers). And statistically speaking, at least one of *them* would have died the next day. Eventually, they would all be dead. Eventually, *we* would all be dead and that would be the end of it. Perhaps it was merely an indication of how unlucky I'd been. Perhaps it was in my mind that if I could somehow quantify my loss, then I could better understand it. Perhaps not. All I can tell you is it got me through the rest of the day and gave me something different to think about. I needed it. My head was dangerously full of Susan. And not just by day, but also by night. She'd invaded my dreams and that too was bothering me.

Five

All throughout our married life I'd never had trouble sleeping. But all that changed once I was on my own. Sometimes it would take me hours to get off and even then I'd simply doze and the slightest thing would wake me. Our road was a cul-de-sac and usually quiet, but at the end was a snicket used by pedestrians and cyclists (myself amongst them) as a short cut onto the main thoroughfare. The passing chatter of those on the early shift at Portakabin started to ensure I was conscious between five and five-thirty every morning. No matter how quiet they tried to be, it was always enough to stir me. Then I might drift back off, the dreams would begin and at six-thirty the harsh rattle of my alarm clock would wrench me from whatever place my imagination had taken me.

It was almost invariably the hospital. Even after the horrors of the funeral and all it had entailed, my subconscious mind continually went back there as if it were trying to get to the root of the mystery. I knew that one day I'd come to accept the fact of Susan's death (all the handbooks on bereavement told me so) but it seemed that I might never know how or why.

Sometimes it would begin (or end – these were dreams and I never knew which) next to the car park. I'd be standing on the pavement, the concrete multi-storey to my left, the hospital building on my right, waiting to cross the road. The little green man would appear but I wasn't going anywhere. I'd stand rooted to the spot, looking at the clouds, light grey patches scudding along in a blue sky. Then I'd feel the breeze riffling through my hair and spots of rain on my cheek.

More often than not it would start in one of the corridors. The hospital appeared to be entirely made up of them. They seemed interminably long but somewhere in the far distance I could make out a T-junction and a notice. Doors would open on either side and nurses would bustle in and out with clipboards. I'd set off in the direction of the T-junction but as I moved towards it, it would retreat further away. I'd start to walk faster but still I couldn't reach it. Then I'd break into a run and soon I'd be flying down the corridor at high speed, brushing the nurses aside as if they didn't exist, but I still wasn't getting any closer.

Then, suddenly, I'd be standing directly in front of the notice but with no idea how I'd got there although my stomach was still in motion from the running. The notice was a set of directions, all pointing to the right – never the left, always the right. I'd turn to look and there was another corridor, exactly the same as the first, stretching away towards the same T-junction and the same notice, the doors on either side emitting and receiving the same plethora of nurses. And I'd set off again with the same inevitable result.

That would usually be it, and I'd continue round and round the same set of corridors until I finally woke up. But occasionally, very occasionally, instead of stopping in front of the notice, I'd career round a corner and *he* would be there in his white operating gown and mask. I could never see his face but I could watch his mouth move so I knew he was talking and I could listen to the words in my head. But they were never the words I wanted to hear.

They were words like 'tests' or 'scan' or 'investigation' and on one occasion, I distinctly remember 'transfusion'. But there was never anything positive like 'result' or 'outcome' or 'conclusion'. I hoped for something simple but I'd have accepted technical expressions like 'infarction' or 'temporal acuity', even if I'd had to go home and look them up in the dictionary. At least it would have been something to work with. All he ever said that made sense was that he was sorry.

Why did *he* have to say he was sorry? Everyone else said they were sorry and I wanted something different from him. I wasn't sorry, I was desperate, but it didn't seem to get me anywhere.

Once, (or was it twice because of her hair – I was confused) I was in the room with her. She was on her own, sitting up and there was a vase of flowers at her bedside; daffodils I think. At first she was bald – they'd either shaved her head or her hair had fallen out, I couldn't remember which. I know she was conscious because I had hold of her hand and she turned to look at me and said, *You will look after the children, won't you?* and I'd promised that I would.

Then she was young again and her hair was back and she was laughing and we started talking about something. We were in the kitchen and the bird feeder was empty and she wanted me to go out and fill it, so I went out in my carpet slippers and filled the feeder and came back to the kitchen for our cup of tea. But when I got back, she'd gone and I couldn't find her. So I started looking round the house, in the utility room, the downstairs loo, the garage, the sitting room. Then I went upstairs and pushed open the door to our room and there was the bed I'd just got out of with the duvet on my side folded back and her side empty. So I went back downstairs, passing each of the children's rooms where I could hear them breathing, and sat at the kitchen table. Then I realised I was actually awake and I'd been searching the house for a dead woman and I started crying again. After a while my alarm clock went off and it was time to get ready for work.

I say I went in to work, but it wasn't as though I did very much of it when I got there. Sitting next to the window in the Goldfish Bowl, I felt far more comfortable looking out than I did looking in. Looking in meant the possibility of eye contact and social interaction and all those things that now made me feel uncomfortable. Looking out meant day-dreaming and a chance to reflect. The panoramic view I'd been granted was supposed to inspire me but in reality it proved distracting. Paper was piling up on my desk and my phone messages were going unanswered.

Work, real work, began when I got home – immediately I got home, in fact. Getting the tea had always been a pink job (bless her) and ready when I walked in, although I'd say in my defence that the clearing up was definitely blue and never shirked. It sounds as if we were a pair of pre-feminist reactionaries, but so what? We each knew our roles and were happy doing them.

Post-mortem, getting the tea was now a job of indeterminate colour. At first the three of us had worked on it together, but then Jonathon went back to university and any sense of togetherness went with him. Philippa had homework and revision and with the prospect of 'A' levels looming there was every excuse to retreat to her room. Rightly or wrongly, we'd brought our children up to expect their parents to provide for them. In the hospital I'd promised Susan I'd look after them and I hadn't the heart to tell Philippa anything different. And so, each day, it fell to me.

As did most things, as over the course of the next few weeks I gradually assumed the mantle of head cook and bottle washer. As comfortable as our old routine had been, it was now shot to pieces and I was forced to invent a new one. But there were simply not enough hours in the day to make it work. In respect of tea I'm afraid to say I reverted to childish things – fish fingers, pizza, chips and salad – and my cooking was anything but cordon bleu. After I'd cleared it away, I didn't have the energy for very much else and the rest had to be left until the weekend. The jobs list was a swathe of blue – shopping, cleaning, washing, ironing – it all had to be fitted into those few precious hours between Friday night and Monday morning.

And to be honest, I couldn't do it. Just as the paper piled up on my desk at work through lack of action, things piled up at home despite it. The wash-basket was forever full while the heap of ironing in the utility room grew ever higher. The cupboards in the kitchen became empty through lack of replenishment and we were always running out of the one thing we needed. On the day the rubber drive-band on the hoover burnt out, I lost my temper and kicked the machine down the stairs where it lay smashed beyond repair in the hallway. Thinking it might have been me that had gone headlong, Philippa rushed out from her room and lectured me in her schoolgirl tone.

"What on earth's going on? Get a grip, Dad, for goodness' sake."

The incident cost me dearly as I was not only forced to go out and buy a replacement but another precious afternoon was lost.

But if there was one job I was determined not to give up on it was filling the bird feeder. It was what had brought us closest together and I was not prepared to lose it. We might faint for lack of food, our clothes might smell a little off and our house might not be as clean as we would like, but the birds would always be fed. I don't know why, but it seemed to chime with Susan's priorities as much as mine. So every morning before I went to work I traipsed religiously across the lawn to ensure the feeder was full, then retreated to the kitchen and stood in memory for five minutes with my cup of tea.

It was now getting toward the end of April, and with each passing day I noticed that the grass was literally growing beneath my feet. I began to dread the onset of the gardening season and the imposition of yet another job. I'd enough to do already, and it was as though nature were mocking me for my inability to keep up. I decided to rebel, and rather than rush out and whizz round with the mower, I elected to stay by the window, clutching my tea, and willed the grass to grow. I wasn't going to cut it. It could grow as tall as it liked but I wasn't going to touch it. Nature was God's invention, not mine. God had got me into this mess and God could get me out of it. Let Him look after the garden, I thought.

Don't get me wrong – I've never minded work, I work as hard as the next man. But work without objective has always seemed pointless to me, and now I had no one to share it with, it no longer served any purpose. Released from the grip of winter, the garden quickly became unkempt. Weeds sprouted up alongside the grass and flowers grew in all the wrong places as God had his way.

From the comfort and safety of the kitchen I watched it all happen with a form of malevolent pride. I'd been challenged and rather than being forced into a form of blind panic, I'd responded in a calm and measured manner. Sometimes it paid to know when you were beaten. Had I rushed round with the edging shears there would doubtless have been an accident, just as there'd been with the hoover, and I'd have ended up snipping the end off a finger instead of a blade of grass.

This too was probably a mistake. My feeling of smug self-satisfaction gradually dwindled away as I began to realise I'd been defeated and I was inadequate. Then the rot *did* set in and the same 'let it go hang' attitude I'd adopted toward the garden began to infect the house. What did it matter if the kitchen floor wasn't swept once a week, if the dusting didn't get done, or if the mirror in the hallway wasn't polished? When it came to the final reckoning, what did it all count for in what Susan used to call 'The Great Scheme of Things'?

And so I let it *all* go hang. I either didn't care about it, or I cared about it far too much, but for whatever reason, I found I could no longer act. If I couldn't do it all, what was the point of doing any of it? Then I started not to care about whether I cared or not. I'd slipped over the edge and began to slide toward the inevitable abyss of self-pity and self-deprecation that had always lain waiting. I no longer cared about the garden, I no longer cared about the house and I no longer cared about myself. I was lost and there was no hope of redemption. I'd been anchored to a rock for thirty years but I'd broken away and my ship was drifting on the open sea. Now that link had been fractured, who knew where it might land?

Weeks went by and nothing got done – not at work, not at home, not anywhere. Although mine was a gradual descent and I sank progressively lower into whatever chair I happened to occupy until at last I disappeared from sight. I wore my depression like a cloud, hiding my head in it and thinking that no one else could see. Some days I shaved, others I did not – there was neither rhyme nor reason to it. If there was one thing I could thank God for, it was the fact that I didn't drink.

On good days I went out for a walk – even if I was at the office. The urge would build up over a period of time and I'd sit there looking out over the city thinking *What in God's name am I doing here?* Until eventually, when I couldn't think of a sensible answer, I'd just get up and leave. If I was feeling particularly self-conscious I might take a detour via the water cooler, but otherwise I'd head straight for the stairs (I still couldn't be doing with the lift). I knew exactly where I was going. I had a set route round the city centre finishing up at a coffee shop at the end of New Street, and I'd sit there sipping my latte, staring out of a different window.

On bad days I stayed at home. Daytime TV was now a godsend and I began to worship Jeremy Kyle because *he knew how I felt*. And believe it or not, there were people on his show in a worse state than I was, although perhaps I didn't know it at the time. And ok, I'll confess, I wallowed in it, soaking up their pathetic stories until I felt sick with it. And if they cried, I could cry too as if my tears weren't for me anymore, they were for someone else, and that made it alright.

Then, if I managed to get through the show without breaking down and disappearing to the loo to recover, I'd challenge myself to see how long I could sit there without switching off. Sometimes, if I tried really hard, I could make it through until four o' clock when Philippa was due home and I'd rouse myself and get tidied up before she got in. She didn't want to see her father like that – and I didn't want her to either.

I was as low as I thought I could get, but I knew my state of depression couldn't last forever. One way or another it would have to resolve itself, although I was incapable of providing the catalyst myself. That came in the form of an interview at work. My regular absences from my desk had not gone unnoticed, and one day toward the end of May I was called into the boss's office.

Six

Our Head Actuary had been with the company considerably longer than I had. It wasn't uncommon for an actuary to stay with the same company all their working life – there's a great deal of stability in our profession. I think it's to do with the fact that we don't like change. For us, change is an anomaly, an unlooked-for and awkward event that disrupts the normal pattern of life. We aren't expecting it and when it arrives it's in our nature to try and explain it and quantify the chances of it happening again. How much easier it would be if nobody smoked at all and every woman died at 86 and every man at 83. But then I suppose there'd be no need of actuaries and I wouldn't have had a job. Although whether I could count on keeping the one I did have much longer was open to question. But I digress.

R.L. Atkins BA. MA. Phd. FIA (or Bob, as I was allowed to call him) was located in a corner position on the same floor as I was. The view from his office therefore gave out in two directions, one downriver, the other across it – twice the fun. It was the ultimate perk and one to which we were all supposed to aspire, although the thought of ever succeeding him petrified me. It was another change I didn't want to contemplate and my hope was that he would stay there forever – or at least until he was 83.

He rarely came out onto the floor of the general office, preferring instead to remain behind closed doors, or if pressed, to use the adjacent conference room. You can therefore imagine how surprised I was to bump into him at the water cooler, and even more so when I realised he'd ventured out specifically to find me. A phone call or an email would have sufficed, but Bob was of the old school and believed in face-to-face contact. It made things seem far more informal.

"Ah, Alan… Could I have a word?"

I nodded. "Of course."

"Good. My office?" He looked at his watch. "Fifteen

minutes?"

I was being given notice and I wondered whether I should go and tidy myself up. Fortunately, it was one of the days when I'd bothered to shave, although it would have been nice to have had on a clean shirt. Somewhere in my desk I remembered I kept a tie for special occasions.

Bob was not alone. To his left and diagonally opposite the interview chair I was clearly intended to occupy, sat a young professional business woman I'd never met before. The Latin word for left is of course 'sinister' and I'm afraid I was already thinking that way. I guessed she was not yet thirty, and over her pristine white blouse she wore a black suit with no hint of adornment or jewellery. Her shoes had heels like six-inch nails and must have been painful to walk in. Her knees were clamped firmly together and on top of them she balanced an open laptop. Given my recent experiences I felt I was in the company of a highly paid undertaker.

"This is Miss Prentice," said Bob, extending a hand in her direction.

Miss Prentice looked up from her computer and gave me one of those simpering smiles I'd come to recognise so well. I'd already decided that if she so much as mouthed the words *I'm sorry* I was going to scream.

"Miss Prentice is from Personnel," said Bob. He'd been there over thirty years but still hadn't got round to the idea of calling it Human Resources. "You don't mind if she makes a few notes, do you?"

Actually, I minded very much but I was hardly in a position to argue. It was rather like going to the surgery for a flu injection and the nurse saying, *This won't hurt a bit. If you just wouldn't mind keeping still…* I was about to be given a painful jab and if I was lucky, a lump of sugar afterwards.

"Shouldn't I have someone with me?" I asked. It was beginning to look like that kind of meeting.

"That won't be necessary," said Bob. "We're all friends here. We've known each other long enough."

We had. Too long perhaps, as our relationship encompassed not just dining at each other's houses but also the regular exchange of Christmas cards. I couldn't decide if this was a good thing or not. If it was, there was a chance he might cut me some slack.

Bob had adopted a deceptively relaxed pose, leaning back in his swivel chair and clasping his hands behind his head. The cynic in me suspected this was a ploy to lull me into a false sense of security. I reacted by folding my arms across my chest.

"So, Alan," he began. "How are things?"

A few feet away, I was acutely aware that Miss Prentice's carefully manicured nails were hovering over her laptop, ready to pounce on my every word. *Anything you say may be taken down and used in evidence...* I decided to give her as little to go on as possible.

"Fine."

Bob smiled, rather graciously. "Good. And how are things at home?"

"Fine."

"What about the children? How are they taking it?"

I could sense he was sparring with me, but this was a low blow. He wanted me to drop my guard but I was damned if he was going to get at me through my kids.

"They're fine."

They *were* fine, damned fine, and I wasn't going to have them dragged into it.

"Good, I'm glad to hear it." Bob paused. He'd finished circling and elected to come straight to the point. "I guess what I'm trying to say is, how are you coping?"

"I'm fine."

I looked toward Miss Prentice and dared her to make a move. Her fingers remained reassuringly stationary over her laptop.

Four balls of the over bowled and I'd blocked every one. I imagined that the next two would be variations on the same theme, e.g. *Is there anything we can do to help?* or even *Mary sends her love,* but it soon became clear that Bob had exhausted this line of enquiry.

"We were pleased to see you back at work." Another pause, during which I sensed the imminent arrival of a 'but'. "How's that been working out?"

"Fine."

Miss Prentice gave an audible sigh of frustration. By now she must have been wondering what on earth she was doing there and in an effort to justify her presence began tapping at her keys. I could imagine what she was saying: *Subject in denial.*

Bob, however, was not to be put off. "What I meant was, you don't feel you came back too soon?"

I shrugged. "Maybe."

At last, a chink of light in the darkness, a breach in the defences. It was as if he'd slipped a knife through a crack in my armour and pricked me into some form of consciousness. I told myself to tighten up. What I didn't want was that knife in my guts, twisting my insides. But I think he knew that and backed off.

"These things can take a lot of time, Alan."

He rose from his swivel chair and casually wandered over to the windows where he stood with his hands in his pockets. The set of Venetian blinds on that corner of the building were half closed to cut down the glare. He pulled at one of the slats so he could peer out over the city.

"Well, we don't want to lose you. You're one of our best people, you know that. One day, I'll be retiring..."

I suppose this was intended to give me hope but there was an element of regret in his voice. I wondered how often he'd stood there, peering out of his windows and thinking about it. He of all people would have known how long he could expect to live and therefore when he should pack up work – but I knew that didn't make a scrap of difference. There was always chance, that terrible cause of disruption that made our lives so unpredictable. Susan had proved that, maybe for him as well as me.

"We have a proposal to make," he announced, suddenly turning round and letting the blind drop. "Miss Prentice here will explain."

Miss Prentice looked up from her laptop. Ever since 'fine' had turned into 'maybe' she'd steadily been making notes, although the talking had primarily come from Bob. Perhaps I wasn't the only one under observation. She had a steely look in her eye and for the first time, I noticed she wore glasses. She couldn't have been a day over twenty-nine, yet here she was recording the fate of two men old enough to be her father.

In what looked like a practised manoeuvre, she swivelled round as if she were preparing to get out of a low-slung sports car and reached into a carry-case at the side of her chair. She fetched out a document, neatly swivelled back and then began reading from it. I was momentarily distracted and missed out on her opening words but I remember they contained the phrase 'the company is prepared to offer'. After that, things seemed to get bogged down in a set of caveats and technicalities and it felt as though I were being read my rights in respect of a mobile phone contract. *Terms and conditions apply.* The exact details passed me by but the gist of it was clear – I was being given a six-month respite on full pay and time to sort myself out. There was even a mention of counselling. I began to lighten up and Miss Prentice took on the aura of a saint. Her blonde bob acquired a radiant glow and I fought back the impulse to kiss her on the cheek. I settled for shaking her hand instead and saying thank you.

Bob had returned to his swivel chair and was pointing himself in my direction.

"You'll give this some thought I hope, Alan?"

"Yes, Bob, of course I will. It's very kind of you."

What I'd thought was going to be a life sentence had been commuted to six months probation. This would be hard to turn down and I left the office with their offer tucked firmly into my pocket and a promise to study it in detail.

As soon as I got in, I showed it to Philippa.

"What is it?" she asked. "You've not been made redundant, have you, Dad?"

"No, sweetheart." I shook my head. "I've not been made redundant. I've just been given a sabbatical, that's all."

"What's a sabbatical?"

I don't know why but somehow I'd expected her to know.

"A long holiday."

"Thank goodness for that. I've been so worried." She wound her skinny, schoolgirl arms around me, tucked her head beneath my chin, and we hugged.

"What are you going to do with it?"

We were standing in my favourite place in the kitchen. I pressed down her hair and looked beyond it into the garden. Spring was as good as over; the grass was as tall as Miss Prentice's heels and the weeds weren't much shorter either. The drowsy heat of summer would soon be upon us and there would be bees and flowers and big blue sky and birdsong and all those other things that Susan loved so much. The thought of her not being there to share it with me was even more painful than the idea of going back to work.

"First," I said, "I think it's time I mowed the lawn – I've put that off for long enough. And there's a few other things that want tidying up around the house. Then..." I hesitated, wondering how Philippa would take it. "How would you feel if I went away for a while?"

I felt her body stiffen.

"Where? You're not going to one of those clinics, are you?"

What other fears lay hidden within her might not be so funny but her unforeseen assumption made me laugh. "No, sweetheart, don't be silly, I was thinking of going to Sweden."

"Sweden?"

"Yes. To spend some time with Uncle Don and Auntie Katerina. You remember they invited me? I thought a few weeks away might do me some good. Somewhere different. It would mean you'd be here on your own of course." (Jonathon was planning on backpacking in France.) "But there's always Grandma."

"Grandma?" There was a note of indignation in her voice. "For God's sake, Dad, I'm eighteen – I think I can manage without Grandma."

"That's alright then?"

"Of course it is."

And so it was settled, I was to go to Sweden and away from it all. No more washing, no more ironing, no more broken hoovers. I was being given the chance to find myself and I was determined to make the most of it.

Part Two

Malaren

One

We'd talked about it before, Susan and I – going to Sweden, I mean. This wasn't the first time an invitation had been issued and we'd often felt we should do it but we'd always found an excuse not to. We usually claimed it was down to timing, just as now when Philippa or Jonathon had exams or when things were 'dodgy' at work, but the underlying fact of the matter was that we simply didn't think of Sweden as a holiday destination.

Holidays were important to Susan. We both worked hard and time off was a blessing to be put to best use. In her case that meant spending time together as a family and relaxing, preferably somewhere warm and inviting. The ideal location would be Tenerife or a private resort in the Med where there was plenty of sunshine and a nice cool breeze off the sea. Our preference was to rent a villa with a pool, and while Susan stretched out on a sun-lounger with her choice of the latest novels, my job was to entertain the children in the water or on the beach and to find a decent restaurant close by where we could enjoy an evening meal.

Sweden, on the face of it, offered none of these things. When we'd consulted the atlas, Sweden was on the same latitude as Scotland, or worse. And as we knew from bitter experience one August Bank Holiday weekend, Scotland was a country where the weather was appalling; it rained for most of the summer and if it ever did warm up it was infested with midges. In Susan's mind, Sweden was tarred with the same brush and with no beach, no pool and no sun, why on earth would anyone want to travel there? I tried to persuade her it was to go and see family – but while family were prepared to come and see her, albeit irreg-ularly, she remained unconvinced.

So I knew I was taking a risk. (Ah yes, risk, that old chestnut – amazing how often it rears its ugly head.) I'd never been to the country before and nor did I know Don and Katerina particularly well. As I say, they were occasional visitors to our home but the infrequency of their visits meant we'd never spent much time together. What little I did know about them I'd pestered Susan into telling me whenever she was in a giving mood, but her reticence on the subject had always frustrated me. I think she felt that when her brother went to Sweden he'd abandoned her and she never forgave him for it. Their story (or as much of it as I'd been able to piece together) went something as follows.

Don and Katerina had initially met in York. It was Don's hometown of course, just as it was Susan's, and thereby a source of regret to his sister that he'd hardly ever been back. Katerina was in her early twenties and reading for a degree in History at the University in Stockholm. She'd come over for a summer school to study some aspects of Viking culture – what better excuse to visit England and one of its most famous cities! Legend has it that one night they'd bumped into each other, literally, in a pub in Micklegate. She was out with colleagues, he was out with friends. The next thing Susan and I knew, they were an item.

Neither of us had any idea that it would last nor as to the depth of Don's feelings. We assumed it was nothing more than just a holiday romance and that when the nights started drawing in and it was time to go home, Katerina would be back in Stockholm poring over her books and Don would be back at the technical college on Tadcaster Road teaching woodwork. You can imagine our surprise when he announced he was buying an aeroplane ticket and proposed going back with her. It was a clear statement of intent – and when a man declares himself for you like that, it must be hard to resist.

Then we heard they'd got married and were living in a small apartment on the outskirts of Stockholm. Katerina continued with her studies while Don looked for work in the building industry. He was originally a joiner by trade and for a man with his skills there must have been plenty of employment to be had in the construction projects of the time. Anything to do with wood, it seemed, and he was happy. A year later their daughter, Lisbet, was born.

In those days I don't suppose the childcare system in Sweden was anything like what it is today. The lack of affordable facilities meant Katerina couldn't work and I think it was that plus the weight of familial responsibility that made Don think he had to better himself. A job came up as foreman in one of the woodyards that supplied the firm he was engaged with. He applied straight away and got it. Then we learnt he'd been promoted and given a yard of his own to manage. We were told of a new address in Uppsala where they'd moved to be nearer his work. Our knowledge as to their steady progress came by way of an annual letter enclosed with their Christmas card each year. And to judge by the photographs that accompanied it, Lisbet grew tall and strong. Katerina's parents apparently had a place in the north and there was mention of going up there in the winter and learning how to ski. In the summer they'd rent a chalet by a lake. For a long while they seemed happy and we were pleased for them.

Then suddenly they were not and the horrid demands of life pressed in on them. Mind you, I don't suppose there's a family in the land where that hasn't happened at some stage or another – I can vouch for that more than most. For them it began with the death of Katerina's parents, killed in a motor-car accident. No one ever knew what caused it as there was no other driver involved. Their vehicle was found upside down, smashed against a tree that had broken its fall at the bottom of a steep ravine, both of its occupants dead. On the road above there were skid marks and evidence that the car had swerved to one side. The supposition was that an elk had run across the highway in front of them. Even if they'd hit the animal, the outcome would have been much the same – the elk is a mighty beast at the best of times. And if that were not enough, there was a rumour that Don had lost his job.

Given the circumstances, we thought it understandable that things would go quiet for a while. Some people like to broadcast bad news but Don and Katerina were not of that type and kept their distress to themselves. But by then of course we had children of our own and our focus was internal rather than on events abroad and for a long time contact was lost. In fact, we heard little at all for the next ten years – but then it came to light that my brother-in-law and his wife owned their own business and boasted both a residence in the capital and a summer retreat in the country.

I was left to wonder as to how all this had happened. Given our lack of contact there'd been little opportunity to find out – plus the fact that Susan had shown no interest and it hadn't seemed right to pry. Despite my wife's jokes about reward, I considered myself a reasonably well-paid professional but any idea of a second property was way beyond us. Had I gone wrong somewhere? The natural assumption was that Don had become a high-powered businessman. He had doubtless acquired a set of correspondingly attendant habits and during the course of my visit I could expect a level of conversation and entertainment commensurate with his new-found position. There was another risk – I wasn't sure I could contend with continual rounds of golf and drawn-out executive lunches. I found myself loath to make an assessment and besides, I was past that form of evaluation now. The thought of drawing up a list of the pros and cons and forming a balanced judgement was exactly the sort of thing I wanted to leave behind. All that was on my mind was that I needed to get away somewhere in the hope that a change in scenery would provoke some change in me.

Looking out of the aeroplane window high above the North Sea, the signs were initially good. Far below, the minute white dot of a cargo ship ploughed across a bright blue sea. Up above, the sun was beating down and I could feel the warmth of its rays against the glass. Though inwardly, I was still questioning my motives – what on earth was I doing here? The issue of timing had at least been resolved since both of my children's exams were now over. Philippa especially had reached the point where she was eager to prove her independence and was looking forward to the prospect of housesitting while I was away. I knew I could rely on her – and in case of emergency there was always Vivienne.

"You know you can call on Grandma if there's a problem," I'd reminded her.

"There won't be, Dad, trust me," she'd replied.

So my only real excuse had evaporated and it left me with little alternative. I didn't want to be at work and the prospect of frequenting our former haunts, either with or without the children, filled me with horror. The beach at La Playa, the pool in Sorrento, these were places stalked by ghosts of the past and I had no desire to bump into them as part of some journey of melancholic exploration. I'd wallowed in enough pathos already and it was time for something new. So Sweden it was – whatever that might bring.

The flight took just over two hours – too short to settle to anything. Apart from that, I wasn't in the mood for reading or any form of study. But it was long enough for the weather to change and as we made landfall, both our plane and the earlier promise of sun were swallowed up by a bank of cloud. We started our descent and half an hour later emerged low above a flat and tree-covered landscape broken by the occasional stretch of water. A fine yet steady drizzle peppered my window pane. Had she been with me, Susan would have been horrified. *I told you so.* All it wanted, I thought, was for there to be midges…

Don met me at the airport as we'd agreed. His short, stocky figure was unmistakable, despite the fact that he'd radically changed his clothing. The dark and sombre suit he'd worn at the funeral had gone, replaced by a red-checked shirt and puffer jacket. A baseball cap now covered his head and along with his greying beard it all conspired to give him the appearance of a grizzled Canadian lumberjack. I had to admit there was a certain degree of style about it – perhaps this was how businessmen dressed in Sweden when they were not on duty. We exchanged pleasantries.

"Good flight?"

"Fine thanks, no problem."

"Here, let me take that." He reached for my suitcase and wheeled it away toward the exit. "This way..."

We soon cleared the terminal. Once outside, the rain was more organised than it had looked from the aircraft and I fumbled with a nylon waterproof from my backpack. Don, on the other hand, didn't seem too bothered.

"Sorry about this. It's not much of a welcome."

"Don't worry," I said. "I'm used to it. I'm from England, you know."

"Ah yes, of course. I remember England – the land of the four seasons. We have exactly the same in Sweden."

"You do?"

We were halfway across the car park, our heads bent to the wind.

"Sure. Winter, winter, spring and winter."

"Don't tell me," I said. "Let me guess. This is spring."

"Unfortunately not." By now we were standing beside Don's vehicle while he searched his pockets for keys. "You missed spring – that was yesterday."

I think I was supposed to laugh but the joke either went over my head or I was too anxious to get in out of the rain. Don opened the door for me and took my suitcase round to the rear while I clambered aboard.

I say clambered as it was a good step up to the cab. Just like my brother-in-law's clothing, our means of transport was not quite what I'd expected as I'd envisaged a large and spacious saloon of the type used by senior executives.

"Ten to one he'll have a Volvo with air-conditioning and all mod cons," I'd said to Philippa before leaving. Instead of which I found myself sitting high off the ground in the passenger seat of a long-wheelbase Land Rover. A cow-catcher type bumper protruded from the front. When Don told me later it was in case we encountered an elk, I readily understood the need.

"This is a bit of a beast," I said as I strapped myself in. "What is it? Three litre?"

"Three point six," Don corrected me. "I doubt we'll get much trouble on the motorway. Things tend to stay out of our way." He turned the key, the engine fired up with a deep rumble and we set off, far more in hope than any form of expectation.

Two

It had been decided to skip Stockholm and head straight for the country retreat. The journey from the airport probably took as long as the flight, though I think I missed most of it. The drama of the last few weeks had taken its toll; I was exhausted and what with the heat of the cab and the mesmeric slap-slop, slap-slop of the windscreen wipers, I must have dozed off. It was already late in the evening and the sky was darkened by clouds but I do remember the motorway and the steady thrum of the tyres, the blaze of headlights down a country road, the sense of being surrounded by cornfields and the occasional group of distinctive red wooden buildings. Then we'd come to a halt and I was aware that Don was nudging me in the ribs.

"Wakey, wakey – we've arrived." He was dangling a set of keys in front of my face and pointing outside. "Your job."

I yawned and forced my eyes open. We were now on a rough and unlit track surrounded by forest, the headlights shining directly onto a five-bar gate secured by a padlock. I took the key and slid down from the cab.

The padlock was fiddly and I made a bit of a hash of it. I was still fuddled with sleep and my hands wouldn't do what I told them to. Don leant out of the cab window.

"Take your time, there's no hurry. I can wait all night."

I was tempted to show him two fingers and suggest he did it himself. I was not yet properly awake, it was cold outside (it may even have still been raining) and I thought he was riding me. It took me a minute or two to work it out but eventually I swung the gate open and he drove on through.

We entered onto a gravelled yard. Behind us lay the pine forest while on either side the trees began to thin out and slope away. In front, just beyond where Don had parked the Land Rover, framed against the night sky was the outline of a single-storey building. This was also red and made of wood. In this part of the world, everything seemed to be made of wood...

A light came on in one corner to reveal a porch sheltering an entrance door. I guessed that the light was operated by a sensor as no one immediately appeared. I swung the gate back and clicked it into place.

"D'you want this locked?" I called.

Don had got down from the cab and was busy unloading my suitcase.

"No need. I can't imagine anyone's going to come in. It's just that Madame likes to feel secure while I'm away."

I dropped the padlock back into place and removed the key.

Then Katerina was there, standing beneath the light in the porchway, the door behind her open and her arms folded against the chill of the evening. She and Don exchanged a few brief words before she turned and went back inside.

"She says supper's ready whenever you are." Don ushered me up the porch steps and held open the entrance door. "Well, come on in – and welcome to Malaren."

My immediate recollection is of the tantalising aroma of hot food. But however nice it seemed, ever since my encounter with cottage pie I'd learnt to be wary and I'd reached the point where I read what it said on the label before I even so much as opened a can of baked beans.

"Hmm... What's that I can smell?" I asked.

"Falukorv," said Don.

I was still none the wiser. "Which is?"

"A traditional Swedish recipe. My favourite. You'll love it."

In the absence of a list of ingredients, I decided to suspend judgement.

Accompanying its meaty odour, Katerina's voice came floating through from the kitchen. "Don? Please make sure Alan takes his shoes off."

"Ah yes – I'd better explain." Don had already removed his

footwear and parked them on a mat next to the doorway. "House rule number one. Madame is very particular about the cleanliness of her floors. There are no paths or pavements here so if it gets wet things can become awfully messy. So, shoes off at the door if you don't mind. You can wander round in your socks – or even your bare feet if you like – but if you need a pair of slippers there's some in the cupboard there."

He pointed to a small locker beneath the coat rack. I bent down to open it and found a collection of white fluffy mules of the type usually found in good-quality hotels. I selected a pair and at the same time wondered if there was a bathrobe to go with them. Don must have seen the look on my face.

"Don't ask," he said.

I changed my shoes and while we hung up our coats, Don took me through the remaining regulations.

"As for smoking, it's quite simple – not indoors. If you feel the need to indulge yourself, you're quite welcome to go out on the veranda." He gestured toward the far side of the building. "Not that you do, I suppose?"

I shook my head. A look of mild disappointment crossed his face.

"Hmm… That's a shame – I have been known to sample the odd cigar… Well I guess that's about it. No, wait a minute, I forgot. Toilet seats must not be left up under any circumstances. And," he cocked an eyebrow at me, "no women in the rooms after midnight." He paused deliberately, as if he were seeing how I'd take it, then added, "Only joking. But seriously, the lady of the house is quite adamant about rules one, two and three, and I'd advise you to stick to them at all times, if only for my sake. The good news is that in exchange for compliance with these minor inconveniences, we get to enjoy certain privileges. Namely, a decent meal at least once a day, a bed for the night, and, if we're lucky, something palatable to drink. Speaking of which," he lowered his voice so that only I could hear, "the sun's over the

yardarm and I'm absolutely parched." He turned toward the
kitchen. "How long have we got, my love?"

"Ten minutes," came the distant reply.

"Time for a quick one – provided Madame hasn't hidden the
key to the drinks cabinet." He gave me a wink. "Why don't you
go and say hello while I get something sorted out. You can join
me in the lounge." He left me to seek out Katerina and disappeared in the opposite direction.

I poked my head round the kitchen door to see my sister-in-
law clad in an apron and with her hands buried deep in a pair of
fireproof gloves, shepherding a roasting tin back into the oven. A
cloud of steam billowed outwards and up.

"Not a good time at the moment, Alan. I suggest you go and
make yourself useful elsewhere. I'll catch up with you in a
minute."

I retreated back to the safety of the hallway and crossed into
the lounge. Experiences at home had taught me not to interrupt
the cook's preparations. Our hello could wait whereas dinner
clearly could not.

The lounge must have been the largest room in the house, yet
it was still of a modest size. Beyond it lay what I assumed was the
veranda, but for the moment the curtains at the picture window
were drawn and there was no external view to be had. The floor
was of a light and polished wood, but if I'd expected the furniture
to be fashionably modern and straight from IKEA then once
again I was mistaken. It was in fact an eclectic mix of old and
new, including a sofa and two armchairs none of which seemed
to match – and yet they all contrived to look inviting. This, I
thought, was a house where style had been sacrificed for comfort
and there was a sense of rustic homeliness about it. In the far
corner stood a wood-burning stove, its encased metal chimney
extending up through the ceiling. I noticed it had not yet been lit.
A pile of logs lay waiting.

Don was on his hands and knees in front of the drinks cabinet, rummaging through its contents. I squatted down beside him.

"So, what d'you fancy?" he asked.

I peered inside the cupboard. There seemed to be an abundant supply of most everything you could think of – scotch, gin, red and white wine, martini, liqueurs – and in most cases, two bottles of each. On the shelf below stood an array of beers, and further underneath, a selection of mixers.

"You're well stocked," I said.

"There's a very good reason for that," Don explained. "It doesn't do to run short here. It's a forty-mile round trip to the nearest supermarket so we'd rather not go popping out for anything in the middle of the night. I'm having a beer by the way, what about you?" He picked a bottle from the second shelf and a glass to go with it from an adjacent cupboard.

"Gin and tonic please, and go easy on the gin." I'd eaten little in the past eight hours and I'd no intention of disgracing myself on my first night. "So, what about your nearest neighbours?" I asked. Mention of the distance to the supermarket had put me on edge. I was used to my creature comforts, plus the idea of readily available company, and the thought of being stranded in the middle of nowhere was mildly disconcerting.

"They're closer than you think." We hauled ourselves up and Don began pouring out the drinks. "There are houses less than a hundred yards away on either side but they're hidden amongst the trees. The Swedes value their privacy, and when they developed this stretch of the waterfront they made sure every-thing was well spaced out."

"Waterfront?" I said. "What waterfront?"

"The one at the back of the property."

"Really? So where exactly are we?"

In my haste to get away I'd neglected to consult any form of directions. My concern had been not so much where I was going, but more what I was leaving behind. I roughly knew the answer of course – Don had told me the place was a couple of hours west of Stockholm and for the time being that had been enough. Now I was confused.

"Here, let me show you." Don pulled open a drawer in the sideboard and fetched out a pile of maps. Some, I noted, were shipping charts. He selected one and spread it out on the coffee table. The central section was a large swathe of blue. "Stockholm is over in this direction." He pointed to the end of the map on the right. "It's about 80 kilometres by boat – that's actually a lot shorter distance than by road. We're here, on the southern side of the lake." Don prodded a thick finger at a point halfway along the line delineating the blue of the water from the green of the landmass. "The nearest place of any significance is Eskilstuna. That's over here." He moved his finger down and across. I was getting the gist of it, but geography had never been one of my strong points. I searched the area he'd originally been indicating.

"So where's Malaren?" I asked. I'd expected to see it shown as an identifiable point on the map, a town or a village or at least something tangible I could relate to.

"Malaren?" Don looked up at me as though I were missing the obvious. "Malaren isn't a place, Alan. Malaren is the name of the lake."

There was a moment's silence before my embarrassment was cut short by a voice from the kitchen.

"It's on the table!"

We took our drinks and went through into the dining area.

Three

Katerina was midway through stripping off her apron. Her cheeks had acquired a ruddy glow and I noticed she'd opened a window to let in some air. A wayward strand of hair had fallen forward and she blew it to one side.

"Phew! Thank goodness that's over. Now we can hug."

We kissed cheeks. The last time we'd met it had been under similar circumstances in the kitchen at the Memorial Hall. Was that a hint of dampness in the corner of her eye? I wondered. She held me close for a moment then stepped back to look me up and down.

"It's good to see you, Alan. You're looking well."

"Thank you. Although not as well as I might be. I'm sorry but I haven't had the chance to get changed." I was still wearing the clothes I'd travelled in and they bore rumpled evidence of my impromptu nap in the Land Rover.

"Oh for goodness sake, don't be silly! We don't dress for dinner here." She pointed to her own outfit of jeans and a T-shirt. "Now come and let's have something to eat before I get all emotional."

We sat ourselves down at a small rectangular table. In the centre rested the roasting tin I'd last seen on its way back into the oven. It contained what looked like a large German sausage surrounded by plum tomatoes and covered with melted cheese. Next to it, slices of crusty bread lay on a wooden chopping board. Plain food perhaps, but for someone who'd hardly eaten since breakfast it was manna from heaven.

Don had already uncorked a bottle of wine and was pouring out three substantial glasses. I'd barely started on my gin and tonic but I thought it rude to decline. Besides, I knew just the one word of Swedish and here was my chance to put it to good effect.

"Skol," I said, bravely hoping I'd got it right.

"Skol," was the affirming reply.

We touched glasses and I was about to take a drink when I felt the weight of Don's restraining hand on my arm.

"In Sweden, when you say 'Skol' and touch glasses you're supposed to look the other person directly in the eye," he advised. "It's about the only time the Swedes ever do, so it's important – the rest of the time they're too busy staring at the floor to make any kind of connection. And Katerina's keen to maintain these ancient customs, aren't you, darling?"

Katerina lowered her glass. "That's not fair," she scolded. "You make me sound like some reactionary traditionalist, which I'm not."

Don chose to contradict her. "You so are! D'you know what? Every year on the King's birthday we have to pay homage to the Swedish flag."

"So? What's wrong with that? A little loyalty to the Crown doesn't do any harm. Somebody's got to keep these traditions going. If it was left to the likes of Don here," she poked her husband playfully in the ribs, "we'd have nothing left to celebrate. Anyway, Skol! So now you know."

We raised our glasses and clinked again, this time giving each other the required amount of eye contact.

"I'll try and do better in future," I promised.

Frankly, I was desperate to tuck into the falukorv – eight hours without food and it felt as if the sides of my stomach were knocking together. Plus I needed something solid to counteract the effects of the wine and the gin and tonic. Don and Katerina fell silent as we began to eat but I still had unanswered questions from the plane.

"So, how long have you had this place?"

My hosts looked quizzically at each other.

"When did we buy this?" said Don. "Middle of 2007?"

"I think so," confirmed Katerina.

"Oh," I said. "I thought it was rented..."

"To begin with, it was," said Don. "But then there was a

property boom, pretty much like you had in the UK. Mind you, we probably bought at the top of the market. That didn't matter though. We had a big house in Stockholm and we sold that at the same time so there was enough to get this and keep a small flat in the city. I was cutting back on my business interests and we wanted to start slowing down, so it suited us. Then last year I was made an offer I couldn't refuse for the company, so I sold up entirely."

Here was another surprise.

"So you're not working anymore?"

"Good Lord, no. Whatever gave you that idea?"

"Ah, you see I was under the impression..."

"Didn't..." Don hesitated, wondering whether to mention the dreaded subject. "...Susan say anything?"

"No, I don't think so. Or if she did it must have passed me by. To be fair, what with everything else going on I was rather distracted."

"Of course... Anyway, I've packed it all up now. Best thing I ever did, wasn't it, darling?" Katerina nodded between mouthfuls of falukorv. "A couple of years ago, I'd have been sitting in some sweaty office surrounded by paperwork and problems. Now, thank God, I'm free of it all and we can spend our summers out here. Well, I'm free of most of it, at least..."

He tailed off and I thought he looked nervously at his wife. I wondered whether there was some issue between them over it. Perhaps Malaren was more his than hers, although there was enough in the idea of a summer cottage by a lake to make me think of Chekhov and how 'traditional' it might be and so appeal to her. I decided it was best not to pursue it. I was a guest in their house and my remit was to smooth the way over such bumps in the road, not to accentuate them.

"Then what?" I asked. "The rest of the year you presumably retreat back to Stockholm?"

"Exactly," Don continued. "This place is pretty much

uninhabitable in the winter. The lake freezes over and it's difficult moving about. And on top of that, the heating system's not really up to it and it gets a touch too cold for Madame." Katerina nodded once again, this time a little more enthusiastically. "So around the end of September we get packed up and head back into the city. I'd stay here longer if I could. I've got an auger for making holes in the ice and I've always fancied doing a bit of winter fishing…" He began to sound rather wistful, as if he were hiding some regret.

I didn't think it wise to dwell on that, either. Apart from that, what was intriguing me was that if Don liked the place so much, what did he get up to all day to justify it? I'd spent the last few months without a second of spare time but prior to that, there'd been far too much of it. The last thing I wanted was to repeat the experience and based on what I'd seen so far, the idea that we were going to indulge in long business lunches and endless rounds of golf was fading rapidly into the distance.

"So what is there to do here, exactly?" I asked.

Katerina cut in before Don had chance to answer. "Yes, do tell us – I'd really like to know." She turned to face me. "D'you know, Alan, I hardly see him all day. Goodness knows what he gets up to; I'd be interested to find out. I think I saw more of him when he was working than I do now."

Don looked sheepish. "Well, it's like any property of this size. Upkeep, maintenance, there's always something wants doing. The painting alone is a full-time job. It's like the Forth Bridge, you think you've finished and it's time to start all over again. And then there's always the lake…"

"The lake?" I repeated. "So you sail then, or something?" That would make sense of the charts in the living room drawer.

"Sail?" Don gave me another of his 'you must be joking' looks. "God no, that's far too much like hard work. Although I do have a boat."

"Two, actually," Katerina was at pains to remind him.

"Ok, so I've got two," conceded Don. "One for speed and one for comfort – both of which you enjoy going out in, so don't pretend otherwise."

"That's true," admitted Katerina. "Occasionally."

"If you're interested, I'll take you down there in the morning and we'll have a look around," said Don.

It was an offer I was happy to accept. I wasn't particularly into messing around in boats, but if it came down to a choice between that and the painting, it had much to recommend it.

After we'd finished our meal, Katerina insisted we abandon the dishes and go straight through into the lounge. Don lit the fire and a series of bright orange flames soon began flickering up the chimney.

"Fancy a liqueur?"

The drinks cabinet was open again.

"No, I'm alright thanks."

Don poured himself one and we made ourselves comfortable on the sofa. Katerina joined us and something passed between them. It caused me to wonder if Don had ever taken lessons in Swedish.

"You must speak the language pretty well after all these years," I said.

"I try my best," Don replied.

"It took him a while," said Katerina, "but in the end he mastered it – although he's never been completely fluent. It's one of the few things I've ever been able to tease him about. When he first arrived he had blond hair and grew a beard and he's always been reserved and kept himself to himself." She turned to face her husband. "Do you remember what I used to say? 'You may look like a Swede and you may act like a Swede. But until you can talk like a Swede, you'll never be able to call yourself one.'"

Don threw his head back and laughed. "Yes. And I'd say, 'Thank God for that. Who in their right mind would ever want to be a Swede?' I'm British and proud of it."

"Then we'd start that old debate about who was best, the Swedes or the Brits, and I'd have to remind him of how it was the Vikings who invaded his country."

"And I'd have to tell her how they got beaten at the battle of Stamford Bridge."

"And in the end we'd fall about laughing."

"Yes indeed. Happy days..." Don smiled at what was clearly a fond memory, although his face quickly clouded over. "Or they were, until your parents..."

It was as if he'd suddenly remembered the seriousness of the times and how happiness was not an emotion we were presently allowed to entertain. Sensing she'd inadvertently led him into it, Katerina attempted to come to his rescue.

"Every cloud has a silver lining, Don, you know that. If it wasn't for the accident, we'd never have had the inheritance when we did."

"That's true."

"Inheritance?" I said. More news for me to digest.

"Yes," said Katerina. "After they... passed away, I sold my parents' house and it left us with a large sum of money (I have no siblings, remember). At much the same time, things were going wrong at the woodyard where Don worked. The owners announced their intention to sell; there were no guarantees as to what might happen and Don's job was under threat. But it's strange how things have a way of resolving themselves sometimes. Don was offered the chance to buy in and it seemed like the right thing to do. Suddenly we were in business for ourselves and life's been different ever since."

I could see that now. Having once been broken apart, it was as if their lives had been parts of a jigsaw that lay scattered on the floor. Then they'd found two pieces that fitted together and the picture had been gradually rebuilt from there. But any suggestion that there was benefit to be found in Susan's demise was not an argument I was open to. My puzzle was still in bits and there was no immediate prospect of repair.

The conversation turned quickly to the well-being of our children. This was a subject with which we all felt more at home. In Lisbet and Philippa we shared something in common and for the next half an hour we traded anecdotes about the difficulties of raising teenage daughters – their hopes, their fears, their problem boyfriends and whatever else ailed them. Lisbet of course was well past that stage by now and I was told of the joys I could expect to come. Jonathon featured little and besides, I knew less of what went on inside his head.

Before long I began to feel drowsy as the length of the day, the heat of the fire and the last of my gin and tonic all took effect. I may even have nodded off and after I'd yawned for at least the third time, Don offered to show me to my quarters.

"I think we'd better get you off to bed. I'll fetch your suitcase. You'll need your shoes on. You're in the guesthouse across the yard."

I got up and went out into the hallway. My exit left the lounge door ajar and it was while I was changing out of my mules that I caught snatches of their whispered conversation.

"Why did you have to raise the subject of my parents? I thought we were going to try and steer clear of that sort of thing. We don't want to risk upsetting him."

"Hmm… Good point. And by the way, what am I supposed to do with him all day?"

"Well you're going to have to think of something. I don't know if you've forgotten, but he is your brother-in-law."

"And? I hardly know the guy."

"Precisely. And that's the way it'll stay unless you're prepared to put yourself out. Things have changed now and it's important for us to keep in touch."

"Ok. So what d'you want me to do?"

"How should I know? You said you were going to take him down to *look at the boats. Invent some kind of man thing the two of you can do together. You're good at that. You were keen to tell us earlier how much work there is to do around the place. Here's your chance to get another pair of hands to help. You spend half your life in that boathouse of yours as it is. You never know, you might find him useful."*

"What, Alan? He doesn't look the outdoor type."

"Well, maybe not, but don't let that be an excuse not to do anything. People can surprise you. Now off you go and get him settled."

Then, before I had chance to think about it, Katerina came through to say goodnight, Don was there with my suitcase and the two of us went outside.

It had grown quite chilly. On three sides of us the forest loomed large and behind the trees lurked a pale and distant moon. We passed the darkened outline of the Land Rover, our feet scrunching on the gravel. Beyond it, I discerned a row of outbuildings.

"It's over here."

In the corner opposite the gate stood a small wooden shack for which Don had brought a key. He opened it up and switched on the light to reveal a single room. It looked comfortable enough (although perhaps a little Spartan) but at least there was a bed, which for the moment was all I cared about.

"You should be alright in here. There's no bathroom unfortunately so if you need to use the facilities there's a toilet in the outbuildings across the way."

"What about a torch?" I said. "I didn't think to bring one."

"A torch?" Another querying look. "Don't worry – you won't need one. This is the land of the midnight sun, remember?"

"Of course," I nodded. My eyelids had suddenly grown heavy and I was too tired to argue.

"Well, goodnight. Sleep tight. You know where we are if you need anything."

Then he was gone and I could sink down onto the bed and

take off my shoes. I was fearful of falling asleep fully clothed so I immediately got undressed and climbed between the covers. The temptation was to try and stay awake and reflect on the events of the day. We'd managed to get through a whole evening without undue mention of Susan and then there was that business of their cryptic conversation as I was leaving. What the next day might bring was still a mystery – for Don as much as for me by the sound of things – but for the time being I was too exhausted to dwell on it and I crashed out as soon as my head touched the pillow.

Four

Tired as I was, I didn't sleep particularly well. I rarely do on the first night in a strange bed and I must have woken up two or three times. On the last occasion I switched on the bedside lamp and looked at my watch. It was 3.30 a.m. and I needed to make myself comfortable (two glasses of wine and a gin and tonic were more than I could carry) so I resolved to get up and visit the loo. I pulled on my shoes, put on a coat and went out into the yard.

Don was right, I didn't need a torch and there was more than enough daylight to see by. The clouds had cleared away while to the north and east the sky was tinged with pink and there was already a hint of blue on the horizon. Beyond the house I caught a glimpse of the lake, flat and calm at the edge of the trees. High above, a pair of seagulls drifted silently by. Nothing else stirred except a slight shimmer on the water, the birds had not yet started singing and all was at peace. I went back to bed and this time fell straight off to sleep.

Then I was wide awake and it was broad daylight. I sat up in the bed, squinting. In the roof space to my left, a narrow skylight was letting in the sun and it was playing across my face. I threw back the covers, got up to draw the blind that should have been covering it, then went to sit back down.

It was the first chance I'd had to survey my room. When Don had said, *You're staying in the guest house,* I'd imagined something grandiose, but now I could see my quarters were quite confined. I'd just the one room – or so I assumed as there were no doors off other than the one I'd come in by. The place was clearly a conversion as, unlike the main house, the fittings were stylish and modern. Again, the floor was wooden, laminate I think, and the bed on which I was sitting was a low-lying futon, a fact which helped explain my slightly cramped position. To my right was a picture window covered by a slatted blind. As to furniture, all I had was a small chest of drawers and the glass-topped bedside table where I'd left my watch. I picked it up and rechecked the time. It was now half past seven. I contemplated going back to bed, but even though I'd masked off the skylight there was still too much light to try sleeping again. I decided to get up, hauled myself to my feet and went over to the window to lift one of the slats.

The window looked out over the yard which was now bathed in sunlight. The Land Rover stood exactly where we'd left it, but the rest of the yard was empty – save for a small black dog padding about and sniffing at the base of the wheels. To go by its floppy ears and curly coat I concluded it was a cocker spaniel. I let the slat fall back into place and sank back down on the bed. No one had told me there was going to be a dog.

There were few things Susan and I ever rowed about (we'd not even crossed swords over the matter of her mother) but a dog had been one of them. I suppose it's only natural for children to want a pet but I hadn't expected my wife to take sides against me, or at least, not quite so vehemently. I'd conceded that they might have a hamster, or any form of animal that was caged. But as to something that could roam free and unfettered about the house, I'd put my foot down. As far as I was concerned, the risk of an uncontrolled animal wreaking havoc with our furniture and messing on our carpets was far too high to be contemplated. Statistically speaking, the probability of disaster was unity, i.e. certain, and on the basis of this evaluation I'd come down on the side of no. I'd been surprised by the strength of Susan's reaction. She'd actually said I was mean and it hurt me. Had she said 'meany' in the way she said 'numpty', I might not have minded but there's a world of difference implied by that one missing letter. I don't think we spoke for a day or two after as I pig-headedly decided to stick to my guns. We slowly got back to normal and the wound healed – but it left a scar and from then on, dogs were a sore point in our house.

But I could hardly let that prevent me from going outside. Sooner or later I'd have to face up to it and I began to think of getting dressed. I'd not yet unpacked my suitcase and to do so now would simply be putting things off. So I pulled on what clothes were available, opened the door and went out into the yard.

It was colder out there than it looked. I thought of going back for my coat, but that would have been to procrastinate still further and besides, the dog had already seen me and I wasn't going to give ground now. I feared it might bark or run and jump up at me, but it simply continued padding about, nose to the floor, gradually making its way over. Once it had covered every inch of the ground in-between, it eventually arrived and began sniffing round my ankles. For one dreadful moment I thought it might cock its leg, but fortunately it made off to a patch of grass beside the house and returned carrying an old tennis ball. It lay down in front of me, stretched out its paws, dropped the ball down between them and then looked up with a pair of imploring eyes.

Oh my God, I thought, *now it wants to play*. But I was not to be persuaded and walking straight past, I set off across the yard. Seemingly undeterred, the dog calmly picked the ball up between its teeth and ambled after me.

The porchway door was closed, the lights were off and there was no sign of life so rather than disturb anyone I decided to explore my surroundings. To the left, an unmade path led down the side of the house. I followed it and quickly found myself at the back of the property. Here the ground shelved steeply away to the lake some distance in front of me.

The view from the top of the bank was stunning. A great expanse of water a mile wide, maybe more, glistened in the sun. On the far side stood a rocky shoreline covered in trees, while immediately below me the lakeside had been cleared of any woodland. To the left, a short jetty protruded into the water and on either side a motorboat bobbed gently in the swell. To the right, a wooden boathouse hugged the water's edge while laid out in-between was a sandy beach. In the middle, clad in nothing more than a pair of speedos and some flip-flops, stood the stocky figure of Don. I set off down the hill to join him. The dog, having initially dropped its ball while it waited, now picked it up again and followed at my heels.

There was a light breeze blowing and a series of small waves lapped against the sides of the boats so I don't think Don heard me coming. He had a towel about his neck and droplets of water were dripping from his beard and catching in the hairs on his chest. The body beneath, I noticed, was equally as bronzed as his face. His whole appearance made me feel a little awkward.

"Morning, Don," I began, as breezily as I could.

He raised one end of his towel and wiggled it in his ear. "Afternoon, Alan."

That's a bit cheeky, I thought. I hadn't got up that late.

"You've been swimming I take it."

"Absolutely." He wiggled the towel in his other ear. "Can't beat it. I'm down here most mornings about now if you fancy trying it."

"Isn't it a bit on the cold side?"

As inviting as the lake might appear, there were goose pimples forming on his upper arms.

"Not once you get used to it. It's very invigorating. The Swedes do it all the time. You should really give it a go."

"I should?"

"Sure. Did you bring any swimming trunks?"

"Well, no, I didn't think…"

"No problem. I'm sure I've got a spare pair I can lend you. We can soon get you kitted out."

"Hmm…" I wasn't sure I wanted kitting out. The breeze had got up and the patch of goose pimples was rapidly spreading.

He began drying his back. "I see you've met Max."

"I'm sorry?" Perhaps it was my ears that wanted cleaning out.

"I see you've met Max," he repeated.

"Who's Max?" I asked.

"The dog."

"Ah…"

I looked round behind me. Max had taken up the same position as he had in the yard, sitting like a guardian lion, paws outstretched, the tennis ball resting between them. A large pink tongue lolled from his jaws and between regular bouts of panting he occasionally looked up at me with that pair of imploring eyes.

"I think you've made a friend there." Don nodded in the dog's direction. "Look, he wants you to play."

"Does he now," I said with a distinct lack of enthusiasm.

"What's up? Don't you like dogs?"

"Not particularly," I said. "Susan and I had a row about them once and they've been a bone of contention ever since." I thought that by invoking the memory of my dead wife he might back off, but I was wrong. I was in a different country now – perhaps the dead-wife card didn't play too well out here.

"Suit yourself," he said, a little peevishly. "Personally, I love 'em. Here, boy." He stooped to pick up the ball and lobbed it into the undergrowth beyond the jetty.

Max got to his feet and faced in the direction of the rapidly departing ball. But instead of scampering off after it he looked enquiringly up at Don as if waiting for instruction.

Don nodded. "Go on."

Max now set off, ambling along in a circuitous route and sniffing at every inch of ground between ourselves and the place where the ball had landed. At this point I felt I should say something mildly encouraging.

"I didn't know you had a dog. How long has he been around?"

"Ever since we bought the place. In fact, he came with the property. He was here on the day we moved in and he's never gone away. We asked around the neighbours to see if he belonged to someone else but apparently this is his home just as much as ours."

"Oh..."

By this time Max had returned with the ball and was lying at my feet again. Don bent down and gently stroked his head.

"Good boy." Then, "He won't hurt you, you know. He's not going to bite."

I looked down and saw that pair of soft brown eyes staring back at me. *No*, I thought, *he isn't*. Then, *Oh what the hell*, and I picked up the ball.

Max stood up in expectation as I prepared to throw. On closer inspection the ball bore the scars of a number of expeditions into the undergrowth and in places the covering had been chewed through. I tossed it carelessly into the bushes in much the same direction as Don had. Max faced round and waited obediently for his signal.

"Go on," I said and off he went, ambling along in his thorough and unhurried way.

"Well done," said Don. "That wasn't so bad, was it?"

"No," I said grudgingly. "I suppose it wasn't."

While we'd been talking, Don had continued to towel himself dry. On the side of the wooden jetty rested a pile of his belongings and he pulled out a watch.

"Ten to eight," he announced. "Breakfast's at half past. We've time to have a quick look round the estate. You ok with that?"

"Sure," I said. I wasn't planning on going anywhere. "Only, are you going to put a shirt on? I don't like the thought of you catching cold."

"No problem." He gave me a curious smile. "This do?" He took a green and white striped top from the pile and pulled it over his head. "And now that we're properly dressed, we can begin. If sir would like to step this way, we'll start at the boathouse."

We set off across the beach. Max, meanwhile, had once more retrieved his ball and was trotting along quietly behind us.

Don's idea of 'a quick look round the estate' didn't work out quite as planned. Or not planned, as the case may be, because if there was anything in Don's head about what we were supposed to be doing at the start, it very soon disappeared once we got going. In fact, of the forty minutes available before breakfast (which I assumed Katerina was preparing up at the house) the vast majority of them were spent in the boathouse. And if it hadn't been for my pointing out the time, I think we'd still have been there come lunch.

It soon became clear that Don was devoted to boating – and once he got started on the subject, he found it difficult to move on. Ok, so the boathouse was an interesting place and I learned an awful lot, but I wasn't quite ready for a crash course in elementary seamanship. He'd just completed a description of every rope and chain in the place and we were about to start on the intricate business of how to tie sailor's knots when I saw it was twenty-five past eight.

"Don," I said, tapping my watch. "I hate to interrupt you but don't you think we should be going up?"

It wasn't just Katerina I was thinking of – my stomach was beginning to rumble.

"Jesus, you're right." He checked the time for himself. "Hmm... Five minutes. I've just got time to show you the boats."

We trooped back across the beach, Max in tow, carrying his precious ball. For the half an hour or so we'd been in the boathouse he'd set his toy to one side and had made himself comfortable on a sheet of tarpaulin with his head resting between his paws. Once or twice he'd got up to shake himself and yawn but had then settled back down. I guessed it wasn't the first time he'd heard Don's talk on the different uses of a sheepshank and a bowline.

We spent another twenty minutes at the jetty by which time I'd become distinctly edgy. But however late we might be and whatever consequences that might have, nothing was going to come between Don and his boats. Their length, breadth, displacement tonnage and horsepower were all explained to me in detail. I'm afraid I took little of it in – except to record that one was a cabin cruiser decked out in cream (used mainly for idling about and the occasional fishing trip) while the other was a speedboat in lurid red and kept strictly for pleasure.

At last I persuaded him to leave and we'd just started up the slope, Max following wearily to the rear, when something caught my eye. Standing on the beach on the far side of the jetty was a large grey pontoon, the top covered with wooden decking. To the untrained eye it looked like a relic from the Second World War, a piece of kit left over from the Normandy landings.

"What on earth is that?" I asked.

"Ah," said Don. "Glad you mentioned it – I almost forgot. That's our swimming platform. Need to get that floated off and set up out on the lake. It'll be our first job after breakfast."

This, presumably, was the 'man thing' Katerina had encouraged him to come up with the night before – although whether he'd given it any thought or just happened to make it up as we were passing, I couldn't really tell. As for the idea of it being a job, nobody had told me there were going to be any. I'd come all the way from England to get away from that sort of thing and I wasn't looking to start again now.

We made our way back up the hill and arrived out of breath, late and almost certainly in trouble.

Five

Walking up the slope, I wondered as to the reception Don might get when we reached the house. I'd come to the point where I didn't much care, just as long as I got something to eat. I was used to breakfast at seven, it was now ten to nine and nothing had passed my lips all morning – although this was probably just as well given the size of the feast Katerina had prepared.

As we entered the hallway Don called out, "Hi honey, I'm home." But if his attempt at comedy was intended to head off any criticism, it didn't work and he received a frosty reply.

"You're late."

"Ah…" Don kicked off his flip-flops and replaced them with a pair of the white fluffy mules. "It's all Alan's fault." He turned and winked at me. "He insisted on a full tour of the boathouse and wanted to hear all there was to know. I'd have come up straight after that but he wanted to look at the boats as well."

"Liar. I don't believe he had anything to do with it, he's far too polite for that. You did tell him eight-thirty?"

"Of course."

"Hmm… Well, it's his first morning and he's forgiven. But next time…" Katerina was standing at the stove, stirring a saucepan full of beans. "How d'you like your eggs, by the way?"

"Just as they come," I said. "I've no real preference."

Don passed by on his way to the dining area, stopping to kiss his wife on the neck. "Fried, please," he called out. "Two."

"Fine with me," I said, shrugging my shoulders. "Anything I can do to help?"

"No, everything's under control. Although you could go and help Don lay the table. I thought we'd eat out on the veranda."

Sheltered beneath an overhanging roof, the veranda stretched right across the back of the house and looked out over the lake. Beyond the balcony rail there was a steep drop down to the ground and the top of the slope.

Barely an hour had passed since I'd first seen the lake that morning but the outlook had already changed. The sun had truly risen and the golden sparkle it had created on the water had been replaced by a constant blue. The breeze had died away and out in the garden below, the Swedish emblem hung limply at the head of one white flagpole while the Union Jack drooped at another. Apart from the occasional cry of a seagull, it was all eerily quiet.

Don whistled jauntily to himself as he laid the table. I helped as best I could. Eventually we both sat down and I was sipping at a glass of orange juice when a thought occurred. I looked behind me then checked at my feet but my constant companion of the morning was no longer there. Max had gone missing.

"Where's the dog?" I asked.

"Max?" Don lowered his glass. "Oh, he doesn't come in."

"D'you mean he's not allowed?" I was thinking of the 'shoes off' rule and the need to keep the floors clean.

"No, he just doesn't come in – he never has. We don't know why but he won't enter the house. Maybe it's something to do with the previous owners. You can leave the door open for him but he won't cross the threshold. He seems happy enough to sit on the porch and wait for us to come out."

"So where does he sleep?"

"There's a basket in one of the outhouses. He kips in there."

"I see…"

Katerina arrived with the fruits of her labour, two plates piled high with food. This was a working man's breakfast – but as yet we'd done no work and as hungry as I was, I knew I'd struggle to finish. Katerina, I noticed, had apportioned herself considerably less and was making do with one egg and a single piece of bacon.

"Tuck in," said Don, eager to make a start.

He was still wearing his speedos and the green and white striped top. Together with the white fluffy mules his outfit looked rather incongruous, but he must have thought it imprudent to delay things further by going to get changed. None of this stopped him from enjoying his food however, and he soon demolished the pile in front of him. As anticipated, I was forced to slow down and eventually gave up.

"Too much for me I'm afraid," I said, pushing aside a sausage, the black pudding and one of the eggs.

Katerina smiled graciously and began collecting up the plates.

Coffee arrived but rather than tackling his drink, Don put his feet up on a neighbouring chair and leant back with his eyes closed.

We stayed like this for a while, Don slumped in his chair while I sat and stared out at the lake. In the far distance a yacht appeared and its tiny white sail slid mesmerically across the horizon. I began to feel curiously relaxed. It wouldn't be long, I thought, before I nodded off myself.

After about twenty minutes, Don suddenly sat bolt upright and looked at his watch.

"Jesus Christ! Look at the time." It had gone ten o'clock. "Come on, we've got work to do." He jumped to his feet and headed for the lounge.

"You'll need to give me a few minutes," I said. "I want to get tidied up."

"Ok. Meet you on the porch."

I nodded and set off for the hallway to pick up my outdoor shoes.

Max was sitting where we'd left him, just outside the front door and with his ball between his feet. He got up, wagged a stubby tail and I thought he might follow me across to the guest-house but he elected to stay put. Nearby, I caught sight of a dog-bowl containing what looked suspiciously like the remains of my breakfast. I wished him good luck with it and walked on by.

The pontoon, or would-be swimming platform, proved stubbornly difficult to move. It seemed such an inoffensive thing, lying there quietly on the beach, grey and forlorn, and if it were at all possible for inanimate objects to have any form of will you'd have thought it would have wanted to get off into the water on its own and make itself useful. But it did not. On the contrary, rather than help it seemed determined to frustrate us and it took us the rest of the morning to get it free.

Don still hadn't changed out of his trunks and casual top. I'd sought out the oldest shirt and pair of trousers I could find – although they weren't the remotest bit suitable and for all his appearance of going off on holiday, my brother-in-law was probably better equipped.

We trooped down the slope in a kind of marching fashion. Don began singing to himself and swinging his arms in time:

"Two men went to mow
Went to mow a meadow
Two men, one man and his dog
Went to mow a meadow..."

And there was Max, loping along at the rear.

We got down to the beach in good order and gathered round the pontoon. Don began giving instructions such as a general might give his troops. I wondered if it was a trait he'd inherited from his mother.

"Right then, chaps. First things first. Our objective, Sergeant Major," (he glanced in my direction) "is to get this swimming platform from here..." (he slapped it playfully with one hand) "...to there." He indicated the water lapping at the edge of the beach, a distance of no more than six feet. "Got it?"

"Got it," I confirmed. It seemed simple enough.

"So, any ideas as to how we might achieve it?"

"I suppose we could always try lifting it," I said.

"Well, there's a thought," said Don with a hint of sarcasm. "I tell you what. You grab that side, I'll grab this and we'll give it a go. And you," he said, looking directly at the dog, "stand well clear." Max stared back at us with his big brown eyes and settled down into his guarding lion pose. "Right," said Don. "On the count of three."

We got into position with our hands beneath the rim and bent our legs.

"One, two...three!"

We huffed and puffed and raised the front end a tad – but we couldn't move it and the pontoon sank back into the sand. We stood aside, hands on knees, breathing hard.

"Well that's enough of that," said Don between two deep inhalations. "We're obviously going to need some mechanical assistance."

We recovered our composure and went across to the boathouse in search of help.

We returned with two pieces of four by four, each about six feet in length. This time we tried the back of the pontoon and while Don raised one corner, I inserted a post underneath. We repeated this on the other side and then tried working our makeshift levers in the hopes of some forward movement. Yet again we could lift it but we couldn't shift it and after a couple of attempts, it was clear we weren't getting anywhere. We sat down on the jetty for a rethink.

"What now?" I said.

"What now indeed," said Don. "Any thoughts?"

"Well, this may seem like a silly question..."

"No problem, at this stage all questions are welcome, silly or not. What we need is some blue-sky thinking."

"Well, how did it get here in the first place? I assume it must have been dragged up the beach."

"Good point. And the answer is, I don't know. You see, it's a bit like Max here." He pointed in the direction of the dog. "It came with the place and it's been stuck here ever since."

"You mean you've never tried to move it before?"

"Nope."

"Why on earth not?"

"Well to be honest, it's the first time I've had any help."

We took a five-minute break, then went back to our task and over the course of the next half-hour exerted ourselves relentlessly in pursuit of the impossible. No matter how we used our pieces of timber, the story was the same – we could get upward motion but none forward. If we lifted the front, the back bogged down. If we lifted the back, the front did likewise – it was all to no avail.

By now it was getting on for half past eleven and we'd just broken off to take another rest when Katerina appeared at the top of the slope with a cup in each hand.

"Uh-oh," said Don, leaning on the jetty. "Here's trouble. She's come to check us out. Beware of Greeks bearing gifts. Or Swedes even."

Katerina picked her way carefully down the hill and passed us our tea.

"You boys looked in need of refreshment," she said. "You seem to be working awfully hard. Having trouble?"

"You could say that," I said between sips.

"No, we're not having any trouble," Don was keen to assure her. "We're just limbering up, that's all. We'll soon have this fixed." He gave a cheesy and rather unconvincing smile.

"Hmm..." Katerina sounded dubious. "Well I certainly hope so. I've banked on taking a swim later and I wouldn't want to be disappointed."

"You won't be."

Katerina looked at the pontoon, then at us, then back at the pontoon. Although the surrounding sand had been deeply disturbed, it was clear that the platform itself hadn't moved.

"We'll see." Then, in what sounded like a pointed remark, "I'll bet the Vikings didn't have these problems."

"Oh ha, ha, ha," snapped Don. "Well we're not Vikings, we're British and we'll sort this out in our own way and in our own time, thank you very much."

"Lunch is at one, by the way," said Katerina. "On the dot, so don't be late. In fact, I'll make Alan responsible for getting you there – he seems to be the only one with any sense of timing."

Don pursed his lips but wisely decided to stay silent.

"Good luck, boys. See you later." Katerina collected our empty mugs and set off back up the hill in apparent triumph.

Don scowled. "That's the trouble with women," he said, as soon as his wife was out of earshot. "You only have to give them the tiniest crack and they'll drive a wedge straight into it. Your remark didn't help, by the way."

"Oh? Which remark was that?"

"The one about 'you could say we were in trouble'. Even if we were, we can't go admitting it."

"Sorry..."

"Never mind – you'll learn." He straightened up and took a deep breath. "Well, we can't allow ourselves to fail now. I don't know about you but I've got a reputation to maintain. The good news is, I've had an idea. Don't you dare tell her this but what she said about the Vikings has given me a clue."

"Go on."

"Well, they used to transport their longboats across short stretches of land by rolling them on logs. Now it just so happens that I've got half a dozen old fence poles stored under the boathouse. They should do the trick. What say we give it a try?"

"Fine with me."

We traipsed across the sand once more. The boathouse, it seemed, was the source of everything useful...

The sun had now reached its highest point, the breeze had dropped away and it had grown warm. Don's reaction was to strip off his top. I too had begun to feel uncomfortable and after the exertions of the morning clad in full-length trousers and thick shirt, sweat had started to dribble. I didn't count myself as being particularly fit. Beyond biking to the office, my only forms of exercise had been housework, gardening and the occasional bouts of sex, and despite Susan's repeated suggestions to the contrary – *You really ought to work out* – I'd never persuaded myself to join the gym. I was a stone overweight and my body lacked Don's muscular tone. It was also unused to exposure to the sun and although my hands were tanned beyond the point at which my cuffs buttoned down, the rest of me remained an insipid white. It was probably this feeling of personal embarrassment rather than anything else which had prevented me from uncovering myself further.

But none of that seemed to matter anymore. Here we were, two men, out in the middle of nowhere, engaged in a task of honest labour in the midday sun. A degree of nakedness would dignify our work and there was a voice inside my head (was it Susan, talking to me from some far-off place?) saying, *Alan, for God's sake take your shirt off.* And so I bared my chest, literally and mentally, and stripped off. As for my trousers, the best I could do was to roll them up above the knee but even that was an improvement. Don, bless him, didn't say a word.

The poles were damnably heavy. It took both of us to carry one and we sweated, even with our shirts off, as we got them into position, one at the front, one at the back and finally, one in the middle. Max sensibly kept well clear. There was an immediate sense of unsteadiness and for a second it looked as if the thing might run away with us – but then it settled and we knew we were on the right track. An exploratory push at the rear suggested it was ready to roll.

"This is looking good," said Don. "We'll get it pulled forward until it's balanced nicely on the front two poles, then whip the back one round. Ok?"

"Ok."

We braced ourselves.

"Ready?"

"Ready."

We bent our backs and heaved, and lo and behold the

platform moved forward a couple of feet, releasing the pole at the rear.

"Whoa!" said Don. "That'll do."

We stopped and took the back pole round to the front. We were already no more than two or three feet from the water's edge.

"One more shove and that should do it," said Don.

We applied ourselves once more and this time the job did run away with us, and what with the rolling motion of the poles and the increasing slope of the beach, the platform careered forward out of control. But by now the front end was in the water and floating free so all we had to do was lift the back in after it. We finished by walking out into the lake with the pontoon in front of us; Don in his trunks and his flip-flops, I in my socks and trainers. We were soon up to our thighs and my rolled-up trousers were soaked – but we'd done it and I no longer cared.

Don let out a whoop and we instinctively high-fived.

"Well done, partner," he added. "Good job."

I can't begin to describe the overwhelming sense of satisfaction I got from seeing that platform out on the water. On reflection it seems such a trivial matter in what Susan used to call 'The Grand Scheme of Things' but it meant a lot to me. Ok, so all we'd done was move a relatively heavy object six or eight feet but it signified much more than that. There'd been effort and teamwork and for a couple of hours my life had known some kind of purpose. True, we were only half done, we'd the poles to replace and Don sensibly suggested we should tie the pontoon off to stop it floating away, but I felt I'd achieved more in that one morning than I had in the previous six months put together.

There was a distinct spring in our step as we ascended the hill. Not only that but we were ten minutes early for lunch and there was time to make ourselves presentable.

"You look pleased with yourselves," said Katerina as she prepared to serve out the salad. She nodded in the direction of her husband. "You realise he'll be insufferable for the rest of the day."

"And why not?" I said. "He's done a bloody good job if you ask me."

Don waited until she'd gone to fetch something from the kitchen, then muttered quietly under his breath. "Bloody Vikings – I always knew we could beat the buggers if we put our minds to it."

Six

Lunch was conducted in much the same manner as breakfast, i.e. a hearty meal followed by a period of studied relaxation. After we'd eaten, Don tipped back his chair and assumed his customary position, feet up, eyes closed and with his hands clasped across his midriff. I don't know what I was expected to do during these moments of post-prandial shuteye. Despite the morning's work, I personally wasn't tired. But it was pleasant enough on the veranda, there were more yachts to look at on the lake and I could contemplate the results of our handiwork as the platform bobbed gently up and down next to the jetty. Lapped by the swell of the waves, its motion was faintly soporific and this time, I too began closing my eyes...

Then I was wide awake as I realised Don was talking to me.

"...love to give you the afternoon off, Alan, but we've got more work to do." I sat up and tried to pay attention. "We've shifted the platform off the beach. Now we need get it onto the lake – I'd say about fifty yards offshore where we can reasonably swim out to it. Now it just so happens there's a white buoy moored in exactly the spot where I think we should be. Have a look." He fetched a pair of binoculars from a hook on the balcony and passed them across so I could scour the area. "Got it?"

I nodded. From where I was sitting it looked like a plastic milk bottle.

"I swam out to have a look this morning. That buoy's got a line attached to it. It's not that deep out there, eight or nine feet at the most, so you can follow it down to the bottom. You can't see a bloody thing of course, it's like swimming in pea soup, but it's tied to a set of chains on the seabed. The chains are anchored to a concrete block and I reckon that's what keeps the platform in position. So, our mission this afternoon is to get the platform out there and secured to those chains. Are you up for that?"

"Ok with me," I said. Another task, another objective, more

teamwork – what was there not to like? "Just one thing. How are we going to get it out there?"

"Good question. We're going to use one of the boats and tow it. Ever driven a boat?"

"Er... no. Unfortunately not."

"Hmm... Well there's no time to learn like the present. And if her ladyship wants to go swimming today, we'd best get on with it."

We gathered ourselves together and headed off down the hill.

The idea of setting foot on a boat, never mind actually driving one, made me distinctly uneasy. Boats, especially of the size and type owned by Don, were inherently unstable and not to be trusted. Irrespective of the state of the water they floated on, as soon as you got into them they wobbled and induced a feeling of immediate insecurity. We British are supposed to be a sea-faring nation but if the desire to rule the waves had ever been present in my family, as far as I was concerned it had skipped a generation and passed me by. Lord Nelson I was definitely not and I began the afternoon with a degree of apprehension.

Our first requirement was naturally to pay a visit to the boathouse and collect a set of tackle. We loaded up a green tote box and took it to the jetty. Max had joined us with his ball although as we were taking to the water, I didn't see how we could possibly play with it.

"We'll use the launch," said Don. "The speedboat's no good for this."

We walked out onto the jetty and set the tote box down. The pontoon was where we'd left it, moored to the side some six or eight feet behind the launch.

"First things first," said Don. He took two lengths of rope from the box, jumped down on top of the platform and began tying them off. After a detour via the jetty, he boarded the launch and secured the other ends. I thought to give him the tote box too but he shook his head.

"No, you're going to want that."

"Me?" I said. "Whatever for?"

Don looked up at me from the well of the launch, his eyes squinting in the sun. "You haven't thought this through, have you?"

"No," I had to confess, "I haven't."

He came over to the side and rested his arms on the jetty. "Well, since you can't drive a boat, I'm going to be in the launch, and you're going to be on the platform." He pointed at the pontoon.

"You're joking," I said. "I'm not getting on that." The idea of riding in the boat had been bad enough.

"So how else do we get this done? What I want to avoid is the pontoon smashing into the back of my boat and buggering up the work of a lifetime. That's why you're going to take this..." (he picked up a boathook from the deck of the launch and thrust it in my direction) "...and fend the boat off if it gets too close. Alright, so you might fall off the pontoon and end up in the water. You can swim, can't you?"

"Well... Just about," I nodded.

"So what's your problem? Don't tell me you're going to get seasick riding on that thing. The lake's as flat as a millpond." He bade me look at the water which, I had to admit, appeared rather glorious. "Where's the risk?"

Where indeed. It didn't take the trained mind of an actuary to see that of the two eventualities, the downside of affairs lay squarely with Don.

"Ok, so what d'you want me to do?"

"Take the box and the boathook, and get onto the pontoon. When I give you the word, cast off the moorings and sit tight. If you look like coming anywhere near the boat, just be ready to fend off. Ok?"

"Ok."

I picked up the equipment and stepped tentatively onto the pontoon. Just as I'd feared, it wobbled precariously and my first instinct was to crouch down. As soon as I did so it settled and I crawled across to the centre.

Max had been left on the jetty and was padding up and down between the launch and the pontoon, undecided as to which was the best option. Eventually he plumped for the pontoon and having sensibly discarded his ball, sprang forward and landed beside me, his pink tongue lolling.

The motor fired up on the launch and Don appeared from the wheelhouse to cast off his moorings. I did the same on the pontoon and our towlines drew taut. Then we were off and clear of the jetty. I had a tote box on my left, a dog on my right and with the boathook clamped firmly under one arm and the pontoon swaying gently from side to side, I looked for all the world as if I were taking part in an episode of *It's A Knockout*. And yet despite my sense of trepidation, I felt a curious level of schoolboy excitement...

We spent the next couple of hours securing the pontoon. The exercise involved Don making a series of dives to the bed of the lake, returning each time with a chain which I helped him shackle to the eyelets on the pontoon. He was clearly working to a plan and his mind was focused on it. Mine was left to wander although it's hard to recall exactly what was going through it at the time.

What I do know is that I wasn't thinking about Susan. On other occasions, in the short intervals that hung between the need for action, my thoughts would usually revert to her and I'd find myself drawn back toward the same dark hole that had once consumed me. But the further I'd travelled from York, the more distant all that had become. Now I'd taken another step forward and ventured onto the lake. Out here, a different set of rules applied. Away from the shelter of the shoreline, a light breeze rippled the surface of the water and wafted against my cheek. It brought with it the warmth of the sun, making it feel almost idyllic. It was as if Malaren were a seductive siren and had put on her finest clothing with the intention of luring me on. Max dozed peacefully beside me, I lost all sense of time and it was only Don's constant reappearances from the deep that kept me in the world.

He finally pronounced us finished and with the platform floating level and everything tied down, we could count the job done. We high-fived again and stopped to admire our handiwork. Up at the house, I wondered whether Katerina was watching while she waited for her swim.

"Well, that's enough of that," said Don. "We can't stand here gloating all day. We'd best get packed up."

We gathered our kit and loaded it onto the launch. Our expedition had taken us deep into the afternoon and I was desperate for a cup of tea but Don had other ideas.

"It's time you had a driving lesson," he said, and opening the throttle, headed out into open water.

Earlier that day, I might have challenged Don's assumption that I was in need of boating tuition. I'd no desire to take to the water, and in fact I'd been in fear of it, but the atmosphere had changed and now it didn't seem such a bad idea. I hadn't fallen in, I hadn't made a mistake and I might even flatter myself to think I'd been useful. We'd achieved our objective and Don naturally wanted to celebrate so it was time to let off some steam. Max thought likewise and elected to join us.

The playground Don had chosen was immense. The lake stretched away for miles on either side while the tree-topped shoreline opposite seemed unimaginably distant. At its right-hand end the trees dropped away and the lake itself became the horizon. There was no telling what lay beyond it.

We cleared the pontoon and Don increased our speed. We'd not yet reached full throttle (the lever he used was only halfway along its slot) but it was enough to give the impression we were making steady progress. The water sped by on either side but far in front of us the shoreline barely moved. We were no more than a tiny dot on one of Don's charts, heading out into the wild blue yonder.

The sun was behind us now, lighting the way ahead. Out in open water, the waves grew in height and the cream-coloured prow of the boat began to bob. A cascade of spray spattered against the wheelhouse window. The wind had got up and Don had to shout to make himself heard above the drone of the engine.

"What we're going to do..." (I leant forward to catch what he was saying) "...is head out toward the island." He pointed to our right then turned the wheel. Some way in front of us a small hump appeared on the horizon. "You can take over and get us round. Leave it on your port side – that's the left to you landlubbers – and keep at least fifty yards off. Take it steady, don't make any violent moves and you'll be fine. Ok?"

I nodded. It didn't sound too demanding. He stepped away to give me the wheel and all at once there I was, in sole command of a boat on the high seas.

It's not exactly rocket science, steering a small launch in a straight line across a relatively calm lake, but it's amazing how focused you can become when you're out of your comfort zone. As soon as my hands touched the wheel I found I was aware of the slightest thing – every rock of the boat, every slap of a wave, the tiniest gust of wind, they all had an effect and I was ready to react in an instant. With enough practice you probably learn to relax, although for the moment I felt acutely alive.

But if I was temporarily on edge, Don was certainly not. I risked a quick glance to the side and saw him resting against the gunwale, arms folded and looking calmly beyond me. He showed not a trace of worry and I drew confidence from his bearing. While he was around, it seemed I had nothing to worry about.

And neither apparently did Max. For just as a dog looks out of a car window, he had his feet on the ledge, his head full to the wind with his ears blown back and for a few precious minutes I felt as though their lives were in my hands.

The island drew steadily closer. As we approached, I saw it was covered in dead trees, a row of thin black sticks pointing up towards the sky as if it had been ravaged by fire.

"That's Cormorant Island," shouted Don. "There used to be a colony of them on it. Then all the trees died off. Nobody knows why. The birds won't go near it now."

He signalled for me to keep out to the right. I adjusted our course and gave him the clearance he'd asked for as the island slid by on our left. There was a strangely eerie feel about it, and beneath the blackened stumps of the trees there was little, if any, vegetation. I sensed a cold chill as we passed.

Once beyond it, Don indicated I should swing round to the left. I made the turn and we began to sweep round the far end of the island in a big semi-circle. He gave me the thumbs up.

Out to our right floated two white buoys, just like the one that had marked the location of our chains.

"Best keep away from those," said Don. I instinctively steered away. "There's a set of rocks close under the surface. The buoys are there as a warning."

Rocks on one side, the island on the other, it was a nervy moment. I thought of Scylla and Charybdis and tightened my grip on the wheel.

We motored on and I began to feel more confident. I'd held the boat steady, negotiated a turn and kept us off the rocks. As I say, it's not exactly rocket science, driving a boat. My heightened awareness remained but I felt I could relax just a little.

We headed back into the sun and the change of direction transformed the appearance of the lake. With the light behind us it had looked a Mediterranean blue, but it now mutated to a silvery-grey. The wind had died away and without its hindrance we seemed to skim along, barely touching the surface. On the land far in front of us I could see the slope cut amongst the trees and at the top of it, the house, standing out against the skyline.

Don had found a pair of sunglasses in the locker beneath the wheel and he'd jammed them on, tilting his head upwards to catch the warmth. He saw my look of envy and took out a pair for me too. Neither of us had as yet replaced our shirts and we must have resembled a pair of ancient sybarites, luxuriating in the afternoon sun.

The closer we got to the shore, the more quickly it seemed to approach and with the pontoon getting ever nearer, I felt a rising sense of panic. If a boat had brakes, I'd no idea where they were. I motioned Don to take over. He took the wheel, shut down the throttle and we instantly slowed to a crawl while I watched and took note.

"Well, did you enjoy that?" he asked.

"Yes, thank you," I said. "I did."

"Good. We'll have another lesson tomorrow."

"Fine. I'll look forward to it."

It had been a pleasant afternoon.

But things were about to take a turn in the opposite direction and as we neared the pontoon we found we were not alone. While we'd been away, Katerina had emerged for her swim and was clinging to the edge of the platform. She did not look best pleased. Her face was streaming wet and she was having trouble keeping the hair out of her eyes. As soon as we were close enough, she waved an arm and called out.

"Where have you been?"

It was not a polite enquiry.

Don leant over the gunwale. "I took Alan for a trip round the island."

"Well, you might have thought to stay here while I took my swim. You'll have to come and help me out. I can't get onto the damn thing." Her voice sounded strained.

"We'll get moored up and come over. Two minutes."

Don brought us alongside the pontoon and cut the engine. We got tied off and climbed out onto the platform.

Katerina hadn't moved. She was hanging on for dear life, her hands had turned white and she was shivering.

"What happened?" said Don.

"I told you. I came out for a swim. I kept trying to get up onto the platform but I couldn't make it." Her voice shook as she spoke. "Then I got cramp and I daredn't risk swimming back. I've been waiting for you to come back ever since. For God's sake get me out, I'm freezing."

We knelt down on the edge of the pontoon, then each of us took an arm and began hauling her out.

Pulling someone even as slight as Katerina over the side of a foot-high steel platform is not a task to be achieved with any sense of dignity or without collateral damage. Needless to say we managed neither and it was only when we'd raised her up that she could get her knee over the edge and roll sideways onto the decking. I winced as she cracked her shin on the way. But then she was standing, still shaking and dripping water, a trickle of blood running down her leg.

"Alan?" It was the first time I'd seen Don look serious. "There's a blanket in the locker. Get it for me, will you?"

I fetched it from the launch and we draped it round Katerina's shoulders. Then she was in Don's arms, his broad hands patting her back.

"I was worried..." she whimpered.

"I know, I know. But it's alright now," he soothed. "Come on, let's get you back to the house."

We coaxed her gently into the boat and sat her down in the stern with the blanket round her. Max came over to lie at her feet. She reached down to pet him.

"Good boy."

I swiftly cast off and we chugged back to the jetty.

Don and I all but carried her up the hill, her arms about our shoulders as she hopped on her one good leg, gingerly protecting the other. Even Max knew something was wrong and looked at each of us in turn as if he were seeking an explanation. As soon as we reached the house, we sat her down on the sofa. We suggested she went straight to bed but she refused and I lit the fire while Don looked for bandages. Fortunately, nothing was broken beyond the skin and when the wound was cleaned up it was apparent we were making more fuss than was needed. A sticking plaster would suffice.

Katerina waved us away. "I'll be fine," she said.

But it was a while before she dispensed with the blanket.

Dinner was understandably late that evening. Don cooked it, much as I would have done had Susan been the injured party. Although, like me, Don had limited culinary skills and we dined on what was effectively a repeat of breakfast.

In fact it worked out well. Nobody wanted salad and Katerina especially was in need of something warming. After half an hour in front of the fire she headed for the shower then changed into some dry clothing. She reappeared at the table with a thick pullover on over her top and one leg of her jeans rolled up to accommodate the sticking plaster which I have a feeling she displayed purposely for Don's benefit. We ate mostly in an embarrassed silence. There didn't seem much we could say.

After we'd finished, Katerina announced her intention of retiring for the night. Don and I cleared up and retreated to the sitting room. The previous evening there'd been drinks and conversation but that night Don offered neither and went to one of the cupboards instead and took out a pad of paper and a pencil.

We spent the next hour in quiet contemplation, Don at one end of the sofa writing and sketching, while I sat alone at the other. I desperately wanted company and I thought about letting the dog in, but I knew he wouldn't come.

The lake was still on my mind. That afternoon I'd been seduced by its finery and I'd entrusted myself to it, skimming across the water at the wheel of a launch. It had been kind to me, I'd enjoyed an exhilarating experience and I'd been grateful. Now I knew it had a darker side, and one that was not to be relied on.

After a while I excused myself and left Don to his notes and his drawings. On my way across the yard I looked in on the outbuildings. Max was there, curled up in his basket and seemingly without a care in the world. I bade him goodnight and went on over to the guesthouse in a thoughtful mood.

Seven

That night I slept like a log. I put it down to the fresh air and exercise. We'd drunk little the night before so there was no middle-of-the-night excursion to the toilet either and I awoke refreshed and clear-headed.

But it was still early, six-thirty; the light was noticeably paler and the beam from the skylight window shone higher up the opposite wall – I'd forgotten to lower the blind again. I made a mental note, got up, pulled on what now comprised my working clothes and went outside.

Max was waiting in the yard, sitting in his guarding-lion position, his forelegs pointed directly at my door. He'd recovered his tennis ball from the vicinity of the jetty and as I approached, he looked down at it and then up at me.

"Hey, boy."

I bent down and rubbed his head as I'd seen Katerina do. His coat had a damp and silky feel, as if he'd been sprayed with oil. I picked up the ball. Max stood up and wagged his stubby tail.

"Go on then," I said and pitched the ball into the long grass at the edge of the yard. Max ambled after it, his nose close to the ground on his usual circuitous route. By the time I reached the house, he'd found it and brought it back. We repeated the exercise.

Once again there were no lights on. Katerina was sure to be in bed nursing her leg, and thinking that no one was up I decided to walk down to the beach. I'd no option but take the dog, so with Max for company I sauntered down the hill.

The lake looked much as it had done the previous morning – flat and calm, although it had yet to acquire that golden sparkle. The sun was still below the trees and there was a bank of cloud, a layer of gunmetal grey to the west, while to the east the sky was a clear pale blue. Behind the house a light breeze ruffled the flags and out on the water, the pontoon rocked gently up and down with the swell.

Don was not out swimming – or at least, not yet, as he was still dressed in his T-shirt and trunks and was rummaging through the woodstore beneath the boathouse. As I came closer, I could hear he was singing to himself again.

"La... La,la,la,la... Norwegian wood."

I hoped this was a signal that his carefree mood had returned and that the atmosphere in the house had improved.

"Morning, Don," I began.

"Morning, Alan."

This was better – yesterday he'd started with *Good afternoon.*

"How's things?"

"Fine."

"And Katerina?"

"A bit too early to tell. She was still asleep when I got up, but I think she had a decent night."

"Good..."

Don continued rummaging.

"Not swimming this morning?"

"Nope – got a job to do. Or at least, I have if I don't want to spend another night sleeping on the floor." He turned and gave me one of his grins. "Only joking."

While we'd been talking he'd selected a piece of timber and stood holding it out for inspection. A pale-coloured plank, it looked about two metres long. He turned it round a couple of times and ran his hand down it as though he were a trainer caressing the leg of a horse.

"Hmm... This should do it."

"Do what?" I said.

"The job we're going to do this morning."

"What job?"

"You'll see."

Max cocked his head to one side.

"Ok," I said. "And is it?"

"Is it what?"

"Norwegian."

"Good question. It could well be actually." Don turned the plank round again then held it up to his nose. "Certainly smells like it. Have a sniff of that."

He passed it across so that I could smell it too. It had a faint but pleasant tang, like a mild disinfectant. I hazarded a guess.

"Is it pine?"

"Near enough. Spruce probably. And I should say it's from somewhere near Trondheim. There's huge forests of the stuff up there."

"You're pulling my leg," I said. "You can't mean to tell me that you know where a piece of wood's come from purely by the smell of it."

"Seriously."

"Seriously?"

"Of course you can. Well, that and the colour of it and how it feels to the touch, the texture of it. Some pine can be rough as a badger's arse – if you know what I mean – but this is quite smooth you see..."

He ran his hand down it again and invited me to do the same. I had to admit that it felt quite sleek, just like Max's coat.

"Hmm..." Don continued musing for a moment but then turned lyrical. "Let's suppose for a moment that you're a wine buff."

"Which I'm not," I said, "but still..."

"Well, let's just suppose that you are. You like drinking the stuff, you can tell good wine from bad and you can probably guess what type it is without being told – you know, whether it's Beaujolais or Merlot or Pinot Noir or whatever. When you go to a restaurant and the wine waiter comes round... What do they call them? They have a fancy name and I can't for the life of me remember it." He clicked his fingers a couple of times. "Help me out here."

"You mean the sommelier."

"That's the chap. Anyway, when the sommelier arrives with your selection, you swirl it round in the glass, hold it up to the light, look at the colour, inhale its bouquet – all that sort of stuff. You never know, you might even sniff the cork. Then, if you're really good, you start talking about where it's come from, who made it, how old it is and the name of the peasant who trod the grapes etc. There are people like that."

"There are indeed," I said. "Fortunately, I'm not one of them."

"Well, it's exactly the same with wood. Think of this plank as if it were a bottle of wine…" (he gave the pine an affectionate pat) "…and the tree that it came from as the grape. You can't drink it of course, but you can see it, touch it, smell it, feel it. And all that gives you clues. A tree grows in soil, the same as a grape, and the kind of soil and the nourishment it gets will determine the nature of the wood. After a while you get to know these things. I may not be right on every occasion, but nine times out of ten I'm not far off."

"That must take decades of practice," I said.

"A few. But then I was in the business for thirty years."

"Of course – though I had no idea you were that close to it. It wasn't something Susan and I used to talk about."

"That's no surprise. Women don't want to get involved in the machinations of business. As long as there's an income at the end of the month, I don't think they're too worried where it comes from – provided it's legal and decent."

"Very true," I said.

"Anyway, I – or rather we (there were two of us, I had a partner) – owned a couple of woodyards, three when the boom took off. We bought stock from all over Scandinavia – and from across the Baltic too, if the price was right. When the wood business went quiet we converted them into builders' merchants to broaden the product range. The whole thing was worth quite a bit when I packed it up. But it all—" He was on the point of telling me something but deliberately changed the subject. "You see that beach there?" He indicated the stretch of sand behind us. "I had that made specially. You won't find another one like it anywhere along the shoreline – it's all rocks and shingle. Five lorry-loads of sand it took to get that done. It was hell's own job getting it down the hill. It was a birthday present for Katerina. When we bought the place she said she was disappointed there wasn't a beach, so I built one. But that's another story." And one he wasn't going to go into at the moment. "Anyway, we can't stand around here chatting all day, we've got work to do."

"Which is?" I said. He still hadn't let me in on the secret.

"What I thought we'd do," said Don, "is build a set of steps for the swimming platform. You know, so you can climb in and out of the water without all this buggering about – and so Madame doesn't go banging her shins again."

"Sounds like a good idea," I said. There was something similar at the back of the launch which he'd used the day before. "Although wouldn't it be easier to buy some?"

"Probably. But they're expensive. Apart from that, it's not half as much fun as making your own."

"After breakfast?"

"After breakfast. We'll get this wood organised first and then we'll go back up to the house."

I helped him pull out half a dozen lengths of the timber. We laid them out on the beach, then made our way back up the hill. Max followed dutifully behind.

Halfway up, I stole a look at my watch.

"No pressure," said Don. "I'm doing breakfast this morning."

"In that case," I said, "I'll stick to just a poached egg and bacon, if it's alright with you."

"That's fine."

Max stared up at me with what I thought was a disapproving look.

"Oh," I added. "And can I have a sausage with that?"

"Sure," Don nodded, and we went indoors.

You might think that spending a morning sawing up lengths of timber is about as interesting as watching paint dry – but you'd be wrong. Actually, watching paint dry can be interesting when it's on film and speeded up – there's something about the patterns and the way the colours change that fascinates me. But then, I'm an actuary and I can see patterns and change in a sea of numbers scrolling down a computer screen, so maybe it's just me.

As for cutting up wood, there's nothing quite like the rasp of the saw as it begins to bite, then that irresistible aroma as a shower of sawdust cascades onto the floor. It's a warm, moist smell, almost like the smell of a freshly mown lawn, and that morning I could catch the tang of the pine. Don't ask me why but there was something undeniably healthy about it.

We set up on the beach outside the boathouse doors. Don made a trestle from some odds and ends to support the timber and we took it in turns to do the work. It wasn't long before he started singing to himself once more.

"La... La,la,la,la... Norwegian wood."

The sun was out in a clear blue sky and it began to get hot. I'd already changed into a pair of shorts – or rather, I'd made myself a pair. The heavy trousers I'd worn the day before were uncomfortable so I'd borrowed a pair of scissors from the kitchen and chopped the legs off a pair of slacks. These were the smart ones I'd brought to play golf in – but there was no way I could see us doing that now. We'd already taken our shirts off and Don had put on his baseball cap to protect his balding pate. Luckily, I had a full head of hair and didn't need one. Max retreated to the shade and took a nap.

Around eleven, Katerina made her first appearance of the day and brought out a tray of refreshments. We stopped and took a break to enjoy a glass of lemon squash and to wipe the sweat from our brows.

"You boys have been working hard," she said, looking at us and the growing pile of sawdust beneath the trestle.

"Terrible 'ard, ma'am," said Don and downed his squash in one.

"Well, I do hope it's going to be worth it."

"It will be, ma'am, it will be."

"How's the leg?" I asked. Spreading from beneath her sticking plaster, a purple stain gave evidence of a nasty bruise.

"Oh, I expect I'll live," she said and brushed the question aside.

Her intervention came at an opportune moment as we'd just finished cutting the last of the wood and were ready to move on to assembly. We were working to the plan that Don had prepared the night before. From time to time he'd get the sketch he'd drawn out of his back pocket and refer to it. By now it had grown grubby and was covered in markings he'd made with the pencil he kept poked up the side of his baseball cap. After Katerina had taken the tray back in, he drew it out again and spread it over the trestle.

"Now, here's what I've got in mind. There's the two side pieces," he pointed at the plan and then at the two corresponding lengths laid out on the beach, "and these are the cross members. We'll screw some small supports on either side to take the weight, here and here." He jabbed his finger at the plan.

"You're not going to glue them then?" I said. I was thinking of my own ill-fated experiences with do-it-yourself furniture.

"Definitely not. That's ok for Katerina, but I'll be using these steps myself and I'm not exactly Cinderella." He gave his broad chest a pat.

I could see his point. I wasn't exactly Cinderella myself and I was still carrying the extra stone I'd sworn I'd get rid of after Christmas. We set to and spent the rest of the morning marking out and drilling ready for final assembly.

Lunch was followed by our usual twenty-minute nap. It was

consequently well into the afternoon before our set of steps was finished – or so I thought. It had taken another couple of hours but at last we could stand and look at a completed structure that replicated our working drawings. I was ready to high-five again, but Don declined.

"We're not done yet."

"We're not?"

"No. This thing's going to spend its life immersed in water so it'll need some protective treatment. I've some ship's varnish in the boathouse so I thought we'd give it a couple of coats. I tell you what." He looked at his watch. "It's nearly four o'clock now. Why don't we go out in the boat for an hour and then we could put the first coat on after tea? It'll dry overnight and we can second coat it in the morning."

We cleared our tools away and walked across to the jetty.

My boating lesson that day was more comprehensive than its predecessor. The course we followed was much the same, out onto the lake then round Cormorant Island, but this time I was shown how to use the throttle and initiated into the mysteries of the compass. By the end of my hour's tuition I could bring the boat to any given bearing and at any given speed, so I felt I was making progress.

Don brought us back in, taking over the controls well before we reached the pontoon. There was no sign of Katerina – she'd wait until we'd finished the steps before taking to the water again. We motored on past and went straight to the jetty.

I wondered what she'd been doing all day. We found her on the deck at the side of the house, stretched out on a sun-lounger in her swimsuit and reading a paperback. The table on the balcony had already been laid and dinner had been prepared in advance. She bookmarked her page, closed up her novel and sat up to greet us.

"Hello, boys. I understand you want to eat early this evening."

"Indeed," said Don. "Yet more work…"

"…for the working man to do." Katerina finished his sentence. "I know, you don't have to tell me. Anyone would think that you didn't enjoy it. Anyway, it's ready whenever you are. Ten minutes?" She slipped on a pair of flip-flops and headed off to the kitchen.

Don and I went to wash our hands and put our shirts on.

The two of us ate on our own that evening, Katerina electing to go back to her book and saying she would dine later on. There was no post-prandial nap either, although we did manage to clear up after ourselves.

Back on the beach, the set of steps lay face down in the sand. Don decided they'd be better standing up and hung a sheet in front of the boathouse doors, then propped them against it. A bank of cloud had drifted across the sun and there was a chill in the air. There was a danger we might lose the light and we hurried to apply our coat of varnish.

Later, when we could no longer see what we were doing, we packed our brushes and pots away and went indoors. Don lit the fire as he'd done on the first night and the three of us sat and chatted over a nightcap. We talked about the house and boating and Malaren and how the noise I could hear at night wasn't birds at all but frogs croaking down at the water's edge. Then we talked about York and my job and how that had come to an end, and Philippa and Jonathon and how they'd got on in their exams. Finally we talked about Susan. We talked about her life, the kind of woman she was and how she was nothing like her mother (*Thank God*, said Don, and laughed) and the idea that if she were sitting somewhere on high and watching us now, how pleased she'd be to see us together and enjoying each other's company. We drank a toast to her and for the first time since she'd gone I found I could say her name without the lump in my throat that usually accompanied it.

It was gone half past ten when I left to walk across the yard to the guesthouse. Behind the bank of cloud the sun still hadn't set and leant against the sheeting in front of the boathouse, our newly-fashioned steps gleamed like a monument in the half light. Through an open door in the outbuildings I caught sight of Max stretched out on a piece of sacking, his tennis ball lying within reach. As I passed, he opened one eye but quickly shut it again.

This time I remembered to pull down the blind, got into bed and fell straight to sleep.

Eight

I woke early again, despite my attention to the blind. I was anxious to go outside and get on with our day – the sun and the steps were waiting and any thought of staying in bed had been banished.

But first I needed to check my phone. The conversation the night before had reminded me how little contact I'd had with my children since my arrival. I'd sent a brief text from the airport to say I'd landed safely but that was all. For Jonathon it was not so important but Philippa I knew would be worried.

I was notorious for my failure to use social media. My excuse was simple – I was male and over fifty. That meant I possessed a mobile phone but rarely turned it on. Philippa, whose life seemed to revolve around the interaction this facility provided, struggled to see how I could exist without it. She tried to tell me about it once in that manner of undisguised hostility teenage girls have when dealing with their fathers.

"For God's sake, Dad, you're so…"

"Neanderthal?" I volunteered.

"Er, no…"

"Prehistoric then?"

"Whatever…"

Her dismissive wave showed she'd given up on me.

My phone was on the bedside table. I switched it on, and sure enough, it pinged to tell me I had a message. It could only be my daughter.

Hi Dad, glad to know you got there safe. How are you? What are you doing? All ok here. Grandma took me shopping! Lul Philx. Say hello to Uncle D and Auntie K.

At least it was readable, despite the code. God forbid that I should ever be called an expert but I did know my laugh out louds from my love you lots. I composed a suitable reply.

Hi sweetheart. Thanks for asking I'm fine. I'm working! Explain

later. D and K send their love. Lul2 Dadx
I clicked on send and closed the phone down.

Max was waiting outside, tennis ball at the ready. We said our good mornings, I started him toward the house and we set off across the yard.

My guess was that Don had already gone down to the beach. As I descended the slope, I saw that the boathouse doors were open and the steps had been put to one side. Don was inside, but instead of singing it sounded as though he was giving himself a good talking to.

"Brackets, brackets, brackets. Where did I put those bloody brackets?" Then, as he heard me arrive, "Morning, Alan."

"Morning, Don."

"How are those steps looking?"

"Fine," I said. "They're dry, I think."

"Good good." He continued rummaging through the box he'd pulled out onto his workbench. "I'm looking for a pair of brackets. I know they're in here somewhere…"

An awkward moment ensued in which I felt I was in the way. Don must have felt it too.

"Tell you what. Why don't you go and stick a second coat of varnish on those steps. They could do with another layer. No point in the two of us being in here." He handed me the tin and the brush we'd been using. "I'll come out just as soon as I've found these bloody brackets."

I took the brush and the tin and went outside. Max followed on.

The application of paint (or in this case, varnish) bears direct comparison to the sawing of wood. Both have a certain therapeutic quality. The steady stroke of the brush resembles the thrust of the saw – and then there's always the smell. With wood it's something to be savoured and inhaled, whereas with paint of course one needs to be careful. Nevertheless, the aroma is not entirely unpleasant, and taken in the smallest of quantities I don't suppose it does any harm. Fumes aside, it leaves space in the mind for constructive thought, and while I gently guided the brush back and forth, I began to anticipate the events of the day.

Don would soon find his brackets, and once we'd fitted them the need would arise for us to transport the steps out to the swimming platform. The steps were here, the platform was there, and in-between rested a significant stretch of water. Therein lay the problem. I'd just got round to a workable solution when Don emerged from the boathouse clutching two pieces of metalwork.

"Here we go, these should do the trick. How's the painting coming along?"

"Great," I said. "In fact, I'm pretty much done. It's got to dry of course."

"Ah… Bugger. Hadn't thought of that. We'll have to wait then. In which case, we may as well go in and have breakfast."

We returned an hour later to find that the varnish had dried. The sun was now well up and it was growing hot once more. Time to strip off. Don had abandoned his after-breakfast nap for once in favour of a trip to the bathroom and had changed back into his speedos.

"The problem is," he mused to himself, "fixing the damn things to the platform. At some stage, somebody's going to have to get wet…"

He offered the brackets up to the wood a couple of times, turning them this way and that, seemingly unable to make up his mind. After a minute or two he grew cross with himself and slapped his thigh.

"Come on, Don, make a decision, we haven't got all day." He settled on a final position and asked me to hand him the drill.

I passed it across and he sank a couple of posidrives. Then he stepped back, made some small adjustments and sank a couple more, the drill fizzing like an angry bee.

"Right, I think that's as good as it's going to get. The proof of the pudding…"

"…will be in the eating."

"Precisely. So let's get packed up and get this thing out there."

We put our tools away and began to organise ourselves. As I was fetching out the green tote box I remembered the words of Don's song and started humming quietly to myself.

"Two men went to mow

Went to mow a meadow…"

Up until that moment Don had been uncharacteristically withdrawn but he now decided to join in.

"Two men, one man and his dog

Went to mow a meadow."

He turned to face me. "You're really into this, aren't you?"

"I suppose I am," I said.

"Well, make the most of it because the next bit's not so easy. Somehow we have to get this," he said, pointing at the steps, "out there." He indicated the far-off platform. "God knows how we're going to do it. The damn things are too big to fit in the boat and it's been worrying me all morning."

"Ah," I said. "I've been thinking about that."

"You have?"

"I have."

"Go on."

"Well, the steps are made of wood, right?"

"Right."

"And wood floats, right? So why don't we simply tow them out there, just like we did the pontoon."

The silence that followed meant I'd either said something incredibly stupid or something incredibly clever. Fortunately it turned out to be the latter.

"D'you know what?" said Don. "You're a genius – an absolutely bloody genius."

"I am?"

"You are. Now let's go and get some towing rope."

We filled our tote box with everything we might need, then loaded it into the boat. We floated the steps, roped them off to the stern and motored out to the pontoon, only this time Max and I travelled on board instead of riding behind. And yes, once we'd moored up, Don stripped down to his trunks and jumped in so that he could position the steps while I knelt on the pontoon and screwed home the brackets into the wooden deck of the platform. Max watched our every move, panting in the heat.

Once we were done, Don tested it out, applying his full weight to every step. Eventually he emerged from the water and pronounced himself satisfied. After he'd dried himself off we sat on the decking for a while, our feet splayed out in front of us while we admired our handiwork – or at least, what little we could see of it, just two short pieces of wood protruding above the edge of the platform like the tips of an iceberg.

"Bloody good job that, I reckon," said Don.

"Yup," I said. "Bloody brilliant in fact."

"I suppose you'll be wanting the afternoon off now."

"Sounds like a good idea."

"And why not, I think I might join you. Tell you what though…"

"What?"

"I could do with a nice cold beer. There's a couple of cans in the fridge up at the house."

"Well that's no good to us now – you should have brought them with us."

"You're right, I should have."

"Maybe next time."

"Yeah, next time…"

We cleared everything away into the tote box and motored back to the jetty.

It grew oppressively hot that afternoon. Whatever breeze there'd been that morning died away and the flags beyond the balcony hung limp and listless. Out over the lake, a few dark clouds had formed and the sultry atmosphere presaged thunder.

Lunch was taken in a sweltering heat. Don appeared clad in nothing save his flip-flops and swimming trunks, Katerina was already in her swimsuit, and after we'd finished eating she went off to the decking to pull her lounger into the shade and began reading while Don assumed his customary post-prandial position.

I'd grown used to his habit of resting each meal. At first it had frustrated me. In our house the daylight hours were filled with activity, not used for napping, and I suppose I must have expected the same in his. But it had gradually dawned on me that Don wasn't necessarily dozing, just resting with his eyes closed, and it was during these periods of supposed shuteye that he was actually planning our next move. Although on this occasion, after twenty minutes waiting patiently for some spark of life I realised he really was fast asleep. With little else in prospect, I took myself off to the guesthouse.

As I say, I don't ever recall sleeping in the afternoon. There may have been moments at work, looking out of that seventh-floor window as the endless columns of figures swam around in my head when I'd closed my eyes for a few short minutes. But I'd never indulged in a proper go-to-bed, draw-the-curtains type session, even when I'd felt shattered on holiday. Siesta was a continental habit and not ever practised at home. Not that I got into bed now. It was far too hot for that, and I settled for crashing out on top of the duvet. If it was good enough for Don, I thought, it must be good enough for me…

I was woken by a ping on my mobile. I looked at my watch. It had gone four o'clock and the shadows on the wall had all moved. I sat on the edge of the bed for a minute to recover, then reached for the phone. The text that had arrived was from Philippa.

Working?! You are so sad though I still lul. Philx

I didn't reply straight away. It would be difficult to tell her what I meant and there was a chance she wouldn't understand. I shut the phone down and went across to the house.

It was deserted and had that curiously eerie feel that empty houses have. The lunch table had been cleared in my absence and in place of our dirty plates lay a pair of swimming trunks with an accompanying note written on the back of an envelope.

Put these on if you're up for it.

The sound of voices floated in from outside. Leaning over the balcony rail, I looked down toward the lake.

Don and Katerina were poised at the end of the jetty, holding hands. They must have been counting – *one, two…three!* – because suddenly they'd jumped and I heard a squeal as warm flesh made contact with cold water. I turned the trunks over in my hands. Much to my relief they were shorts rather than briefs of the type that Don wore. With thoughts of Alice in Wonderland and a bottle marked *Drink Me* in my head, I went to get changed.

I'm not, and never have been, particularly good at swimming. In fact, I've never been particularly good at anything really. Except I will admit to a certain facility with numbers, although that's not a skill that endears me to the population at large. Suffice it to say I can manage the breaststroke and I get along quite happily on my side or my back – but any attempt at the crawl is beyond me and I wouldn't even dream of diving in. What Max made of me as I walked back from the guesthouse, I can only guess. I don't suppose I cut an especially attractive figure – I was middle-aged, overweight and sported a mild case of sunburn and someone else's swimming trunks.

My arrival at the lake was greeted as if I were some kind of celebrity. Don and Katerina were engaged in horseplay in the shallows and I was almost at the bottom of the hill before they realised I was there. They stopped splashing each other and turned to welcome me.

"Hey, hey!" called Don. "Look who's here. It's Mark bloomin'

Spitz! Come on down!"

"Are you coming in, Alan?" asked Katerina. She was standing up so I knew neither of them were out of their depth.

"If I must," I said, squirming my toes into the sandy beach. Beyond the edge of the water, the bottom shelved away to a stony ledge. I dipped my toe in. It felt freezing.

"You'll never get in that way," said Don. "Come to the end of the jetty and jump off like we did."

I went out along the boardwalk and stood at the end of the planking.

"What's the water like?" I said.

"Fabulous," said Don, drops of it glistening on his bald patch.

"You lying bugger. You know you're only saying that."

"Actually," said Katerina, "it's not bad once you get in."

Once you get in. I wriggled my toes again.

Then all at once I'd jumped and I was in. The shock of it hit me as the water closed over my head. Beneath the surface, tiny pieces of black peat went floating by. I came up and blew out but there was no panic – I could stand. I pushed the wet hair back off my forehead.

"Welcome to Malaren," said Don. "You can't say you truly belong here until you've been christened."

"Is that it?" I said. "And I thought I'd jumped in the deep end."

"Oh ha, ha, ha!" said Don.

We gathered in a circle, our toes touching the bottom and pretended to tread water.

"What next?" I said.

"Well now we're all together, we can have a go at swimming out to the platform."

"How far is it?"

Down at the surface it seemed a lot further off than it did from the boat.

"I reckon it's about fifty yards."

"Yes, but what does that mean in terms of an indoor pool?"

"About two lengths."

"I think I can manage that."

Don took the lead with a prolonged and easy crawl while Katerina and I followed with a more sedate version of the breast-stroke.

I was the last to arrive at the pontoon. Beyond the immediate shelter of the shoreline, there was a chop on the surface of the water and I had to turn my head to one side. Don was already helping Katerina up the steps.

"This is a lot easier than the last time I was here," she said.

I managed to get out unaided. The steps felt rock solid and as reliable as you could wish. We lay on the decking for a while to catch our breath and watched the rivulets of water draining off our swimwear and away between the lines of planking.

The sweltering heat had abated. Out on the lake there was the hint of a faint breeze and the dark cloud which had earlier threatened thunder had moved off to leave the sun shining down out of a clear blue sky. It promised to be a glorious evening.

"I don't think it gets much better than this," said Don.

"No," I said, "I don't think it does."

"What I want to know," said Katerina, "is what on earth you boys are going to get up to now you've fixed this up?"

Don waggled his toes. "D'you know what? I'm really glad you've asked me that question."

"In other words," said Katerina, "you haven't a clue."

"Precisely."

"I'm sure you'll find something."

"Oh, you can bank on that," said Don. "We'll find something, that's for sure."

And lying there, with the sun beating down and looking up at that cloudless sky, I had every confidence that we would.

Nine

That night we held an impromptu barbecue on the beach. We gathered in the hollow where the pontoon had been, Don found a pair of breezeblocks at the back of the boathouse and with a grill-shelf from the kitchen he fashioned something to cook on. The meal itself was not as inventive; breakfast sausages which arrived somewhat charred, but when hidden between slices of crusty bread and garnished with lashings of ketchup, they proved extremely acceptable. Max didn't complain, anyway.

Digestion was aided by a generous supply of alcohol. The beer we'd missed that morning was retrieved from the fridge and placed in a bucket loaded with ice in the shallows next to the jetty. We helped ourselves at regular intervals. Katerina preferred wine and we soon dispensed with social niceties, Don and I drinking straight from our cans, she straight from the bottle. By the end of the evening we were all a little drunk.

I'm sure I was. I'm sure Don was too, a fact which became clear when we linked arms and danced round the fire to our third chorus of "Two Men Went to Mow". And I can't remember who tripped over first but all of a sudden there we were, lying horizontal and laughing ourselves silly, the beer dribbling out of our cans and staining the sand. By this time Katerina had seen enough and gathering up her bottle and her blanket, retreated back up the hill.

"I'll leave you boys to it…"

We picked ourselves up and rearranged our limbs into some kind of sensible order.

Don waited until the lights had come on in the house, then reached into the pocket of his shorts and drew out a keychain which he dangled in front of my nose.

"You must be joking," I said. "It's a bit late at night for a boating lesson".

It must have been nearing twelve, though there was still a

glimmer of light to the west.

Don shook his head and pressing a finger to his lips, motioned me to follow him. Given what he had in mind, how he expected Katerina not to hear us I shall never know.

We stumbled along the jetty but instead of going left and to the launch, he drew me to the right and the speedboat. God knows what induced me to follow him, but when he invited me down I clambered into it, just as though the idea were my own.

We sniggered like a pair of errant schoolboys as we unclipped the covers and drew them back. Don turned the key and began firing up.

Chick-a-boom, chick-a-boom, chick-a-boom.

At the first time of asking there was nothing. Nor at the second. But at the third came a throaty roar as the power of the outboard motor burst into vibrant life. Something wild and dangerous throbbed and bubbled at the back of the boat.

I cast off at the stern, then at the bow and I barely had time to hop down behind the windshield before we were off, clearing the jetty and out into open water in a matter of seconds. Don swung round onto our usual course and pushed the throttle wide open. We shot forward into the night and I felt the front of the boat lift as Don adjusted the trim. We began to skip across the waves, great gouts of spray spattered the windshield and I found it hard to keep my balance as we bronco'd up and down.

The same cowboy spirit that infected the boat had also infected Don and I heard him shouting above the roar of the engine. "Yi ha! Ride 'em on out, boys!"

I wasn't offered the wheel – nor had I any desire to take it as I was completely engaged in clinging to whatever piece of the superstructure I thought might survive the journey.

Cormorant Island loomed up on our left surprisingly quickly, rising out of the water like a dark mythological beast, its back covered in prickly spines. All at once we were beyond it and Don was swinging the wheel hard over as we lurched into our turn. A sheet of spray shot up from our starboard side, disdainfully showering the pair of white buoys that marked the rocks.

Then we were back on a straight course and heading for home. We approached the pontoon at breakneck speed, missing it by inches, and for a second I thought we were going to plough straight into the beach. Heart in mouth, I pressed my feet hard against the bulkhead in a vain imitation of braking, but at the very last moment Don shut down the throttle and swung the wheel hard round. Thrown violently forward at first and then to one side, I overbalanced and fell backwards in the boat, sprawling onto the plastic cushions covering the seats in the stern. We suddenly lost way and slowly drifted in to the side of the jetty.

Don jumped out and started tying us off, then landed back beside me with a thump. "Enjoy that, did you?"

My heart was pounding like a jackhammer and I was immediately stone-cold sober. "Don't you ever do that to me again," I said.

Don gave me the broadest of grins. Reaching into the top pocket of his T-shirt, he produced two cylindrical tubes and handed one of them to me. "Here, have a cigar."

I unscrewed the tube and took it out. It was Cuban, Havana, one of the best and the tip had already been cut. The guttering flame of a lighter appeared and before I knew it the thing was between my lips, aflame, and I'd inhaled.

We lay for a while on the plastic cushions, smoking our cigars and blowing the smoke up into the darkening sky.

"You won't tell Katerina, will you?" said Don.

"About what?" I said. "The cigars?"

"Yeah. Or the boat trip."

"No, I won't."

Although she was bound to know – the noise of the outboard would tell her and the smell of cigar smoke would linger on his breath long after he'd gone to bed. But these were our secrets and

I was bound to keep them.

Back at the guesthouse I sat on the edge of the bed and cried. God knows why. Maybe I was tired again, maybe it was relief at having survived the boat trip, or maybe it was that awkward thing you keep deep inside and have to let out now and then. I soon dried up and told myself not to be so stupid.

My phone was still switched on and lying on the bedside table. I remembered I owed Philippa a text. This time I could send her something she'd understand.

Went swimming and had a barbecue. Eat your heart out! Lul Dadx

Don was not up early the following morning. Max and I searched for him in the boathouse and along the beach but we could find no trace. It was the first time he'd failed us, even when Katerina had hurt her leg. The easy explanation was that he was suffering from the effects of the night before, but I liked to think he was made of sterner stuff and that he'd simply decided on a well-deserved lie-in. Why ever not? He'd earnt it – the pontoon was afloat, the steps were finished and he'd already enjoyed his swim.

So the dog and I were left to our own devices and with a couple of hours to ourselves before breakfast, we spent them exploring the estate and the forest that surrounded us. Of course, Max walked much further than I did on this excursion since we took his ball and the process of finding it after I'd lobbed it into the undergrowth involved numerous long diversions.

At first we headed west and discovered a footpath between the trees. Now and then we came across breaks where a house had been constructed and in deference to the Swedish way, we kept our heads down as we passed. When the path petered out onto a rocky shore, we doubled back east and walked along the beach. Our way seemed blocked by the boathouse but once we'd pushed beyond it we found ourselves on a small promontory jutting out into the lake. At the water's edge the trees thinned out, and as it narrowed to a point we came across open ground.

Facing toward the water, someone had erected a swing-seat of the type you might find on the porch of an American house. Long-forgotten and neglected, it had grown weather-beaten and tatty, but it was comfortable nevertheless and afforded an open view of the lake. I was glad of a break and sat for a while in contemplation as Max rested at my feet.

In front of us lay the broad expanse of a reed bed. I can't have been there for more than a few minutes when the breeze got up and I was sure it carried with it the sound of someone's voice. I looked around, thinking I'd see a figure emerge from between the trees behind me but no one appeared. Then the breeze returned and I knew it had to be Susan, her low whisper hidden amongst the rustling of the reeds and the shaking of dry leaves.

I'd thought for some time she'd been with me. I'd be halfway through sawing a piece of wood, or in the middle of a post-prandial doze and I'd suddenly get the feeling someone was watching me. I'd turn, half expecting to see a shadow. Sometimes it had been while I was out with the dog or once, when driving the boat. Then there was that occasion when I was sure she'd told me to take off my shirt.

Even without these constant reminders, I was never going to forget about her. Work is a therapeutic thing but you can't do it twenty-four hours a day and besides, I wasn't trying to block her out. The time I was spending with Don, I valued for itself and if she wanted to share it with me that was fine.

But here was a chance to be alone with her and I could tell her how much I missed her. She asked me how I was doing and I told her I was fine and that everything was alright. Her next enquiry concerned the children and I told her what I knew – how Jonathon had gone to France and how Philippa kept in touch and there wasn't a day went by that I didn't get a text of some description. I told her about Don and Katerina and how kind they'd been, and then about woodwork and boating, and of course I introduced her to Max. She laughed and said she knew she'd been right all along about a dog and how glad she was I'd finally come round to her way of thinking. I reminded her of how she'd called me mean and how much that had hurt me and she said she was sorry and could we still be friends. I said of course and I told her I still loved her and she said she still loved me. Then I went back to the house.

After that I began to visit the swing-seat as often as I could, at least once and sometimes twice a day. I took a lot of comfort from being there. And having made my peace with Susan, I found I could go to work with a clear conscience.

Work – ah yes, there's the irony. I'd come to Sweden to escape it and now I couldn't get enough. Although this was work of an entirely different kind. For years I'd been employed for the sake of my brain but this required use of my hands – hands, incidentally, which at first became raw and blistered through unaccustomed use but gradually hardened as the days went by.

I'd discovered that I shared Don's fascination with wood. He was right and there was something undeniably special about it – the touch of it, the feel of it and the thought of what might be done with it. Then there was the smell of it too, a smell that surrounded me wherever I went – the scent of pine that hung in the air from the trees whenever I stepped out of the guesthouse, the warmth like a sauna in my little room as soon as the sun got up, and the bittersweet odour of the smoke from the logs that snapped and crackled in the fire we lit each night.

And just as his wife had foreseen, Don had any number of projects up his sleeve with which to keep us occupied. We began by mending the boathouse roof (a job he told me he'd been meaning to do for years) and then we repaired the fencing on the western boundary. We painted the front of the balcony and lopped the trees that kept the sun from Katerina's piece of decking. There seemed no end to it but I was a willing accomplice in all his schemes and in pursuance of my new employment I wielded the saw and the paintbrush to my heart's content.

Time progressed and we'd all but exhausted the tasks on our list when Don came up with his master plan. He was thinking of upgrading the jetty. Why have an elaborate platform with a set of steps in the middle of the lake, he argued, when we were forced to jump in and make such an undignified beginning? An extension was required which could act as a proper setting-off point and there was even talk of a sundeck down by the water.

I heard these plans expounded over the coffee table as we drank our nightcaps in front of the fire after dinner. Before long, a hand-drawn sketch appeared and then a proper working drawing. The contents of the woodstore were deemed insufficient so we started visiting woodyards and bought countless quantities of wood. We took the Land Rover (and the dog) and piled the roof rack high. When we got home, we stacked the lengths on the beach where the pontoon had been. Getting it all down the hill was a long and laborious task but we managed. Driving the piles for the foundations into the bed of the lake was more problematic. We resorted to hiring a machine and waited on the veranda while its continual *thump, thump, thump* drove us all mad. Katerina complained bitterly at the noise.

"You'll be glad of it in the end," Don told her.

But at last it was done and we could start erecting the superstructure.

The sun shone and we sweated. I was continually outside with my shirt off. I told Philippa about it. The reply she sent me was worthy of her mother.

Be careful. Put on plenty of suncream and don't get burnt. Lul Philx

But I didn't have any suncream, I hadn't thought to pack it. And neither did I need any, as after a while I simply didn't burn any more and I gradually acquired a tan. Soon, I was as bronzed as Don.

And, just as fit. What with all the bending and stretching and the heaving of heavy wood, I was getting all the exercise I needed. At the end of each day every bone in my body ached but

I started toning up. I lost weight too and that additional stone I'd been carrying began to slip away.

The swimming must have helped. Every afternoon we had an hour of it. When Katerina came down in her costume around four o'clock, that was our signal to pack our tools away and join her.

We fitted the boating in whenever we could. I was never allowed near the speedboat but bit by bit I gained mastery of the launch. The day I took charge from the moment we stepped on board to the moment we landed back safe was marked in red on the calendar.

"Well done," said Don.

His approbation meant everything.

There were times when it rained, but they were few and far between. Sometimes, if it was just a shower, we didn't even bother to stop working. At night, after dinner, we'd light the fire in the lounge and the three of us would gather round the coffee table and play countless rounds of gin rummy.

The days went by – a week, a fortnight, maybe a month, I really wasn't counting. I was in a good place and I'd no thought of calling an end to it. I was amongst friends and frankly, I didn't much care what I did.

Then came the telephone call – and that changed everything.

Part Three

Visitors

One

I hadn't realised there was a telephone in the house. Had I known, I'd have asked to use it to call home instead of all the texts I'd been sending Philippa. But I didn't and I hadn't so that was that, and later on I didn't feel like using it at all.

It was one of those hot and sultry days and we were sitting out on the veranda having lunch. I suppose it was somewhere between one and half past (no one was concerned as to the time) when there was a muffled *brrr* from out in the hallway. I think the handset must have been hidden behind one of the coats on the coat rack, none of which had been touched in a while.

My hosts exchanged a look of surprise; Don loaded another fork full of salad (a clear signal he had no intention of answering it) so it was Katerina who put down her napkin and pushed back her chair.

"I'll go."

I continued eating. This was no business of mine.

Katerina quickly returned, bearing a message of stark simplicity. "It's Kurt."

She and Don exchanged another look, much as I'd seen them do once before, which I thought contained an element of nervousness. Then it was his turn to put down his napkin and stand up.

"Excuse me..."

Katerina resumed her seat, although she neither looked at me nor offered any explanation. As a result, we could both overhear what was being said in the hallway.

"Hello? Oh, hi, Kurt... No, no, we were just having a spot of lunch... Yes, yes, we're fine... I see... What, this afternoon? Well, what time is it now?" Don consulted his watch. "Say, about half past two then? At the marina? What mooring are you in? Ok, got it... Yes, we'll see you later then. Bye..."

There was a click as the phone went down and Don returned

to the table.

Bar the clattering of cutlery and plates, there was silence for a moment until Katerina enquired, "Is Anna with him?"

"I guess so," said Don. "I didn't think to ask." Then he remembered there were three of us and that to exclude me would be rude. "Sorry, Alan. This is Kurt and Anna. They're friends..." (another look between him and Katerina) "...of ours. They have a yacht they keep on the lake and they sometimes come and visit. The thing is, we never know when they're going to turn up. They're at the marina just up the coast. They wanted us to go over there for lunch. I said it was a bit late for that, so we've been invited for a cup of tea. I hope that's alright."

"Of course," I said. I was hardly in a position to object.

"We'll take the launch. It'll be easier than going by road – it's only twenty minutes over the water."

It was actually less than fifteen. But by the time we'd finished eating, cleared away and got ourselves changed (we could hardly go visiting in swimming trunks or a pair of cut-offs) it was already time to go. We assembled on the jetty, Don and I in our best T-shirts and shorts while Katerina came equipped with a wide-brimmed straw hat as protection against the sun.

Max followed us down, his tail wagging furiously as he sensed that something was afoot, but we were forced to leave him behind. I have to say he looked rather forlorn when he realised he wasn't coming. As we motored away, he turned and trotted mournfully back up the hill, presumably to find some shade and the comfort of his sacking.

We headed east at a modest pace, but instead of our usual course toward Cormorant Island we kept close in to the shore. A row of the familiar white buoys marked the channel. I wasn't asked to drive.

I don't know what kind of image the word 'yacht' conjures up in your mind, but for me it's invariably associated with power and privilege. Amongst his many other ships I don't doubt that Aristotle Onassis had a yacht, several in fact, although I'm sure they would have been of the motorised kind, the type you see moored up at Monaco or Cannes. Personally, I tend to think of sailing vessels, of the America's Cup and Cowes and Ted Heath and of ploughing through six-foot waves with nothing but a twelve-knot breeze to push you along. But then, I have to admit to a fascination with wind power and the idea that you can go anywhere in the world without so much as starting up an engine.

Still, these things are the toys of the rich and famous. For mere mortals such as ourselves, the most we can aspire to is a two-handed dinghy at the local club, and if we're lucky, a decent stretch of water to sail it on. Not that I ever have done mind, although I've thought about it a few times – there's something inherently appealing about the challenge of taking on the elements. But Susan was never the sailing kind and preferred the comfort of her own home to the storm-tossed misery of an open boat. So in the end nothing got done and I was obliged to observe sailing from a distance.

Remember that old saying – you can't judge a book by its cover? Let's adapt that a little and say you can't tell a man by his boat. I for one would disagree with that and I'm sure Don would too. The fact that a man *has* a boat tells you something – and the fact he has a yacht a lot more.

There were plenty of yachts at the marina. They came in all shapes and sizes and to be truthful, Kurt's yacht wasn't the biggest. But it was big enough and sleek and white and modern, with a forty-foot mast and polished silver winches for hauling the sails, although at the moment they were all neatly furled away. You couldn't fail to be impressed by it and although it wasn't overly ostentatious, it did make you wonder as to the kind of man who owned it.

Well, just like the mast on his boat, Kurt was tall and imposing and as he waited at the end of the quay to welcome us aboard, my instant reaction was to think of Robert Redford and that scene from *The Great Gatsby* where he stands on the lawn in his tennis whites, the sleeves of his pullover draped casually over his shoulders. Kurt too was blond and good-looking, although his face lacked Redford's boyish charm and was rather more craggy and possessed of a fixated sneer about the lips that made him appear rather cruel. It was doubtless a face that was attractive to women, although possibly for all the wrong reasons. I know it was wrong of me and I know you're going to tell me that I shouldn't jump to conclusions, but I took an instant dislike to him and I guess that coloured our relationship from there on in.

I didn't see Anna at first. She must have been below in the cabin or in the well at the stern of the boat because it wasn't until we'd arrived that she showed herself. One thing I remember for certain – she wasn't waiting on the quay with Kurt.

We'd been to the harbour-master's office to check the location of the mooring. There'd been a queue which had delayed us and I suppose Kurt had grown anxious as to our whereabouts. Anyway, he seemed keen to get us on board, giving Katerina a quick kiss on the cheek before handing her down into the stern, then shaking Don by the hand. After I'd been introduced and acknowledged by a brief nod of the head and that abrupt *Hey* that passes for hello in Sweden, I was the last to go down onto the boat.

Katerina had already removed her hat and she and Anna were engaged in a long and sisterly hug. It required Anna to stoop to put cheek to cheek. She wasn't as tall as Kurt (I don't think he could have endured to be with a woman he couldn't dominate) but her height was significant nonetheless. Although just like Katerina, she appeared far from typically Swedish. She might be tall but she was no willowy blonde, having a full figure and straight black hair that went no further than her shoulders. The women sat down, we settled into our places on the cushioned seating, and the talking began.

There's a certain predictability about social conversations between couples in the Western world. The men gather in one corner and talk about sport and motorcars while the women gather in another and talk about fashion, weight loss and family matters. It's no different in Sweden, although whereas Don and Kurt nattered on about boating and business, at least they spoke in English. The chitchat between Katerina and Anna was conducted entirely in Swedish so I could only guess at what was said – though I don't suppose I'm very far wrong.

Sandwiched between the two, I was part of neither one conversation nor the other so I was forced to endure both without making a single contribution. I heard my name mentioned a couple of times (at which I nodded my head and smiled obligingly) but other than that I was a passenger.

Anna did glance at me once and I thought her eyes flickered occasionally in my direction, but I thought nothing of it at the time. I was more concerned with the idea of tea, or at least *something* to drink as I'd had nothing since lunch and my throat was parched from the heat. But despite the professed reason for our visit, nothing was forthcoming and I was obliged to suffer in silence.

I consequently withdrew into my shell and indulged in thoughts of my own. I'd nothing to add to either boating or business and as I didn't speak Swedish, participation with the women wasn't possible. Did I yawn at one point and look at my watch? I sincerely hope not, but I can honestly say I have no recollection of anything meaningful that was said save for the closing lines.

We'd been sitting there for the best part of an hour when there was a lull in affairs. The women looked across at the men and the men looked across at the women. *Great,* I thought, *this means we're either going to leave, in which case we can get back to work, or someone's going to suggest we have a pot of tea.* Much to my dismay, it turned out to be neither.

"I've been thinking," said Katerina. (I was immediately filled with trepidation – in my experience when a woman says she's been thinking it usually leads to some unwanted consequence. With Susan it was invariably a domestic chore of some kind, e.g. *I've been thinking – we could do with an extra shelf in the spare room.*) "Why don't we invite Kurt and Anna to come and stay with us for a few days? Anna says they can leave the boat here – they've already booked the mooring for the week. We've no plans to go anywhere, Alan could move into the back bedroom for the time being and they could have the guesthouse. What d'you think, Don?"

Don, damn him, was his usual affable self. "Sounds ok to me – if Alan doesn't mind?"

Actually, Alan did mind. Alan minded a lot, but was too polite to say so. I gave a shrug of my shoulders and tried to look as non-committal as possible. I hoped I might get some support from Kurt and I looked in his direction – but he simply shrugged too and looked as non-committal as I did. It seemed we were both cornered.

"Good," said Katerina. "That's settled then. It'll be nice to have some company."

I found her remark quite hurtful. She'd implied that I wasn't company enough, and even though she may have been thinking of me just as much as she was of herself and of Don, the cut went deep. Yet I can see now why I should have been more under-standing. Don and I had no need of more company – we had each other's – but Katerina was alone for long periods of the day and there must have been moments when she yearned for compan-ionship. With Anna she could share time with another woman and they seemed particularly close. But at the time the thought did not occur to me and I remained selfish and resentful.

Don was of no help whatsoever. The social consequences of his decision had passed him by and he was already dealing with the practicalities. "Why not come back in the launch with us now?" he suggested. "There's plenty of room on board."

I must admit I'd have found this difficult to cope with. Fortunately, Anna declined. She said she needed an hour to pack and didn't want to keep us waiting. But Don was not to be put off that easily and immediately offered to come and fetch them in the Land Rover. Kurt would have none of it.

"Not necessary," he countered. Apart from taking the mooring for a week they'd also booked a car for excursions and would drive themselves over. It was agreed that we'd see them later.

As we walked back to the launch, Katerina slipped her arm through that of her husband and gently patted his wrist. "Thank you."

He responded with a benevolent smile. There were no sides to Don. His strategy was inherently simple. Whatever made Katerina happy made him happy too – he needed no more than that. Arm in arm, I let them walk ahead of me and while Don helped his wife down into the launch, I began casting off the ropes. For the time being I'd become no more than a boatman – but I could still do my job when required.

Our journey back home was a quiet one.

Two

Preparations for the arrival of our visitors began as soon as we returned to the house. There was a lot to do in a short space of time and tasks would have to be delegated. Despite my temporary detachment even I knew that, based on my experience of such events at home.

A palpable sense of panic set in. Having surveyed the contents of the larder, Katerina decreed there was not enough food to feed five people for a day, never mind a week and that she and Don would have to go to the supermarket in Eskilstuna and fetch some supplies. As Don had already told me, that was a forty-mile round trip and they'd be gone for at least two hours. While they were away, could I do them an immense favour and move myself out of the guesthouse and into the back bedroom? This would be extremely helpful as barring their own, the guesthouse was the only room with a double bed. They would willingly have done this themselves but Katerina had in mind a special meal for the evening and needed time to get it ready. A traditional dish, it was Kurt's favourite. She cooked it for him every time he came, and if she didn't serve it he would be disappointed. Not wishing to be the immediate cause of any dissatisfaction on Kurt's part, I readily agreed. I was damned if I was going to clean the guest-house afterwards mind, but I could at least ship out in good order.

The moment they'd gone and I heard the Land Rover depart up the drive, I bunked off and went to the kitchen to make myself the cup of tea I'd been denied all afternoon. Moving accommodation, I decided, could wait.

I soon discovered that my new quarters were far from ideal. The back bedroom to which I'd been relegated was windowless and decidedly pokey, and it must have originally been intended for children as a pair of bunk beds had been erected against the right-hand wall. The bottom bunk was empty but the top one was piled high with pillows and duvets and a variety of spare linen. I made up a bed as best I could.

The place was now in use as a store room. The opposite wall was crowded with cardboard boxes and plastic bags packed full of goodness knows what and by pushing these up into one corner I was able to create enough space to accommodate my suitcase. Deprived of a set of drawers, I guessed I'd be living out of it for a while.

I was obliged to make at least two trips back and forth across the yard. On the first of these I was accompanied by Max who ran enthusiastically up and down with his head cocked to one side. On the second occasion he lost interest and returned to the outbuildings and his piece of sacking where he'd presumably spent the afternoon dozing. It seemed I was no longer headline news.

Our guests turned up soon after eight. Their arrival had been preceded by an hour of what I can only describe as intense activity, Katerina spending the large part of it in the kitchen, an area from which Don and I were banned despite our willingness to help. She did manage to find five minutes to get changed, and for the first time ever I saw her in a skirt and top instead of the jeans or swimsuit I'd grown used to. Don swopped his T-shirt and shorts for a smart shirt and a pair of slacks. I took my cue and followed suit although my attire was somewhat creased, having spent the last two hours in the bottom of my suitcase. So much for Katerina's proclamation about not dressing for dinner.

I say 'cue' as if I were an actor in a play. I felt as though I was, but my part was distinctly limited and to tell the truth, I actually felt in the way. The lead roles were already taken as Don and Katerina went through what looked like a set routine – while she cooked, he laid the table in the dining area and organised the drinks cabinet. I considered excusing myself and taking the dog for a walk but I sensed that would have been rude.

Eventually Don took pity on me, and rather than see me stand around with my hands in my pockets, he gave me the task of filling a number of wooden bowls with nuts and crisps and setting them out on the balcony table. It at least enabled me to retreat off-stage and I could keep myself to myself.

Before we had time to think, there was a knock at the door and suddenly the hallway was full of people. They'd come bearing gifts – a bouquet of flowers for the hostess and a bottle of wine for the host (coals to Newcastle this, I thought). The elaborate ritual of shaking hands and kissing cheeks was performed for the second time that day although thankfully, I was for the most part excluded. I got the briefest of nods from Kurt but I'd yet to receive any such acknowledgement from Anna – except there was another quick glance of the eyes. I responded with my best attempt at a smile. She too had changed, also into a dress, although I was not given long to admire it as she disappeared straight into the kitchen with Katerina. Their departure left the three of us men to wander out onto the balcony and wait to be called to the table. Don poured some drinks (gin and tonics, I think) and we began to make inroads into the bowls of nibbles I'd so slavishly prepared.

Kurt must have thought himself already smartly dressed as he'd not bothered to change and was still in the same set of whites he'd worn at the boat. The collar of his shirt was deliberately turned up in a pose which appeared particularly pretentious, although to give him the benefit of the doubt it may have been to enable his pullover to fit comfortably round his neck and shoulders. A pair of designer sunglasses was pushed to the top of his head. His whole demeanour was one of extreme nonchalance and I don't think he cared whether he was spoken to or not. There being no other party to divert my attention, this time it was hard to see how I could be excluded but it took a positive effort from Don to bring me into the conversation. I was dreading any form of introduction which involved Susan and use of the word 'sorry'.

"I didn't mention it before, but Alan works in insurance."

I nodded gracefully.

"Oh really." The permanent sneer that affected Kurt's lip made him sound naturally contemptuous. "And what does he do in insurance?"

"Good question," said Don, turning toward me. "D'you know, Alan, I've never really understood just exactly what it is you do."

"I don't think I've ever really understood it myself," I said, trying to make a joke of it. "Although in fact I'm an actuary."

"An actuary?" said Kurt. "And what the hell is that?"

"Well, I specialise in risk, but generally speaking we make predictions about how long people are going to live given certain pre-existing conditions."

"You mean you can tell me when I'm going to die?"

"Barring complete accidents, I can give you a pretty good estimate, yes."

"That's ridiculous."

"Maybe – but true."

Kurt leant back in his wicker chair and gave me a long hard look. "Ok," he said slowly, "so you tell me how long you think I've got left."

"Why? Are you suffering from any particular illness?"

He shook his head.

"Alright then. How old are you?"

"Forty-eight."

I began to make a quick mental calculation. While he was waiting, Kurt reached into his trouser pocket and fetched out a packet of cigarettes and a gold lighter and proceeded to light up. I had a swift rethink.

"And how many of those are you on a day?"

"What does that matter?"

"It all counts."

He shrugged. "Thirty, forty, I don't exactly keep score."

I reworked my figures and then took a couple of years off for the hell of it. "Well, you might make seventy if you're lucky."

He shrugged again and looked away and out over the balcony. I had the impression he wasn't really bothered how long he lived. It might be today, it might be tomorrow, but when he was gone, he was gone, and that was it. In the meanwhile there was time for another gin and tonic and another cigarette. Don replenished the drinks.

I was desperate to know what *he* did for a living. I think I already knew the answer but I just wanted to hear him tell me himself. Whatever it was, he certainly didn't work in insurance – that would have been far too mundane. I doubted he was even employed. He was probably a self-made millionaire, a bucca-neering entrepreneur with a story to tell about how he'd left school at fourteen with no qualifications and pulled himself up by the bootstraps. Or perhaps he'd just got lucky. Either way, it was a story I knew it would hurt me to hear and I felt I would regret putting the question. But what little devil there is in me was driving me on so I decided to do it anyway.

"So, tell me about yourself, Kurt. What do you do then?"

He was sitting opposite me, side on, with his legs crossed and facing toward Don. They looked at each other for a second and I was sure something passed between them, much the same as had passed between Don and Katerina earlier.

It was Don himself who answered. "Kurt and I used to be in business together. You could even say we still are."

"You mean woodyards and builders' merchants and the like?"

"Indeed. And the like... In fact, Kurt is still quite involved. Aren't you, Kurt?"

Kurt, who'd remained side on and hadn't looked at me once since I'd pronounced on his truncated life expectancy, declined to give any form of answer and blew a cloud of cigarette smoke up toward the ceiling.

Don waited patiently for a moment and when nothing was

forthcoming, looked at his watch and turned his head hopefully in the direction of the kitchen.

"I think dinner should be just about ready..."

Three

It was a squeeze to get everyone seated round the table in the dining area. There were five of us crammed into a space originally designed for four. Katerina sat at the head, partly because she needed access to the kitchen and partly because she took it on herself to assume the most awkward position. Flanked by Don and Kurt, I thought her a rose between two thorns – although it wasn't Don who was the prickly one...

This awkward ad-hoc arrangement left Anna and I squashed up against the far wall, facing each other. My guess was that we'd been put there as we weren't going to be called on to leave our seats. The one benefit of our position was that we could look out of the small side window. I had a view to the west and the setting sun, and during the course of the evening (which seemed extraordinarily long and protracted) I was treated to a fabulous display of colour. Anna faced east and was presumably confronted by the pair of flagpoles.

I spent the larger part of my time trying to avoid making contact with her knees beneath the table. I can't say it was deliberate on her part, she was tall and long-legged, but it seemed that whichever way she pointed them, they got in the way.

I could not, however, avoid making contact with her eyes. If I found her looking at me (which I occasionally did) I could obviously look away, but during the continual round of toasts I could not, and it meant we were forced together.

I was already well-schooled in the Swedish practice of toasting and how it requires you to engage with your opposite number by looking them squarely in the eye. The Swedes are a Nordic people and generally keep themselves to themselves, but to bottle out on a toast is considered rude.

That evening I found myself looking into Anna's eyes rather a lot. In her desire to maintain her traditions, and also to satisfy Kurt, the special meal Katerina had been planning was Kräftskiva

– which translated into English means crayfish party. This would normally have involved the use of bibs, silly hats and lanterns but there were none to be found in the shops (thank God). It was not quite crayfish season either, but there'd been enough of the little critters in the freezer section of the supermarket to feed five of us, and together with some knackebrod and a couple of cheese pies we were about as close as you could get. The main thing was, there was alcohol, plenty of alcohol, and with it, many, many toasts. Hence the repeated eye contact and the general slide into oblivion.

We were drinking akvavit, a form of schnapps. It comes in a shot glass, it's clear and seemingly innocuous – but in reality, it's lethal. It smells, and tastes, like aeroplane fuel. Not that I've ever drunk aeroplane fuel but if I had, I'm sure that's what it would have been like. It had been the subject of a standing joke between Susan and I. One year, we'd ventured to Greece for our annual summer holiday. After every evening meal we were presented with a complimentary glass of the local version of the stuff. We were never quite sure what to do with it, but Susan finally suggested we should collect it all together in a bottle and hand it in at the airport as a contribution toward our passage home.

The advantage of drinking akvavit at a Kräftskiva is that it masks the taste of the crayfish – or rather, the soup that it comes in. Although it's not so much the taste that's the problem, it's the way you're supposed to drink it. The idea is that everyone selects a crayfish from the central pile (they're meant to be served cold – ours were still warm as they hadn't had time to cool off) and the first thing you do is suck out the juice from its intestines. Yes, that's right, *you suck out the juice from its intestines*. It's only then that you're allowed to eat the meat. Well, you can call me squeamish if you like, but I baulked at the idea and personally, I couldn't wait to wash it down with the schnapps, aeroplane fuel or not.

All this takes place to the accompaniment of an appropriate

drinking song. There were several sung that evening, but there was one that particularly stood out. The Swedes call it "Helan går!". I have no intention of repeating it here but suffice it to say I had no idea what it meant (and I've no idea now) but that didn't seem to matter as long as you sang it with gusto and downed your schnapps afterwards. Needless to say I stumbled through it at first, but I gradually got the gist.

We took it in turns to propose the next song. "Helan går!" was the favourite, but when it came to my choice I was obviously stumped.

"I don't know any Swedish songs," I protested.

"That doesn't matter," said Don. "Give us an English one instead."

I'm afraid to admit that in the heat of the moment all I could think of was "Two Men Went to Mow" – at least I was confident of the tune and the words. It evoked a great roar of laughter, although whether it was the content or my rendition of it that provoked the hilarity round the table I'm not too sure.

As soon as I'd finished I decided I wasn't going to have any more akvavit. I'd rather injudiciously stood up to sing, and immediately I did so I felt dizzy. Not only that, but when I sat back down for the toast, I was disconcerted to find that Anna's eyes were beginning to appear very deep, very blue, and very, very enticing...

No one seemed to enjoy the evening's entertainment more than Kurt. He was the first to take his crayfish, the first to start his song, and the first to down his schnapps. He was also the last as he seemed to drink two to everybody else's one.

Although I have to say that Don ran him a pretty close second. I'd already spent an evening drinking with Don that night we'd barbecued on the beach and I can tell you he's a hard man to keep up with. I hadn't managed it then and I couldn't manage it now (not that I was trying). And whether he was simply drawn into it, or whether he was determined not to be left behind, but he appeared to want to match Kurt drink for drink. One bottle of akvavit soon bit the dust, closely followed by a second. When this was emptied Don lumbered off to the drinks cabinet in the lounge and produced a third.

By then, the rest of us had had enough. I'd become acutely aware of my own limitations, as I'm sure had Katerina and Anna, and so this third bottle remained permanently between the two men and didn't do the rounds. And with each additional crayfish and each additional song, its contents gradually diminished.

When the central plate had finally been cleared and there was nothing left to toast, we gave a round of applause to the hostess and there came a lull in proceedings as we sank back in our chairs and enjoyed a reflective silence.

But it didn't last long. Kurt soon broke ranks and without so much as an *excuse me*, rose from the table and went out onto the balcony, taking the half-empty bottle of schnapps and a glass with him. Don immediately followed. I was happy to stay where I was. At that particular moment, the more distance there was between me and that bottle the better.

Katerina got up and began clearing the table. With half her guest list gone, there seemed little else she could do. I sensed a look of disapproval on her face.

Anna waited patiently for my reaction, then pointed in the direction of the balcony. "Aren't you going to join them?"

"No," I said. "Not yet. Perhaps later. I think I need a few minutes to recover."

There was another short silence, punctuated by the clattering of dishes, then she said, "I liked your song very much."

"What? 'Two Men Went to Mow'?"

"Yes, I thought you sang it very well."

"Really?" I affected surprise although I was sure it had gone down well. "I think the schnapps probably had something to do with it."

"Ah yes," she murmured, "the schnapps..."

It was the first time I'd heard her speak other than in the Swedish she'd used to talk to Katerina. She carried the trace of an accent, but otherwise it was excellent.

"Your English is very good," I commented.

"Thank you. But you shouldn't be surprised. Almost everyone with any kind of education in Sweden learns to speak English."

"That sounds like a very middle-class thing to do. I suppose the next thing you're going to tell me is that in Sweden, the upper class all speak French." It was a terribly crass and supercilious thing of me to say and I suppose I was trying to be clever, but as soon as the words left my mouth I regretted it.

"I think you're mistaken, Mr Harrison. There is no upper class in Sweden."

"It's Alan," I said. "The name's Alan."

Katerina arrived and took away the rest of the plates. She returned bearing dessert – strawberries (fresh that day) and slices of pineapple with yoghurt. As an alternative, she offered to make up a cheese board. I'd already eaten enough of the cheese pie so I settled for the fruit. I still needed to allay the effects of the schnapps, plus I felt she was in need of support. As we ate our pudding, the continual sound of laughter percolated through from the veranda.

My loyalty was soon rewarded. When we'd finished eating I was told I was excused and that Katerina and Anna would complete the clearing up. They disappeared into the kitchen and left me at the table to make my decision – should I go out onto the balcony or not? The alternative (an early retreat to the spare bedroom and its windowless gloom) was equally unappealing, and in the end it was curiosity that took me out there rather than the desire for company. I'd done enough carousing for one evening.

Don and Kurt had installed themselves in a pair of the wicker easy-chairs with their feet up in the after-dinner snoozing position. But they were far from asleep and if anything, more awake than the rest of us. Kurt had been telling some anecdote or another, and as I opened the door from the lounge I was in time to catch the punch line.

"...and then he said I should try it the other way round and I'd see exactly what he meant. Can you imagine that?" He gave a huge guffaw and slapped his thigh.

I'd expected to see him smoking. And so he was, but instead of a cigarette he'd appropriated one of Don's cigars. As I entered he looked up, pointed straight at me and burst into song.

"Two men went to mow..."

There was another roar of laughter. Don turned round to look.

"Ah, Alan, do come and join us. Pull up a chair. I'm afraid we seem to have run out of schnapps." The bottle on the table was now completely empty. "You wouldn't do me a huge favour, would you, and fetch a bottle of scotch from the drinks cabinet?" I turned back in the direction of the lounge. "Oh, and a fresh set of glasses wouldn't go amiss either."

I fetched the bottle and a pair of glasses and returned them to the balcony table. Don slopped out two measures of whisky and set the bottle down.

"Aren't you having one?"

"No thanks." I held up a restraining hand before taking a seat. "I think I'm done for tonight."

"Suit yourself. Anyway, cheers." He and Kurt leant forward to touch glasses and threw back their shots.

There comes a moment in an evening of sustained drinking when you reach the point of no return. Well, there is for me at any rate. It's the point at which I know I've had enough and I make a conscious decision either to stop altogether or to go on and get drunk. I'd already made my decision that evening, and with the aid of a couple of slices of knackebrod and a bowl of fruit and yoghurt I'd managed to regain my composure. On the night of the beach barbecue I'd allowed myself to go on and get drunk and it was only the shock of the boating trip that had brought me round.

That night was different. That night there were three of us and I was the odd one out. And it's edifying how your perspective can change and you see things in a completely different light when those around you are drunk and you're not. What at first might be described as a harmless piece of fun becomes childlike and ridiculous behaviour. What was merely light-hearted banter comes across as trite and completely banal. And once that thought gets into your head and you begin to think how foolish it is ever to get drunk at all, it's easy to assume a position of self-righteous superiority and condemn all drunkards for the rest of time. As I did now.

On the beach, Don and I had tripped over each other and laughed. Tonight, Kurt overbalanced and fell out of his easy-chair, but all I could do was sneer. On the beach, we'd thrown back our heads and sung our silly songs into the night and thought nothing of it. Tonight there were stories and jokes and laughter – but there was nothing said of any consequence and I didn't find a shred of it funny.

I'd endured half an hour or so of their nonsense when I became conscious of a movement in the lounge behind me. I turned to look through the picture window and there was Katerina, plumping up the cushions on the sofa and tidying away the magazines on the coffee table. Then Anna came in and stood stock-still for a moment in the middle of the room looking out at the scene on the balcony. The lamps had been turned off indoors and the patch of her face between jaw and cheekbone shone pale in the twilight. The effect was to imbue her with a strange and haunting beauty, as if she were the melancholic heroine in some 19th-century novel.

I turned back to see if any of this had registered with my companions – but neither Kurt nor Don had looked at her; they were far too busy drinking. I hoped she might come out and bid us good night but she did not. When Katerina had finished her bit of housework, the two women hugged and said something to each other, then disappeared out of sight.

I stayed on until midnight. I'd no hope of anything sensible happening but I was curious to see how it might end. After ten the light began to fade and although it would be a while before it got dark, I lit one of the hurricane lamps and hung it from a hook in the ceiling. Moths began to gather in its glow. Beyond the balcony, the outline of the flagpoles rose up like the masts of a ghostly ship. Eventually, the moon came out as a sign that we should all go to bed, but only I took notice.

They were still at it when I left.

Four

The repeated application of fresh air and exercise had been doing wonders for my sleep, but that night I reverted to the habits I'd acquired after Susan had died. Whatever alcohol I'd drunk was enough to stimulate my senses but not enough to dull them and a thousand different thoughts were running through my head. Foremost amongst them was the continually returning image of Anna's eyes and what that might imply.

The broom cupboard to which I'd been relegated didn't help. At home it would have been euphemistically referred to as the box room but in fact it was less like a box and more like a sauna. During one of my many sleepless hours I deduced that the wooden outer wall faced south and it was this that made it feel warm to the touch. When I'd arrived it had gone twelve, but the place was still baking hot and without a window there was no way of getting any air into the room. I tried propping the door open but it had little practical effect – other than it let in the hall light. And to make matters worse, in the small hours of the morning I could hear someone snoring through the thin partition wall. I assumed it had to be Don.

I must have had some sleep as I recall looking at my watch at regular intervals and seeing the hands steadily advance – two, three-thirty, five – until eventually my body clock cut in, I was wide awake and it was half past six. I was used to the sun streaming in through a set of blinds but here there was just a vague sensation of daylight from somewhere beyond the doorway.

I sat up on the edge of the bed – and immediately cracked my head on the rail of the upper bunk. Cursing violently under my breath, I got up and instinctively pulled on my cut-offs and T-shirt, then ventured out into the hall. The pile of white fluffy mules lay undisturbed by the front door (our guests had been excused wearing them) so I slipped a pair on and padded off in search of company.

It seemed there was none to be had. The kitchen was empty (save for a pile of pots left inverted on the draining board) and the lounge was equally deserted. Out on the veranda, two dirty glasses and an empty bottle lay randomly on the table as testament to the previous evening's party, and on the floor next to it was a seat cushion that had come adrift from one of the wicker chairs. I opened the lounge door and went out to replace it but I couldn't bring myself to fetch in the bottle and the glasses. A breeze had got up and was ruffling the flags on the flagpoles.

I decided to go out and see what was happening outside. The sound of snoring from the room next to mine had ceased and there was a chance that Don might have got up early and gone down to the boathouse. I traded my mules for a pair of trainers and stepped out onto the porch.

It had been raining overnight. The gravel in the yard had a dark, damp look and here and there were pools of lying water. Next to the Land Rover stood what I assumed to be Kurt and Anna's hire car, a Volvo estate. I looked over toward the guest-house but the blinds on the window had been pulled down and there was no discernible sign of life – except for Max, who was sitting immediately outside it in his customary guarding-lion position, feet pointing squarely toward the door. Whoever came out couldn't fail to notice him. His battered tennis ball lay motionless between his paws, ready to play.

I tried calling softly to him, "Come on, Max, come on boy," and patted my thighs in the full expectation that he would pick up the ball and trot across to me in that ambling gait of his. He did look round, tongue lolling as he panted, but decided against moving and resumed his vigil at the door.

I didn't push it. I didn't want to risk waking anyone up, and besides, I might not have been the best of company myself. I walked down to the beach on my own.

Don had not got up early, that was now obvious. The doors to the boathouse were locked and there was no sign of him on the jetty.

The extension we'd been building was progressing nicely. After the piles had been sunk, we'd pulled them together with three-metre boards and used them as a base for mounting the superstructure. Our next task had been to build a frame onto which we could secure the decking. We were well advanced and it only wanted a few more days work and we were done. There was never any need to ask what we were going to do each morning – this was our regular meeting place and it was where I reported for duty.

Although today it was obviously not. Perhaps I'd been given the day off and no one had thought to tell me. Or perhaps the boss just hadn't bothered to turn in. I stood with my hands in my pockets wondering what to do next. I couldn't work on my own, nor should I, for a number of very good reasons. Eventually I settled for a walk and set off in the direction of the headland.

My intention was to spend some time on the swing-seat. A moment of reflection was called for and that was the best place for it. The reeds would be rustling, I wanted to hear what they were saying and here was a chance to talk to Susan.

But someone had beaten me to it. As I approached the seat through the trees I saw a lone figure sitting at one end, staring out over the lake, and although she had her back to me I instantly recognised it as Anna.

What the hell, I thought. *There are no toasts to distract me out here.* I walked on and sat myself down on the other end of the seat. My arrival must have surprised her as she suddenly turned her head and greeted me with a puzzled frown. She had a faraway look and the wind had blown strands of straight black hair across her face.

"Oh," she said. "I didn't see you." Then she got used to the idea I was there and added, "Hey."

"Hey."

"How are you?" she asked.

My reply was a little brusque. "Tired, frankly." I was not in a conciliatory mood and I could still feel the bump on my head where I'd clattered into the bunk bed.

"Didn't you sleep well?"

"To tell the truth, no, I didn't. I don't think the box room was made for sleeping in. Storing junk, yes, but sleeping in, no, definitely not."

"Oh, I'm sorry. It's probably our fault. Katerina says you gave up the guesthouse for us."

"I did, but hey." I shrugged my shoulders. "It can't be helped."

She looked out at the lake as if expecting the waves to lend her some excuse. Here and there the breeze had given rise to white tops. She turned back and brushed the hair from her face.

"I don't suppose it's any consolation, but I didn't sleep well either."

"No?"

"No. Kurt sleeps heavily after he's been drinking and he's prone to snoring."

"Ha!" I had to laugh. "So is Don."

"Really?"

"Yes, he's in the room next door and I could hear him quite clearly."

"Well, at least you don't have to sleep in the same bed."

"No, I suppose not..."

"Were you up late?"

"Not really. I left just after twelve."

"Oh. Kurt came in sometime between two and three. I didn't get much sleep after that."

There was a short intermission while we listened to the reeds. A seagull flew lazily by, calling as it went.

Then she said, "I was sorry to hear about your wife."

"That's alright. Don't worry about it." She'd rather caught me on the hop. Katerina must have told her the story, probably while we were on the yacht the previous afternoon. I tried to brush it aside. "These things happen. That can't be helped either."

"Were you very close?"

"You could say so, yes."

"You must miss her."

"Yes, I suppose I must."

"Do you mind me talking to you about it?"

"Not in the least. It's been a while. If I can't talk about it now, I probably never will."

"But you'd rather I didn't?"

"Yes, I think I'd rather you didn't."

Another interval followed, filled with more reed-rustling. She was facing away from me once more, offering the same profile I'd seen in the lounge the night before. It was a minute or two before she spoke again. "I like it here."

I immediately wondered what she meant. Was she referring to the house? Or the lake? Or did I imagine it was being with me?

"You mean Malaren?" I said. "Or what?"

"I like Malaren too, but I mean here, this place. It's peaceful."

She was right of course, it was, a fact which explained why I liked it too. Perhaps it was something we shared, something that brought us together...

Overhead, another grey cloud scurried by, accompanied by a few spots of rain.

"I think I'm going in now." She suddenly stood up, upsetting the balance of the swing-seat. I made as if to get to my feet, but she motioned me back down. "You don't need to come. I'll find my own way."

Then she was gone and it was just me and the reeds and the persistent rattle of dry leaves. I tried listening for Susan but for the moment, she had gone too.

After a while I followed Anna back up to the house.

There were just the three of us for breakfast that day – Katerina, Anna and I. The other two members of our party were reportedly lying in and unlikely to be around for some while so there was no point in waiting. In their absence, normal rules were suspended and instead of half past eight, the start time was advanced to accommodate our latest guest – her early-morning dose of fresh air had apparently made Anna hungry.

There was also a change to the menu – no egg, bacon and sausage, but a far healthier offering of cereal with an assortment of fruit and yoghurt. This was no 'working man's' breakfast – but then, there were no working men present to enjoy it. I wondered how Max might fare without his regular morning treat. If he was set on waiting for Kurt to appear from the guesthouse, he might be going hungry for quite a while.

I helped the girls clear away. But then they moved on to chores and I couldn't join in so I was left to my own devices. I'd already been out for a walk and I'd no intention of going back to skulk in the Black Hole of Calcutta. The veranda seemed to be the obvious alternative and I wandered out there in the hope of finding something to do. The weather was still fresh and breezy, the flags on the flagpoles were blown tight against their halyards and there remained a hint of dampness in the air. I pulled one of the easy chairs round to face the lake and sat down.

After ten minutes of energetic thumb-twiddling I went back indoors. It had actually grown quite chilly and if I was going to stay outside, I'd need the addition of a pullover. Returning from the box room I checked for any sound of life next door, but there was none. As I passed by the coffee table in the lounge, I spied Katerina's hoard of trashy novels. One of the covers jumped out at me so I picked it up and went back out on the balcony. Just like Max and his sojourn outside the guesthouse, I'd have to wait until the master appeared.

Five

The Nordic crime novel is allegedly the cream of its genre. This was the time of Stieg Larsson (although I'd never read any of his work) and also Jo Nesbo (tried them but couldn't get on with it). Then there was a TV series Susan and I used to regularly watch. I'm damned if I can remember the name of the author, but I can remember the name of the detective – *Wallander*. He was played by Kenneth Branagh and the whole thing was so utterly depressing it made you want to slit your wrists right there and then.

The good thing about the book I'd selected was that it was written in English. The not-so-good thing was that it was equally depressing as the rest, and we were barely halfway down page three before someone had died in the most miserable of circumstances. I'd never heard of the author (it was neither of the above) but they definitely had a unique way of portraying blood and gore. Why anyone so innocent as Katerina would want to read that kind of thing was quite beyond me. Anyway, it was sufficiently engaging to keep me occupied for the next hour or so.

A series of murders had taken place in a travelling circus. The finger of suspicion was immediately pointed at Franco Zapata, the South American knife-thrower. He had a fiery and unpredictable temperament and often beat up on his girlfriend, an acrobat, and one of his knives had been found embedded between the shoulder blades of Maxi the clown. Now it appeared that one of the trapeze artists had become entangled in their safety gear and had been found strangulated and hanging upside down in the centre of the main tent. Although, given the fact that he'd been having an affair with the acrobat, nobody thought it was likely to have been an accident.

From time to time, when it was convenient to tear myself away, I looked up and checked the lounge for any signs of movement. Other than an occasional appearance by one of the girls, there was nothing to report and I was able to continue reading. I'd reached chapter eight and the body count was beginning to rack up (the ringmaster had just been shot in front of a full house – someone had loaded one of the clowns' pistols with real bullets in place of the usual blanks) when Don finally emerged. It was just after eleven and I'd been up for four and a half hours. I marked my page, lay the book down on the table and went indoors.

For a man who'd spent the previous night on the lash, Don looked remarkably well – tired yes, but definitely well. And as if to prove the point he gave a huge yawn and extended his arms in a stretching exercise. He was not yet properly dressed and in addition to a pair of the fluffy white mules, he had on one of the matching white bathrobes. It was far too small for him and the ends of the sleeves finished just below his elbows.

"Morning, Don," I began.

"Morning, Alan."

"And how are we this morning?"

"Me?" The returning look he gave me suggested that the question I'd just put to him was entirely superfluous. "Why, I'm just fine. Couldn't be better. Fit as the butcher's dog. Raring to go. Great, smashing, super. I could climb mountains." Another yawn. "Although first, I think I could do with a strong cup of coffee."

"Would you like me to get you one?"

"No, it's alright – I'm sure there'll be one in the pot. Katerina always makes one before breakfast. Where is she by the way?"

"She's around somewhere." At least, I assumed she was – with my head buried deep in my book I hadn't been keeping tabs.

Don looked to see if anyone was within earshot, then inclined his head toward me and lowered his voice. "So you wouldn't happen to know how the land lies then this morning, by any chance?"

"No, Don, I don't. And I have no idea what you're talking about."

"Hmm…" Another quizzical look. "How many years was it you were married?"

"Thirty," I said, rather abruptly. I didn't need reminding.

"Sorry."

"That's alright."

He went off to the kitchen in search of his coffee.

I looked at my watch. It was quarter past eleven. With a bit of luck we could get in an hour or so's work before lunch. I went back out onto the balcony, re-opened my book and picked up where I'd left off while I waited.

Half an hour went by. The electric shower in the bathroom came on and then I heard the sound of its occupant cheerfully singing.

"*Arrivederci, Roma. Goodbye to Napoli. La, la, la, la… La-la… La, la, la…*"

I smiled to myself and continued reading.

Shortly after twelve, the door to the lounge opened and someone came out to join me on the veranda. Although it wasn't Don, as I'd expected, but rather Kurt who'd surfaced and was in need of fresh air.

This time he'd changed and instead of his regulation tennis gear had put on a pair of khaki shorts and some brown loafers. As for socks, he'd either forgotten them or preferred to do without. He'd already equipped himself with a cup of black coffee which he put down on the other side of the table together with his cigarettes and lighter, then pulled the remaining easy-chair round to face the lake and sat down. If I hadn't have said something, I don't think he'd have spoken to me at all.

"Hey."

"Hey."

And that was as much as we could manage. I went back to my book while he lit up and drank his coffee. It seemed we had nothing in common to discuss.

Once or twice I sneaked a look across at him although he

showed no interest in me whatsoever. Don had appeared tired but well, whereas Kurt most certainly did not. His face was tanned, but drawn and haggard and the area beneath his eyes was deep in shadow. He was either unused to drinking and took it badly or, as was my suspicion, far too used to it and bore the marks of extensive practice.

It wasn't long before he lit another of his cigarettes, then another. I had the misfortune to be sitting downwind and caught the full effect of his smoke. Soon it began to annoy me and I packed up my book and went indoors.

In the small dining area next to the kitchen, Katerina and Anna were starting to lay up the table for lunch. It was clear there'd be no work done that morning.

Nor was there to be any done that afternoon. God knows where the suggestion came from (I must have been away at the time) but it was decided that we would all go swimming. I was the last to wash my hands before lunch and when I returned to the table it had already been agreed. Perhaps it had been Kurt, pleading boredom, although I doubt that as he could quite happily sit and do nothing but drink coffee and smoke cigarettes for over an hour. More likely was the idea that Katerina had volunteered it on behalf of her friend – but for whatever reason it was a done deal and there was nothing I could do about it. Why couldn't Kurt and Anna arrange their own entertainment and go out sight-seeing for the afternoon? Wasn't that why they'd hired a car? In a fit of pique I declined to join them.

"Aren't you coming, Alan?" Anna's eyes flickered constantly.

"No, I think I'll give it a miss, if you don't mind. Swimming isn't exactly my forte."

"Oh..."

Two was company and four could make a party, but five was definitely a crowd.

I told myself they were making a mistake and they wouldn't

enjoy it. The weather was chilly, there was too much chop on the water, and since we'd not yet finished the extension to the jetty, there was no convenient setting-off point.

I was completely wrong, of course. The breeze had subsided and the sun was out, drying up the patches of water in the yard. The lake looked as calm as I'd seen it and, I have to say, wonderfully inviting. As for the jetty, they all found a way of getting in, although I comforted myself with the thought that they'd all find it difficult getting out. I was not in a charitable mood.

I elected to make myself a cup of coffee and watch from the balcony. Everyone went their separate ways to get changed then congregated at the corner of the building before trooping off down the hill, their towels wrapped around their necks or slung over their shoulders. Don had made up a backpack (though I'd no idea what was in it) and Anna carried a beach bag. Max tagged along behind, tight on Kurt's heels. They all had their costumes underneath and stripped off when they got to the beach. Don wore his usual set of speedos while Kurt sported a similar pair – although his were noticeably smaller, presumably in an attempt to show off everything he had. I was already familiar with Katerina's one-piece of course.

What made me think I'd have trouble with Anna? The sight of a woman in a bikini wasn't new to me – the beaches in Greece or Spain or wherever we'd been on holiday had been littered with them – but I knew this was going to be different. She'd started out in a lacy white top and a summer skirt that clipped around her waist. These soon disappeared into her beach-bag and the swimwear this revealed did not leave much to the imagination. But I'm a normal red-blooded man and imagination was a trait I possessed, so it bothered me. Her white bikini matched her top and beneath it her body was tanned and perfectly shaped. It was a relief when she disappeared into the water and all I could see of her was her head.

Two by two, they headed out to the pontoon. Don and Kurt

took the lead while Katerina and Anna followed behind. When they got close, Kurt put on a sudden spurt and boasting an extravagant crawl, easily won the race to the steps. Given the number of cigarettes he consumed, I wondered how long he could keep it up.

I waited until they'd all clambered out onto the pontoon and lay down in the sun to dry off. Watching Anna emerge was a torture. I knew I shouldn't do it, but so what? I'm only human. Then I couldn't bear it any longer and I got up and went indoors.

I'm embarrassed to have to admit it, but I took myself off to the box room and sulked. The alternative was to remain on the veranda and read. I was now well into my piece of Nordic noir and eager to find out who'd done it. I guessed it wasn't Zapata – to shine a light on someone so early in proceedings was always a red herring. The potential suspects were dropping like flies, but I knew I wouldn't be able to concentrate. The thought of seeing Anna get back out of the water and towel herself off was enough to convince me of that.

So I stretched out on the bottom bunk and dozed. The day had caught up with me, the box room was stiflingly hot and I simply lay down and let go. I was feeling unforgivably sorry for myself and there was really nothing else for me to do. Under the circumstances, the dream that followed was entirely predictable.

We all dream, but I suspect I dream more than most – my experiences with Susan had taught me that. Although it's probably the fact that I can recall mine. Somebody told me once that you have to wake up unexpectedly during the course of a dream to remember it. Now I was sleeping fitfully again so maybe that explained it.

Fortunately, this one didn't involve Susan at all. I was at the circus and the whole of the action took place in the ring inside the main tent. A full house packed the stands and I had the sense that the audience was closely scrutinising everything I did. Franco

Zapata, the evil South American knife-thrower, was on the prowl and every so often I'd hear a high-pitched whistling as one of his knives whooshed perilously close by and thudded into one of the wooden tent-poles. He bore a remarkable resemblance to Kurt.

High up above, Katerina and Anna had taken on the role of acrobats, performing a series of death-defying gymnastic moves on the trapeze or the tightrope. At the end of each trick it seemed certain that one of them would fall and become entangled in the netting. But at the very last second, one would miraculously rescue the other to the great 'oohs' and 'aahs' of the crowd. Instead of circus costumes they were both wearing swimsuits.

Don was the ringmaster. Broad-chested to the point where his neck seemed to be bursting out of his shirt collar, he wore a top hat and tails and carried one of those long-handled whips you'd use to control a lion. He'd apparently survived the deviant bullet by cleverly catching it between his teeth and was now showing it to the crowd to rounds of rapturous applause.

God knows what part I was playing in all this – be it clown or juggler, I really hadn't a clue. All I could tell was that every time I looked at my hands they had blood on them, and before too long, someone else was going to die. But I didn't know who – or why.

Don't ask me what it all meant, you've probably got far more idea than I have. Personally, I don't place much store by it. As I said before, I'm possessed of a vivid imagination. That can play terrible tricks and as far as I was concerned, that's all it was – imagination.

I must have surfaced between four and four-fifteen. It was probably the sound of voices that woke me. The swimming party had returned and had gathered on the balcony where the remains of their tea and cake lay scattered across the table. I fetched another chair from the dining area and joined them.

The rest of that afternoon and evening passed without incident. When I got back to the box room after dinner there was a text waiting for me from Philippa.

Hi Dad. Great to hear you're having a good time. How was the swimming? Lul Philx

I decided not to answer it.

Six

I didn't bother looking for Max the following morning. I knew exactly where he'd be – sitting outside the door to the guesthouse waiting patiently for Kurt. They'd been together most of the previous day – or at least for as much time as Kurt was out of doors (Max didn't come inside if you remember). I don't think Kurt realised he was being followed. Even when Max was right at his heels he didn't turn round and I never saw him toss the tennis ball once. Talk about blind obedience. But still, you get that in a dog.

I wondered why he didn't follow Anna. She'd obviously been the first to emerge the previous day and must have walked straight past him but he'd chosen not to move. It puzzled me. Maybe Max was a man's dog. My grandparents had owned a cat like that. Every time we visited, it would come to me or my father but wouldn't go anywhere near my mother. Perhaps Max was the same. I'd never seen him with Katerina either and my guess was that when there were no guests, he'd follow Don. But for the moment he'd abandoned me and it was Kurt who was flavour of the month.

I didn't even bother going outside. I could tell Don wasn't up, courtesy of the deep rumbling noises from the room next door, so I didn't see the point. I'd woken early again, although life in the Black Hole had markedly improved. I'd got used to the bed and the temperature had dropped sharply overnight on account of the fresher weather. Despite the recent fitful nature of my rest, I'd enjoyed a decent night's sleep and I felt almost human.

The white bathrobe Don had been wearing was hanging from the coat rack in the hallway. I pulled it on, together with a pair of the fluffy mules. My plan was to make myself a cup of tea and go out onto the balcony and read. After my dream the previous afternoon I was driven to discover how many more deaths there were to come, who'd perpetrated them and why.

My book had originally been cleared from the table to make room for afternoon tea, but someone had thought to replace it and it now lay awaiting my pleasure. Outside it was still quite fresh – but the flags lacked wind, there was sun instead of rain and all looked very pleasant. The lake had acquired that early-morning sparkly look and the sky was a blaze of uninterrupted blue.

I was just about to go back indoors when a movement caught my eye down below. Beyond the end of the jetty, a head was bobbing in the water. It was a head I immediately recognised – Anna had gone out swimming.

I set my book back down on the table. It wasn't a difficult decision. I'm not impulsive by nature – it doesn't do to be when you're an actuary; everything has to be carefully considered – but I knew from the moment I saw her that I was going to go and join her. I returned to the box room and changed into my trunks.

I could hardly make it sound accidental. At seven o'clock in the morning, using the line *I thought I'd come out for a swim, fancy seeing you here* simply didn't stack up. If I was going to proffer a reason, I'd have to concoct something more original than that. But why should I concoct anything at all? I was a grown man, I'd no one to answer to (other than myself) and I could go swimming when I liked, where I liked and with whomsoever I chose. And it was with that thought in mind that a few moments later I took a deep breath and slipped quietly into the water.

It felt numbingly cold. My preference would have been to jump off the end of the jetty and get it over with, but I didn't want to make a splash and attract attention. Such exhibitions of showmanship, I thought, were best left to Kurt. Apart from which, Anna was well on her way to the pontoon by now and I didn't want her to stop and turn round. Using my casual breast-stroke, I pressed on as quickly as I could.

She reached the steps well before me and hauled herself out

onto the platform, then turned and sat facing the shore. I was some minutes behind and she must have seen me coming but she showed no sign of recognition or surprise. I pulled myself up and sat down beside her.

"Hey."

"Hey."

A lick of wet hair lay plastered across my forehead and I pushed it back out of my eyes. Even in the weak morning sunshine she looked to be partially dry, although I noticed that a rivulet of water had drained down into her navel.

She began by taking me to task. "I thought you said you didn't like swimming?"

"I never said I didn't like it. I merely said it wasn't my forte."

"Oh, I see. And now it is?"

"I'm sorry, but I wasn't in the mood yesterday."

"In the mood? What does that mean?"

"It means, I didn't feel like swimming."

"But today you do?"

"I guess so. I need the exercise." That at least was true – a whole day hanging around the house had made me feel restless. "Anyway, did I miss anything important?"

"When? This morning?"

"No, yesterday."

"I don't think so. We just came out here and talked." She looked up and watched as a seagull sailed by, heading up the channel to the west. "Are you and Don good friends?"

"I guess so."

"He was telling us that the two of you built all this." She indicated the platform beneath us.

"That's not strictly true."

"No?"

"No, we didn't build the pontoon – that was already lying on the beach when I got here. All we did was float it off and add the steps." I was keen to stick to the truth – although it made the whole thing sound terribly inconsequential, which of course it wasn't.

"You must have worked hard though, all the same."

"Perhaps. Don't go getting the wrong idea by the way. Don's the brains behind all this. I'm just a pair of hands."

It had been in my mind to say 'unpaid labour' but that would have been unfair. I'd received plenty of rewards – they just hadn't come in the form of an hourly rate.

"I see…"

I wasn't convinced that she did. It was the same problem I'd had in trying to explain things to Philippa. I decided to let it pass – there were other, more pressing issues I wanted to discuss.

"I see Kurt's a good swimmer."

She shrugged. "He likes to think so."

"But you don't?"

"Maybe. Kurt likes to think a lot of things. We don't always agree on them."

"Oh, like what, for instance?"

"Politics, religion, family – anything you care to mention really."

"Really?"

"Really. We don't see eye to eye on a lot." For a moment I thought she was going to open up, then she suddenly clammed shut as if she realised she was giving too much away – but the damage had already been done. "Anyway, I don't see what business it is of yours what Kurt and I talk about."

"You're right, I shouldn't pry. I'm sorry."

"That's alright."

She looked away again. It seemed to me that she didn't want to talk about Kurt any more than I wanted to talk about Susan. It didn't surprise me. What did was the fact that she and Kurt had any form of meaningful conversation at all. In all the time they'd been there (we were now thirty-six hours and counting) I don't think he'd spoken to her once.

My body had begun to warm up and I was starting to dry off. I lay back on the pontoon to soak up the sunshine and closed my eyes.

Although Anna wasn't in the mood to relax. "I'm hungry."

"You were hungry yesterday. I expect it's the fresh air," I said without moving.

"I don't suppose you brought anything to eat?"

It was a silly question of course – there was nowhere to store provisions on the pontoon and I'd no means of carrying any.

"No, unfortunately not," I replied, eyes still closed.

I listened as a seagull cried in the distance. Then came the sound of movement as I sensed her scrambling to her feet. I opened my eyes and sat up.

"Are you off?"

"Yes, I'm going to have breakfast." She was staring up toward the house.

"I'll come with you," I volunteered.

"If you like," she said, although it was a lukewarm, offhand invitation, as if she didn't really care one way or the other. "I'll see you up there."

She didn't wait but dived straight off the side, the arc of her white bikini two-piece curving into the water.

I watched as she surfaced and her head began to bob athletically in time with her strokes. I would have loved to emulate her diving skills but it was far more than I dare. I lowered myself carefully down the steps in reverse and followed at a safe and respectful distance.

Judging by the rate at which she ascended the hill, Anna's contention that she was hungry held true. I most certainly was not – at least, not enough to warrant sitting down with her at the table in the dining area. My suspicion was that at this hour there'd be no one else about and I was beginning to feel that it wasn't safe for the two of us to be left alone together.

I guessed she'd go straight to the guesthouse to dry off. If I was quick, I could retrieve my belongings from the balcony and make it back to the box room before she returned. At this stage I wasn't sure I trusted myself, never mind her.

I was right and the house appeared empty. I stopped in the hallway to collect the undersize bathrobe and a pair of fluffy mules, then headed outside where I collared my book and my half-finished cup of tea. I came back via the kitchen to use the microwave and pick up a couple of biscuits from the biscuit barrel before making it safely back to the box room and closing the door. Left in the dark with my hands full, I was careful not to spill anything while I groped for the light switch.

I had a sudden premonition that she was already there. You can call me vain if you like, or arrogant, or just plain stupid but it occurred to me that instead of going off to the guesthouse to change, she'd come directly to the box room and was lying there on the bed, waiting for me.

I nervously turned on the light. The bed was empty of course, the duvet thrown back just as I'd left it, and after a surge of relief (or was it disappointment?) I cursed myself for being so delusional. Here I was, allowing my vivid imagination to run away with itself and take me to places I had no business going. I sat down on the edge of the bottom bunk and finished my tea and biscuits in an attempt to remain calm.

After ten minutes or so I turned out the light and lay down in the dark. I'd meant to read my book but the prospect of more circus deaths and the guilt (or otherwise) of Franco Zapata were no longer enough to distract me and I knew I wouldn't be able to concentrate.

I was thinking about Anna of course – it was only natural that I should. I wondered whether she was thinking of me, and if so, just exactly what was going through her head. I'd convinced myself I knew, but perhaps I was fooling myself. What signals had she given me? For that matter, what signals had I given her?

Surely the fact I'd gone out swimming that morning and had joined her on the raft was indication enough? But this was all rampant speculation – what did I know of these matters? It had been over thirty years...

I tried telling myself to stop these wild fantasies and think in a practical vein. After all, I was an actuary, not a Lothario, and actuaries dealt in the real world. I hoped this would bring some improvement but in fact it made matters worse. My mind inevitably turned toward risk and I began to evaluate the dangers involved in having an affair with another man's wife. At least, I'd made the assumption she was his wife – no one had ever told me whether Kurt and Anna were married. Although, on the face of it, that wasn't really the issue...

So what *were* the dangers? That was the first thing to decide. I'd no experience of affairs, either personally or amongst my friends, and in fact I'd little idea of how to start one off, let alone how to manage it. One assumed that cuckolded men like Kurt could get angry, even violent, and some, like Franco Zapata, might be inclined to take things into their own hands. What were the factors that might induce such a reaction? Age? Upbringing? Social class? I went through all the possibilities but none seemed material to the case. Did smoking have anything to do with it? Well, it did betray a certain level of nervousness. And then there was the influence of alcohol...

There was always a chance that infidelity would produce the opposite effect and as opposed to violence, would result in continued indifference. I could just as easily believe that of Kurt too, and I wondered what it would take to shake him out of his current state of apathy. If such a betrayal did not, then there were other implications to consider. It seemed to me that one was damned either way – it wasn't much of a choice.

I must have been lying there for an hour, trying to figure it out. I was loath to leave the room until I was confident of the company and eventually there were stirrings next door. Someone got out of bed (Katerina to judge by the lightness of the footsteps) and soon there were voices in the kitchen. I waited for another five minutes then sauntered out, empty cup in hand and wearing the bathrobe and mules as if I'd only just surfaced myself.

Katerina and Anna were both fully dressed and in the midst of organising a shopping expedition.

"We're just going out," said Katerina. "We're running short of a few things and there's some bits and pieces I need for tonight. Anna's already had breakfast and I'm just grabbing a quick something…" (she held a cup of coffee in one hand and a piece of toast in the other) "…and then we'll be off. You can sort yourself out, can't you, Alan?"

"Yeah, no problem." I manufactured an artificial yawn. If having an affair meant deception, then I'd need to get in some practice. "Don't worry about me," I assured her. "I'll be fine."

They gathered up their shopping bags and moved out into the hallway, then Katerina went to fetch the car keys from her room. Anna was left standing alone. *If this is going to work,* I thought, *she'll turn and look at me now.* A few agonising seconds passed in which she did not. Then Katerina was back with the keys, but not before Anna had lifted her head and given me the benefit of her eyes.

"Come on, let's go", said Katerina, ushering Anna out of the door.

I waited until it had closed behind them then cast around the kitchen for something to eat. Now I was hungry too.

Seven

I fancied getting myself something cooked à la Don's Boy Scout breakfast. I'd been up for almost three hours and after my bout of early-morning exercise I was feeling decidedly peckish.

I'd managed to assemble an egg and a couple of rashers when Don arrived in person. I thought this might save me the trouble but I could tell he wasn't in the mood. He was fully dressed (although not in working clothes, I noticed) and eyed the white bathrobe and mules with suspicion.

"Morning, Don," I chirped.

"Morning, Alan." His response was courteous if not overly cheerful.

"You breakfasting?" I asked.

"No, not just now, thanks." He looked at his watch. "I'll wait until Kurt gets here. You go ahead though. You should know where everything is by now. Help yourself."

"Will do."

"Any chance of a coffee?"

"I think so." The red light on the percolator blinked intermittently. "There should still be some in the pot."

"Thanks." I poured him out a cup and he took it through into the lounge. "When Kurt arrives, tell him I'm in here." He settled onto the settee and began rustling the pages of a magazine.

I pressed on with my egg and bacon – I'd no intention of waiting for Kurt. Had our roles been reversed, I'm sure he wouldn't have waited for me. And anyway, he didn't look like the type who'd enjoy a working-man's breakfast. To tell the truth, he didn't even look like a working man…

My instincts proved correct and it was another hour before he materialised, during which time Don grew ever more restless. And when Kurt did finally appear, not only did he decline a fry-up but he wanted no breakfast at all and settled for the same diet of coffee and cigarettes as he'd enjoyed the previous day.

I have to say I felt rather sorry for Don – it saddened me to see him kept waiting that way. I was inevitably reminded of the dog. Max had no doubt been in a similar position outside the guest-house, paws extended, tongue lolling. Neither of them would get anything out of the deal. Life, it seemed, was on hold as we all waited for Kurt.

So it was clear we weren't going to get any work done that morning either, although this wasn't entirely on account of Kurt's tardy nature. The weather had turned against us and despite the day's promising start, a squall had blown in from the west and was peppering the roof of the veranda.

Mind you, it wasn't enough to deter Kurt and Don from going out there. They drew their chairs up to the table and Don came in to fetch a pack of cards from one of the drawers next to the drinks cabinet. For one horrible moment I thought he was going to reach in and take out a bottle, but it was deemed too early in the day for that. He asked if I wanted to join them but that would have made things awkward and I sensed they were set on a game of their own. They fell to playing what looked like cribbage with a pegboard and coloured markers. Their game was punctuated by frequent bouts of laughter, the occasional oath and numerous cups of coffee. Some money changed hands, although not in great quantities. I excused myself and resorted to occupying the space that Don had vacated on the settee and continued reading my book.

Soon, I hoped, the rain would clear and we'd be able to go outside.

Seeing that the men had skipped breakfast, it was inevitable that lunch would be taken early. Katerina and Anna duly returned from their shopping trip and began laying up the table in the dining area and by just after twelve we were sitting down to eat. As a result of their expedition there were significant additions to the menu and so it was quite a spread.

After it had been cleared away, Don and Kurt returned to the veranda. I was convinced they'd resume their game of cards, but I was mistaken. Don was a man of habit and could not resist the practice of taking a nap after a heavy meal. He arranged his chair into its customary position, put his feet up and closed his eyes, and within a few minutes he was, to all intents and purposes, asleep. Kurt followed suit and a quiet calm descended on the scene.

In some respects this gave me hope. Outward appearance might suggest otherwise but in my experience these periods of rest were usually a prelude to action. Don might be asleep – or feigning it while he thought – but after a short break he'd be wide awake again and ready for whatever came next.

I retreated into the lounge. Beyond the balcony rail the rain had long since ceased and there was a freshening breeze to dry up the ground. It was only a matter of time…

A frustrating hour went by in which little or nothing happened. I'd long since finished my book. My surmise proved correct and Franco Zapata turned out to be a private detective in disguise, hired by the circus boss to solve the spate of murders. How a private detective also happened to be an expert knife-thrower was an interesting question, but hey, this was fiction and I was prepared to suspend my disbelief for the sake of the story – although I wasn't quite so credulous over the question of the culprit. Zapata had concluded that the crimes could only have been committed by a dwarf. And just by chance, a whole troupe of them had recently joined the outfit immediately prior to the murders. One of them now broke ranks. A chase ensued on horseback (circus horses, naturally, complete with those waving pink head-plumes) after which the dwarf was captured and confessed – although his motives were entirely unclear. It was all highly unsatisfactory, but at least it had succeeded in occupying my time. Now I lacked diversion and I was beginning to feel bored.

I looked out onto the veranda but there was still no sign of movement. Short of actually going out there and waking Don up there was little else I could do. Eventually I took to rattling the coffee cups and rejuvenating the percolator in the hope of provoking some reaction. It worked as Don stirred and jerked himself awake. I poured out a coffee and took it out as a peace offering.

"Here," I said. "I thought you might need one of these."

He opened one eye and hoisted himself up on an elbow.

"Cheers..."

"You've been out of it for a while," I said.

"Have I? Not used to all this rest and relaxation I suppose. Why? What time is it?"

I already knew the answer, having followed the hands on the lounge clock as they made their way laboriously round the dial, but I checked my watch all the same. "Half past two."

"Is it really? Jesus Christ!"

"Yup. And the weather's faired up. Another twenty minutes and I thought we could make a start."

"Make a start on what?"

"You know – the jetty. Finishing off that extension we were building."

"Ah. Glad you mentioned that." He was sitting upright now. "I've promised to take Kurt out in the boat this afternoon. I hope you don't mind, but I'll have to take a rain check on the jetty for the time being."

"Oh..." I said. "Kurt... Out in the boat... Well, you've certainly got a nice afternoon for it, I'll say that."

I hope the two of you are very happy together.

"You're welcome to join us if you like."

"That's very kind of you, Don, but you know what they say – two's company and so on. I'll..." *just sit around here and twiddle my thumbs while you go out and enjoy yourself* "...be fine."

"Ok, if you're sure."

I was sure, absolutely sure. The way I felt, I'd rather sleep with a dead policeman than go out in a boat with Kurt for the afternoon.

Don glanced across the table at his companion. "Is he awake by the way?"

"Is who awake?"

"Kurt."

I looked reluctantly round. Kurt was not awake and lay sprawled in his easy chair, head back and mouth open. It was not the prettiest of sights.

"Give him a nudge, will you?" said Don. "If we're going to go out, we'd better get started."

I stared at Kurt's recumbent form. The idea of giving him a nudge struck me as rather repellent. The best way of waking him up and getting him down to the boat, I thought, was to bundle him over the balcony rail and let him drop the ten or twelve feet to the floor so he could roll all the way to the bottom of the hill. I resorted to tapping my foot against the leg of his chair instead.

"Wakey, wakey, old chap. Apparently you're going out in the boat."

Kurt gave a cough, then sat up with a distinctly disorientated look on his face. *The first thing he'll do*, I thought, *will be search around for his packet of fags...*

Don had already stood up and was going through some stretching exercises. "Right, come on then. Let's get cracking."

Kurt hobbled to his feet and yawned.

"Are you sure you're not coming?" Don asked.

"Sure," I said.

I wouldn't have lasted five minutes.

I forced myself to watch the whole affair from the balcony – I even borrowed Don's binoculars so I could do it.

They began by trailing down the hillside, Don (who'd changed into boating gear), Kurt (still in his shorts and loafers) and Max, following slavishly at the rear. No breakfast sausage for him now for a couple of days – plus the prospect of being left behind when the boat set off. Poor bugger.

I'd assumed they'd be taking the launch – but they were not. Don fetched the keys out of his pocket and began unclipping the covers to the speedboat. I should have guessed – the launch was far too dull for the likes of Kurt, he needed his excitement.

Chick-a-boom, chick-a-boom, chick-a-boom, boom, boom.

I'd heard that sound before. The engine spat out a puff of oily smoke and began its throaty bubbling. Then they were off, with Kurt ensconced at the wheel.

I'd not yet had the pleasure of driving the speedboat. Despite all my training in the launch, I guess Don didn't think I was ready. Or perhaps he was just protective of it, but for whatever reason, I'd only been out in it the once. Watching Kurt drive it at the first time of asking wasn't easy.

They set off at a steady pace, but as soon as they'd cleared the swimming platform, Kurt slammed the throttle forward and the boat leapt into the air. With the power full on, the bows reared up and it looked as if the thing might stall – but then he adjusted the trim as the prow came down and the boat shot forward across the lake. It roared off, bucking like mad over the swell.

It's a good job it's not rough, I thought. *Then there'd be trouble...*

They headed off in the direction of Cormorant Island, presumably under Don's guidance. I'd have kept a steady course, but Kurt could not resist a few flamboyant manoeuvres, throwing up great sheets of spray. They reached the turn in what seemed like record time, and my heart was in my mouth as they careered around the tip of the island and out of sight.

I don't know why I didn't put the binoculars down there and then – I'd seen enough to make it hurt already. But I didn't, and like a fool I waited until they re-emerged from the far side, the boat bounding up and down across the water.

And of course, it wasn't enough for Kurt to come straight

back, even at that speed, but no, he had to go off on a jaunt of his own, out into the middle of the lake where he could perform every trick imaginable – up, down, round and round; boating turns that would make your hair stand on end. It was a good job I wasn't there or I'd have been sick as a dog.

I think it was then that the full implications of Kurt's visit came home to me. Don would pander to him for as long as he was around and I'd be left to one side. Woodwork, the jetty, all of the plans that we'd made – none of that was on the agenda. We'd got no work done that morning, nor indeed that afternoon, and it was becoming clear that we'd get no work done at all while Kurt was still on the premises.

Eight

"Need any help?"

I'd grown bored with watching the boating shenanigans and being at a loose end had wandered into the kitchen. Katerina was out there alone, preparing dinner.

"That's very kind of you, Alan. Yes, I could do with a hand. There's some potatoes want peeling."

A pile of vegetables and two empty saucepans lay waiting. I rolled up my sleeves. "So where's Anna?"

"She's gone to lie down for an hour."

"Couldn't bear to watch, eh?"

"I beg your pardon?"

"Couldn't bear to watch." My hands were now immersed in water and I could only nod in the general direction of the lake. "The boys with their toys."

"Oh, I see what you mean. No, I just think she was tired, that's all. She doesn't always sleep very well."

"So I understand."

It was an ideal opportunity to have mentioned Don's snoring but I thought better of it. Katerina was still digesting my comment of earlier.

"Boys with their toys... That's a strange expression. English, is it?"

"Something like that. You haven't come across it before?"

"No, I can't say I have. I rely solely on Don to keep me up to date with what goes on in England and he doesn't always tell me everything."

"He doesn't?"

"No, not always."

This might explain why Susan never had as much contact as she'd have liked. It seemed to me that her brother had never been overly forthcoming.

"Still, it seems to fit the bill though," I said.

"What does?"

"The boys with their toys."

"Yes, I suppose it does."

I let my bait drift for a moment, then cast again in the hopes of getting a bite.

"So how do you feel about it? All this charging about."

Katerina was busy at the chopping board. She lay down her knife and looked thoughtfully at the wall. "I get used to it."

"Doesn't it worry you?"

"Of course it worries me. But if I let myself get upset by everything that worried me I wouldn't have much of a life. Excuse me."

I pulled in while she squeezed past to put a pan on the stove. It looked to be some kind of stew. I continued peeling potatoes.

I was hoping she'd open up to me. My initial probing suggested I'd have to work a bit harder but I decided to stick at it – I had an inkling she might be an ally.

"You don't like this any more than I do, do you?" I said.

"I don't like what?"

"This thing going on between Kurt and Don."

"What thing?"

"You can't pretend you haven't noticed. This old pals' act they put on together – you know, the cards, the drinking and so on. And now this." I freed up a hand so I could point outside.

"Oh, that. Well, no, I'm not keen on it. Mind you, it hasn't always been that way. In fact, it's only in the last couple of years…"

Suddenly she dried up. Either there was something she didn't know or wasn't disposed to tell me. I decided to keep pressing.

"So what's the story?"

"About Kurt and Don? Hasn't Don said anything to you about it?"

"Not really. He may have mentioned something in passing."

"Well, all I can tell you is that just after my parents died, the woodyard Don was working at got into some kind of financial difficulties. Kurt was the sole owner at the time. The creditors threatened it with closure and stipulated that it should either be sold outright or that someone come on board with some money. Don stepped in with my inheritance and that was that."

"So you're telling me that Kurt was forced to take a partner?"

"As far as I understand it, yes."

"That's probably just as well."

"What d'you mean?"

"Well as far as I can see, Kurt couldn't run a bath, never mind run a business."

"That's not a very kind thing to say."

"Maybe not – but I'll take a bet it's true."

There was no reply. In our house, silence had always been assumed to signify consent. If the same applied here, Katerina's lack of response meant she agreed with me. I waited for a moment to see if she might raise some objection – but she did not and then it was time to move on.

"So how long d'you think they might stay?"

"What, out there?" Katerina glanced up at the window at the end of the dining area. From way out on the lake came the grating whine of a propeller as it lifted clear of the water. "Another half an hour maybe. They'll get bored with it eventually and come in wanting something to eat."

"No, I meant Kurt and Anna, staying here."

"Oh, that. Could be days, could be weeks. I never know, frankly. Last year they were here for a fortnight. At the end of the day, it's all down to Kurt. He's the one who makes the decisions."

"Ah…" The prospect of spending the next few days, never mind weeks, cooped up in the Black Hole under the same roof as Kurt was decidedly unappealing. Although his wife was an entirely different matter… "Doesn't Anna have any say in it?"

"Anna?" Katerina had appeared quite comfortable with our conversation up until now, but here there was an edge to her voice. "Anna does as she's told. Haven't you noticed?"

N.E. David

I'd not yet had the pleasure of seeing Kurt speak to his wife so there'd been no opportunity to observe. But, if that were the case, it came as no surprise.

"But the two of *you* seem to get on well together."

"Yes, I suppose that's why I put up with it all. Anna and I are old friends. We go back a long way."

"Really?"

"Oh, yes. We've known each other for over twenty years."

"As long as that? I see…" This was an interesting aside, but not quite what I was angling to know. "So tell me, how did Kurt and Anna get together?"

"Hasn't Don told you that either?"

"No, I'm afraid he hasn't."

"Sometimes I wonder what you men ever do talk about. You spend all that time messing around in boats and playing with pieces of wood but at the end of the day you never seem to know anything of any consequence."

"Fair comment. Well, this is your chance to educate me."

Katerina continued talking while she stirred the stew. "It's quite simple really. When Don bought into the woodyard, I worked part-time in the office while we got started. One day there was a knock on the door and there was Anna asking if we had any vacancies. We were short-staffed so we took her on."

"She and Kurt were bound to meet, then."

"That's right."

It was enough to be getting on with, I suppose, but a little more detail would have been good. I still couldn't rid myself of the idea that Katerina was holding something back. I tried another tack.

"Do Kurt and Anna have any children?"

This time my question was met with stony silence as Katerina busied herself by searching for implements in a drawer.

"Let me guess," I went on, "and say that they don't. My suspicion would be that Anna wanted them but Kurt said no. Am

189

I right?"

The drawer slammed shut and Katerina turned to face me. For a split-second I thought she'd be brandishing a carving knife but it turned out to be a harmless-looking ladle.

"I really think you should focus on peeling potatoes, Alan, and stop being so nosey."

"Sorry..." I said, as innocently as possible. "Just curious, that's all."

But that was it, and for the time being my fact-finding mission had come to an end. I'd pushed it as far as it would go and if I wanted to discover more, I knew I'd have to be patient.

I resolved to pay particular attention at dinner that evening – if there were some nuance I could pick up from the gathering it would all be grist to my mill.

As I've already made clear, we were not expected to dress for meals. You came to the table clothed in whatever you were standing up in at the time you were called, be that dinner jacket, shorts or speedos – there was no requirement for ceremony. True, on the night of the crayfish party there'd been some attempt at formality, but that had been natural on the part of the guests rather than enforced on behalf of the hosts. By pure coincidence, the turnout that evening was the same and there was a noticeable improvement in our standard of clothing.

There'd been more time available than usual for the girls to prepare themselves – we'd had no break for afternoon tea and the extra hour had made all the difference. Anna would always look stunning anyway, and with the benefit of my help in the kitchen, Katerina had been able to sit down at her make-up.

As for the boys, their watery gymnastics had resulted in a soaking and they'd been forced into seeking a change. Kurt reverted to his white tennis outfit. It was hardly haute couture but it was at least a step up from khaki shorts and loafers. Don put on some smart slacks and a casual shirt. I followed suit and so we all arrived in the dining area looking pretty much as good as we could get.

I'd hoped for conversation to match, but I was initially disappointed. Katerina and Anna had barely seen each other since lunchtime so they'd much to catch up on. Don and Kurt were still mentally out on the water. After I'd listened for the umpteenth time to their version of how to perform the boating equivalent of a handbrake turn or their thoughts on the top speed of a powerboat with a 110 bhp outboard motor, I began to get agitated. Soon I found myself perched on the edge of my chair and eager to break in. As an opening gambit *So, Kurt, how are the kids?* was certain to attract attention but was probably a bit too provocative, and besides, Anna might find it offensive. Waiting my moment, I settled for something less brutal although it still had a cutting edge.

"So, Kurt, how's business these days?"

"Business?"

He made it sound as if this were a question no one had the right to ask – least of all me.

"Yes, you know," I persisted, "business. That thing with the woodyards and the builders' merchants and the like."

He glanced at Don, then back at me and gave a nonchalant shrug of the shoulders. "So-so."

"So-so?" I queried. "What does that mean? So-so good or so-so bad or so-so what?"

"Just so-so."

"What I'm getting at is, are you making any money at it?"

I guessed this would be a tricky question for him to answer. His ego would desperately want to say yes, but there were people sitting round the table who probably knew otherwise. Fortunately for him, he had a ready-made retort.

"After the crash? In Sweden? You must be joking."

"I'll take that as a no, then – which surprises me. I'd have thought that a man of your undoubted entrepreneurial talent would have been able to make money just about anywhere."

Kurt seemed to take this as a compliment. *Perhaps they don't do irony in Sweden*, I thought.

"Of course. But here, it's difficult."

"Oh really? Why's that?"

From his post near the head of the table, Don leant across to top up our glasses of wine. This interruption ensured that if they'd not been doing so before, everyone was now tuned in to our conversation.

"The country's run by socialist bureaucrats," said Kurt. "They don't understand business. They have no interest in it. All they care about is social equality."

"Socialist?" I said. "I thought your government was a centre-right alliance with liberal economic tendencies. Am I not correct?"

I was smirking a little as I looked around the table for support. I might not be an economic guru but I did at least read the newspapers. My assertion was met with a general nodding of heads.

"They say that," Kurt responded, "but really, they're not. Every Swedish government is socialist – it's always been that way. Whoever's in power takes money from those who can make it and gives it to those who can't. That's socialism. They can call themselves what they like, but it's still socialism."

"I gather you're not a fan of social equality."

"Social equality? Pah! No, I'm not. And I'll tell you why." If my intention was to get Kurt animated, I was certainly succeeding. He'd moved forward from his normal recumbent position, his elbows were on the table and he was pointing a finger at me. He was gradually raising himself up onto a high horse – and with a bit of luck he'd fall off any minute. "Social equality makes people lazy. When you have social equality nobody wants to work. What's the point when we're all equal? It's crazy."

"Wait a minute," I said. There was an inconsistency here I could exploit. "I thought Sweden was supposed to be a great place to come and work. I thought people were travelling from all over Europe to come and work in Sweden."

"You mean the immigrants? Don't fool yourself." Kurt's voice descended into a snarl. "They haven't come here to work. They've come here to scrounge off our welfare system. We invite them into the country, give them free housing and social assistance, and then what do they do? Nothing. Most of them don't have jobs. And who's paying for all that? Hard-working people like me."

"You could always employ some of them," I suggested. "I'd have thought they'd be ideal workers to have around a woodyard – great big strapping lads from Poland and Romania. I'd have thought they'd be right up your street – cheap, immigrant labour like that."

Kurt chose not to reply. He'd either not thought of the idea (which, as a self-professed industrialist, would infuriate him), or he was already doing so – a move which seemed to contradict his previous statement. It was probably also illegal.

It was a fact that was not lost on Don. Rather than take sides, he'd remained quiet during the whole of our exchange but now he must have felt I was in need of some restraint.

"Alan, this is Sweden. You can't go round hiring anyone at whatever salary you like. We have laws that govern such things and there are minimum wages. It's not as easy as you think."

It was a sign for me to back off. If Don was going to take sides against me I wasn't prepared to fight the both of them. I resumed eating my stew and the mashed potato I'd spent so much effort on that afternoon.

Underneath the table, Anna's knees were pressing hard against my leg. This time, I didn't resist.

I was in two minds as to what to do with myself after dinner. The company had split into its usual formation – Don and Kurt were out on the balcony, Katerina and Anna in the kitchen, washing up. I'd distanced myself from one group and I was in danger of getting too close to the other. In the end I joined neither and opted for some fresh air, going out through the front door and onto the porch.

Max was waiting faithfully in the yard. He looked up at me as I passed, but then looked away again, completely without apology. I knew better than to try and tempt him – apart from which, I was in the mood to be alone. I turned to the right and the pathway that led down the hill. As I rounded the building I could hear the sound of laughter emanating from the balcony and I caught the pungent whiff of a cigar.

I thought I might walk along the beach. My head was spinning and I was desperate for some kind of clarity. And if my mind was turbulent, then so was the lake. Down by the shoreline, a stiff breeze had sprung up and was ruffling the surface of the water. Angry flecks of white dotted the blue beyond the swimming platform.

At the end of the jetty our proposed extension remained gallingly incomplete, its unfinished timbers sticking out like the exposed ribcage of some dead and decaying beast. On either side, Don's boats bobbed with the swell, their cleats and moorings clinking in the wind, here the launch, beige and bulky, there the speedboat, red and sleek, fresh from its afternoon excursion.

I headed toward the boathouse. I wanted to go out onto the headland and see if I could find Susan. I needed to let her know I was alright and I owed her an explanation. She, more than anyone, would be the one who'd be entitled.

The swing-seat was swaying violently back and forth. I sat down and swayed with it, listening for her voice in the swishing of the reeds. Before long I began to talk and I tried to tell her what I was thinking of doing – and, more importantly, why I was thinking of doing it. I waited patiently for a response, some sign of recognition at least, if not approval.

But there was nothing beyond the whisper of the wind, the trees shook their leaves at me and I knew then I was on my own.

Nine

I'm not sure what I was thinking of that morning. In fact, I'm not sure I was actually 'thinking' at all. And by that I mean the strange process that goes on in your subconscious, that part of you that makes those odd decisions when you're not looking and then announces them to you when you least expect it. My conscious mind was quite clear. I knew exactly what I was doing – *I'm going down to the lake to see if she's there*. Any premeditation had been done the night before on the swing-seat and there was no *Shall I or shan't I?* about it. But as to the subconscious and what was going on inside – well, who knows?

I'd made sure my swimming trunks were ready. They'd still been damp from their outing the previous day and before I went to bed I found a warm spot on the wall of the box room where they could dry off. I knew what clothes I was going to wear, too – a T-shirt and a top in case it was chilly. As to footwear, I'd decided against shoes and socks (too fiddly when you want to get into the water quickly) and I'd settled for flip-flops instead. It was all laid out on top of my suitcase – there was no more 'thinking' to be done.

I'd also decided on a time. My body clock was tuned to six-thirty, but I'd thought that a little bit early and I'd resolved to wait until seven – I didn't want to take the risk of arriving first and be seen to be hanging about waiting. And, as on every occasion when there's a deadline to meet, my internal alarm went off an hour early and I was awake from half past five and lay there, breathing gently. Next door, the sound of Don's snoring vibrated gently through the wooden partition.

She *was* there, of course, and from the look of things she had been for some while. From the top of the hill I could make out the distinctive shape of her head and shoulders in the water beyond the end of the jetty. On top of the stack of wooden planking we'd been using for our project lay a neatly-folded towel and a pile of white clothing.

I made my way carefully down the hill. The morning itself was dry and bright but there'd been a heavy dew and the grass was slippery underfoot. I had to concentrate fully and kept my head down until I reached the safety of the beach so it was only then I realised that Anna was actually on her way back and instead of clambering out onto the pontoon as I'd expected, was now at the end of the jetty approaching the shallows. She was also completely naked and the pile of white clothing I'd seen on the planking was the bikini she'd chosen to discard.

Like other continentals, Swedes will often swim without clothing (skinny-dipping as we call it) particularly after a hot sauna – but that wasn't Anna's intention. It was clear from the speed of her arrival that I wasn't supposed to join her but rather that she would join me, and she emerged from the water like a modern-day Venus, her straight black hair dripping wet and her breasts dimpled with goose pimples from the morning chill.

And oh, how I wanted her! I was swept away on a tide of desire and at that moment there was nothing I would not have given for possession of her body. Had she asked me, I'd have taken her there and then, on the beach, but fortunately sense prevailed. I watched as she walked deliberately by and collected her towel and clothing from the planking. A small rivulet had formed next to her spine and was making its way into the small of her back. As she stopped to pick up her belongings she turned toward me and I saw these words cross her lips.

I'll be in the boathouse.

I waited until she'd gone inside and gave her a minute to make herself comfortable. I remembered how I'd felt when I'd imagined she was in the box room and I realised now, as I opened the boathouse door, how that could not have been possible. Just like my room it was dark, but there was that unmistakable scent that comes from the warmth of a woman's body and I cursed myself for having missed it before. Somewhere in there, lying on the tarpaulin...

I closed the door behind me and dropped the latch. It had been a long time.

Afterwards, we walked to the headland and went to sit on the swing-seat. I'd already made the right-hand end of it my own and Anna curled up on the rest, her head nestled on my thigh where she could look out over the lake. She was now fully dressed, although her hair was still damp to the touch. A strand of it lay flat across her ear, leaving that curve between neck and shoulder exposed. It was an inviting place to rest my hand.

We sat in silence for a while, rocking gently back and forth. The sun climbed steadily through the trees, dappling the surrounding ground and with it, our thoughts gradually crept into the open. Eventually, Anna's curiosity got the better of her.

"When we were in the boathouse..."

"Yes?"

"Were you thinking of her?"

"No."

"Oh, I thought perhaps..."

"Of course not."

I tried to sound as positive as I could. It was, of course, a lie, but under the circumstances, a necessary one. Apart from a few short moments when I'd been absorbed in sawing wood or when I'd contrived to lose myself in work, Susan had never been far from my mind and to imagine that I could dismiss her from my thoughts purely because I was making love to another woman would be to deny the happiness and existence of thirty years of married life. It was too much to ask of myself but I knew I would have to pretend otherwise.

It was natural for Anna to be curious, but to be told I was thinking of my wife when I was with her was not what she wanted to hear. She wanted to be made to feel special and to know that she was of some value in the world. Her friendship with Katerina would help – just as my friendship with Don had helped me – but that on its own wasn't enough. Anna needed to be held and touched and loved in a way that only a man could, a way that her husband was either incapable of or unwilling to do. And yes, I was a man and I was readily available and so the task had fallen to me. Was there any more to it than that? Or were we on the verge of something else?

As for myself, I can imagine what you're going to say. You're going to tell me I only did it in order to spite Kurt. Well, I can't deny that there's a certain degree of truth in that. The idea that while he was snoozing away in the guesthouse, sleeping off another night of schnapps and cigarettes, I was in the boathouse making love to his wife had given added spice to what was already a pleasurable encounter. But that's only half the story.

If Anna had needs that were not being catered for, then so did I – and I don't just mean those of the physical kind. I'd been used to the companionship of a woman for over thirty years, and that had been taken away. I'd replaced it, briefly, with that of a man, and now that had been taken too. I was not an island (no man is) and I could not exist in isolation. Perhaps Anna wasn't the only one in this relationship who needed to be held…

Meanwhile, the sun had continued its upward climb and was showing above the tops of the trees. The thoughts that had emerged into its light began to evaporate in the burgeoning heat as our minds turned elsewhere. Anna stirred and raised her head from my thigh.

"I'd better be getting back."

"Yes, you go on," I said. "I'll give it ten minutes and then I'll follow you up."

She hauled herself to her feet and adjusted her dress, then shouldered her beach bag and towel.

I watched as she set off up the hill. Not once did she turn and look back, or smile or wave. I could understand – and I was thankful for it. This was not first love, we were not sixteen and behaving like children at school. We'd grown too worldly for that and we liked to think that we knew what we were doing.

I stayed for a while on the swing-seat, listening to the music of the reeds – but there was no voice amongst them, just the occasional cry of a seagull drifting out to the east and over Cormorant Island. I wondered whether Susan was there and if she'd heard what we'd been saying. If so, she'd chosen to remain ominously silent.

Then I felt a few spots of rain and it was time to go in and face whatever came next.

Ten

If I'd expected any repercussions as a result of our early-morning escapade, they were an awful long time in coming. Up at the house, nothing seemed to have changed and we began what I came to call our affair quietly, slowly, and, I think I can claim, with some element of dignity. No one made a fuss and there were no dramatic scenes – although every time Anna entered the room I felt a frisson of tension that was quite undeniable. Instead of which we just got on with it as if it were an everyday occurrence. And if Anna had any expectations of where it might lead, she certainly didn't show it at the time.

It wasn't as though we had to put ourselves out to be together. To all intents and purposes we were living under the same roof and saw each other every day. And we'd no need to look for opportunities as they came naturally enough. Kurt remained inattentive, Don was oblivious, and Katerina showed no signs of knowing – or if she did, she contrived to keep it to herself. If we met, it was always by accident, never by design, so there was no clandestine passing of notes or the need for secret trysts. We were in each other's company most of the time anyway, but if we wanted to be alone one of us would take themselves off to the swing-seat in the hope of finding the other, or we'd go out for an early-morning swim. And more often than not, that's all it was – just a swim and a sun-bathe on the pontoon. Although, if we were in the mood, we could always repair to the boathouse…

There was almost a sense of routine about it. Other than at the meal table, Don and Kurt could reliably be found in one of two places, sitting on the veranda playing cards and drinking schnapps, or out on the lake charging about in the speedboat. Katerina and Anna would then be left together, either to work in the kitchen preparing whatever we were to eat next, or when their tasks were done, to find somewhere warm to sit and read. One day it was suggested we take the launch and go out to one of the islands for a picnic – but the men showed absolutely no enthusiasm for the idea and so it was subsequently dropped.

I began to feel much more relaxed. I knew when I awoke each day that I wasn't going to work, there was no prospect of carpentry and the jetty would remain in its current state of unresolved completion. And there'd be no boating lesson either. I won't say I forgot about these things, but rather that I learnt to put them to the back of my mind while I focused on other affairs – most notably, spending time with Anna.

I began reading another book from Katerina's slush pile – and found myself enjoying it. It was the next in the series of crime novels featuring the famous Swedish detective, Sven Wonderström. If you remember, he'd previously been disguised as Franco Zapata, the demon South American knife-thrower. Now, the victims were all members of a football team – one found dead in the shower, one found hanging in the dressing room, one dying of overexertion on the field of play – but with the added complication that the team were close to winning the league and with their leading players being gradually killed off, things were getting tight. I could see what was coming of course, having got the gist of things from the first book. Sven was transferred in under an assumed name and took to the field as a top striker – yet another accomplishment to add to his knife-throwing skills. So he'd not only solve the murders (I already suspected the boss of a rival team) but he'd also score the goal that would eventually win the league. It was all completely predictable but there was satisfaction in seeing it play out. You could say much the same about our affair.

I took to sitting at the end of the sofa in the lounge. It was a place from which I could observe almost all that went on in the house. In front of me, the large picture window gave out onto the balcony where Don and Kurt played cards, while to the left was the entrance to the kitchen where I could hear the girls at their chores. Occasionally, one of them would come through to fetch something, a magazine for instance, or a cup. If it were Katerina, she might ask how I was getting on with her book. If it were Anna, there might be a glance and the faintest hint of a smile, but there was never much more to it than that. It was a way of keeping in touch.

In the afternoons it would invariably grow hot and there'd be swimming parties, but for me they were out of the question. As an alternative, the girls would change into their swimwear and go out onto the deck next to the balcony where they could lie on their sun-loungers and read. Most times I dared not join them (the very thought of seeing Anna in her white bikini would torment me and I would yearn for the next time we could be together) so even in the warmest of weather I would force myself to stay indoors and endure the company of Sven. He, at least, provided no such distractions.

As much as I enjoyed our visits to the boathouse, I took an equal amount of pleasure from the time Anna and I spent with each other on the swing-seat. Hidden away amongst the trees and out of sight of the house, it was a refuge from worldly events and gave us the peace and seclusion our relationship seemed to require. I drew comfort from her presence and she, I think, from mine and we could spend long periods looking out over the lake in quiet contemplation, I in my adopted spot while she nestled close beside me.

But we couldn't sit in silence for ever – nor should we – and it was inevitable some form of conversation would arise. We were both carrying baggage so there had to be ground rules. An unspoken law grew up between us – I wouldn't talk about Susan and Anna wouldn't talk about Kurt. I was happy on both counts – neither was a subject I particularly wanted to explore.

It left us with the balance of our respective families – areas we both seemed happy to discuss. Once I'd told Anna that I wasn't thinking of my wife when I made love to her, it ceased to be a subject of interest and she asked about my children instead. As she'd none of her own, it was natural she should be curious. I told her all I knew – which in Jonathon's case wasn't much. He'd always kept to himself and since the death of his mother had grown ever more introspective. As far as I was aware, he was still deep in the countryside of France although news was hard to come by – a marked contrast from my daughter. Philippa wore her heart on her sleeve – and most any other place she could find – so her hopes and fears were laid out in full on Facebook and the like. We were still exchanging texts; her exam results were through and she'd done well. And by way of comic relief there were always her ongoing relations with Vivienne which one day blew hot, the next day cold. It was these differences, these object lessons in personality, that helped keep us entertained.

Without the benefit of offspring and denied access to the present, Anna harked back to the past. What she told me delivered some surprises. My first discovery was that she wasn't Swedish at all. Her dark and brooding looks should have been a clue but it transpired she was actually from Estonia, a boat ride across the Baltic. She claimed to be a refugee, although technically speaking she must still have been classed as an immigrant. I wondered how Kurt might have viewed that, though I suspected she may not have told him. The rest of her story went as follows.

She'd been born and brought up in one of the poorer districts of Tallinn. She barely remembered her parents. At the time, the country had been part of the U.S.S.R and they were political dissidents, taken away, she said, when she was still at an early age and sent to Siberia to see out their time in some god-forsaken gulag. An only child, she'd been left to live with her grandmother, an ancient and spiteful woman who eked out a pittance as a flower-seller on one of the city's street corners. When the wall fell in Berlin in '89, she'd taken the first opportunity she could to get away, not merely from the oppression of her guardian but also from the country altogether.

Her escape had required an accomplice. She'd chosen a young student named Stephan. They were of much the same age (Anna was just nineteen) and he apparently harboured the same convictions as her parents. From her brief description I imagined him bearded, good-looking, overly idealistic and frightfully principled. He probably wore a duffel-coat and carried a copy of a certain political tract in one of the pockets. He was convinced that a life of Western decadence was ideologically preferable to staying in post-Soviet Estonia, even when the yoke of communism had been removed. Whether Anna shared his beliefs was immaterial – the barriers to freedom were down and she was determined to take advantage. It still wasn't easy. After several abortive attempts, they eventually found a route and she persuaded him to help her stow away on a steamer bound for Stockholm. They'd landed sleepless, broke and with nowhere to stay.

One might have thought that finding a solution to these immediate difficulties would have been a priority. They were for Anna but not, apparently, for Stephan. The very fact of being in Sweden seemed to satisfy any sense of ambition he might have fostered and as soon as he set foot on Western soil, he pronounced himself content. The idea that the right to personal and intellectual freedom were granted in exchange for hard work seemed to have escaped him and in practical terms, he did nothing. He was, as Anna soon discovered, ethically industrious but physically lazy and the problems of daily living were left entirely up to her. But she was used to that. A childhood spent in the company of her grandmother had taught her much and she knew how to graft. She found a refuge that would take them in and get them through those first few days. Once established, she could register them for benefits and begin the search for employment. It was a long, hard road with many twists and turns but one that eventually led her to the woodyard and Katerina's door. If it hadn't been for her comfort and kindness, Anna said she might never have survived.

And as for Stephan, what had happened to him? Anna didn't know; they'd eventually gone their separate ways and she'd never seen him again. Had she been in love with him? I wondered. It was a question I could not resist asking. Perhaps, she said, she wasn't sure, it had been a long time ago, over twenty years, long enough to forget what love was like – twenty years she'd spent living with Kurt...

Eleven

Of the two distinct groupings in the house it was readily understandable that I should gravitate more toward the women. Don
had shunned me and I couldn't bear being with Kurt – but the
girls were altogether more welcoming and I felt much more
comfortable in their company. Besides, it meant I could spend
more time close to Anna and these were precious moments.

I began to invent excuses to be with them. I offered to help out
in the kitchen and laying the table for meals became one of my
permanent employments. If something wanted fetching from an
outbuilding, I fetched it, and I soon became competent at
watering the flowers. It was a far cry from woodwork, but I
needed occupation and as much as I enjoyed Sven Wonderström's
efforts at detection, I couldn't bring myself to sit and read books
all day.

Over a week had gone by after our visitors had arrived when
Katerina announced that another shopping expedition was
required in order to replenish supplies. We were running low on
everything, although of most concern to the boys was that they
were almost out of schnapps. Kurt was also in need of cigarettes
and with no immediate prospect of our guests departing it
seemed sensible to get stocked up. To allow Kurt a modicum of
credit, he did volunteer to pay for it as a means of contributing
toward their keep. *Put it on my card,* he said, only he'd no
intention of going himself and with a dismissive wave of his hand
delegated his wife to do the dirty work. So the girls were
dispatched to the supermarket, and attracted partly by the idea
that we were spending Kurt's money and partly for other, more
obvious reasons, I said that I'd go with them.

I thought I might make myself useful. There'd be a trolley to
push (perhaps two) and heavy bags to lift in and out of the
vehicle. I fancied a go in the Land Rover and even suggested I
should drive, but the Volvo was thought more practical and with

only Anna on the insurance, she was the one to take the wheel. Katerina sat alongside her so I was relegated to a back seat and delegated to hop out and operate the gates.

We were out for the whole of the morning. Food shopping can be a time-consuming process (I should know, I'd done it often enough with Susan) and over the years I'd developed a means of coping with it. I'd confine myself to pushing the trolley and lifting the bags and skilfully avoid any involvement in the decision-making. With two women there to debate the issue it's easier to remain aloof, but it was still half past eleven before we were done. With the best will in the world we'd not be back at the house and everything put away before one. Lunch seemed a distant prospect.

We decided to reward ourselves with a break for coffee. On the return journey Katerina detoured to a small town with a harbour and cafés along the waterfront where we could sit and watch the world go by. We parked up and ordered drinks, but we were not there long before Katerina asked to be excused. She claimed she had errands to run (a watch to collect from the repairers or some such thing) and hoped we wouldn't mind. Could we meet back at the car, say in an hour? Within minutes she was gone and Anna and I were unexpectedly left to our own devices.

For once we were truly alone and free of the restraints the house imposed on us – even on our swing-seat we always ran the risk of discovery. Now we really did behave more like school-children. We walked along the promenade holding hands. We browsed the tacky gift shops and in an arty-crafty jewellers she tried on countless pairs of earrings until I finally persuaded her to keep a pair. She proffered Kurt's card but I insisted on paying for them myself. The satisfaction that it gave me was immense.

We bought each other ice cream, hers adorned with a flake, and we sat on the harbour wall to eat them. The sun did its work, we fought the drops and I kissed the chocolate from her mouth.

We laughed, and for a brief but blessed moment we were happy.

But there was no way it could last. Katerina was waiting at the car.

I should have known that she'd find out – and to tell the truth, it was only ever a question of when and not if. Now she had, and I knew I'd have to deal with it. I was sure that Anna had remained silent but they were far too close for Katerina not to have guessed. A woman's instinct is a finely tuned instrument and their social antennae can pick up the smallest of vibrations from some distance away.

The showdown (if you can call it that) was not long in coming. We returned to the house, put the shopping away and set about getting lunch. While we were eating, it was suggested we spend the afternoon swimming and the general consensus was in favour. As per usual I declined and volunteered to clear up while everyone else was excused. I fully intended to work on my own but when the others went off to change, Katerina lingered behind with the apparent purpose of helping. We were soon in conversation. She began by asking if we'd had a nice time.

"I beg your pardon?"

My instant reaction was to try stalling though I knew exactly what she meant. Our trip out was still at the forefront of my mind but I wanted time to steady the ship.

"I said did you have a nice time? This morning… With Anna."

"Yes, very nice, thank you."

A deliberate silence ensued. I'd no intention of amplifying my answer, I was washing up, my hands were deep in the sink and I had little room for manoeuvre. Katerina, however, was not to be deterred.

"She showed me her new earrings."

"Yes, lovely, aren't they."

"It's not often a man buys a woman earrings. I can't remember the last time Don bought me a pair."

"Well, I'll bet he has at some stage. Anyway, I thought I'd treat her. She doesn't seem to get much fun."

"No..."

Another silence.

Then, "Is there something you want to tell me, Alan?"

"No, not especially. Why?"

"I'm sure you'll correct me if I'm wrong, but I just have this feeling there might be something going on between the two of you."

"Really? And whatever gave you get that idea?"

"Call it intuition. And anyway, it doesn't exactly take a detective..."

I immediately thought of Sven Wonderström and wondered how he might deal with the situation. His primary problem would be the lack of a corpse to investigate. What was dead was any form of relationship between Kurt and his wife, and that had no tangible form. He'd therefore need a confession and I was not yet ready to give one.

"I see... Is it really that obvious?"

"Oh I think so, if you're prepared to look hard enough. I don't know where you go, or what you get up to when you get there, but it hasn't escaped my notice that the two of you have been away from the house at the same time on a number of occasions. To begin with I thought it was just coincidence – but then, when it kept happening..."

"You put two and two together."

"Yes. And then there was this morning."

We were still beating around the bush, despite Katerina's attempt at directness. Perhaps it was time to come clean.

"Has she said anything to you about it?"

"She hasn't had to. And anyway, Anna doesn't talk much about her personal life."

I liked Katerina immensely, but as much as I might trust her I found her assertion hard to believe. It seemed inconceivable to me that Anna would not confide in her best (and possibly only) friend, not least concerning the state of affairs with her husband. I had to assume that Katerina knew about that too if I were to continue. After all, as she herself said, it didn't exactly take a detective...

"So, what if there was?"

"What if there was what?"

"Something going on between us."

Katerina shrugged. "I just wouldn't want to see anyone get hurt, that's all."

"I have no intention of hurting her."

"I'm sure you haven't, Alan – you're a kind and considerate man, you always have been. And anyway, I can assure you that Anna's quite capable of looking after herself. It's not her I'm worried about – it's you."

"Me?" I exclaimed with incredulity.

"Yes, you. You may not know it but you're playing with fire."

I have no doubt that Katerina spoke with the best of intentions but I was a grown man and the insinuation that I was out of my depth rankled.

"Oh, I am, am I? Well, I appreciate your concern but if you think I'm in any way bothered about Kurt, you can think again. He doesn't scare me one iota. Not after the way he's treated her."

"Kurt?" said Katerina. "I think you've got hold of the wrong end of the stick here, Alan. Isn't that another of your English expressions? No, it isn't Kurt you should be wary of – it's Anna."

"Anna?" Another expression of disbelief.

"Yes, Anna. I don't know how much she's told you."

"Well, quite a bit about her background – so I know she's not Swedish, if that's what you mean. She told me she comes from Estonia."

"Ah. So you've heard that story, have you? She said the same thing to us when she arrived."

"I gather you don't believe her. Although I can see how you

might think it was a bit far-fetched."

"Put it this way – I've learnt to take everything Anna says with a pinch of salt. Did she mention Stephan, by any chance?"

"As it so happens, yes, she did."

"Well that part of it's true if nothing else. We met him; she had him in tow when she knocked on the woodyard door. He seemed a nice enough lad but as soon as she sensed there was something better on offer, she dumped him."

"Really?"

"Oh yes."

I assumed she was alluding to Kurt, but it turned out not to be so.

"She made a pass at Don to begin with, you know."

"Don? You must be kidding!"

Of all the people Anna could have chosen, he seemed the most unlikely.

"Don't sound so surprised. Twenty years ago my husband was a very attractive man. He still is of course."

"Of course. All the same..."

"Well, it happened, trust me. After she'd been at the woodyard for a couple of weeks I found she was spending more time in his office than she was in mine. Don, bless him, was completely oblivious – you know what he's like. I wasn't though. I warned her off and as soon as she realised he wasn't available, she started looking round elsewhere. That's when she went after Kurt."

"She went after him? I'd always thought it was the other way round."

"It's easy to see why, she's very clever. But no, and once she'd set her mind to it, it didn't take her long to get her claws into him. They were sleeping together within a week and by the end of the month she'd moved into his apartment. Sometimes she can give you the impression she's no more than a child, but she can be very clinical when she wants to be."

Something horribly cold and clammy descended my spine. I'd

been warned I was playing with fire – but suddenly it felt more like ice. If Katerina was right, I'd come perilously close to being duped, although I still found it hard to accept. Surely there must be some element of truth in what Anna was saying? She'd lost her parents at an early age, she'd been uprooted in her teens, she'd met and married an older man (most likely for security), and now she felt abandoned, emotionally if not financially. It was the easiest thing in the world to take pity on her and take her in my arms and comfort her and I sensed there was a part of me that was doing that even now.

But maybe there was more to Anna than met the eye. She could appear tremendously naïve but beneath that innocent exterior, a calculating mind was potentially at work. Even supposing her story was true, you couldn't escape the tyranny of Estonia without a great deal of nous and determination and one way or another, maybe she was exercising that now to escape the tyranny of her husband. Perhaps she used men for a purpose. Perhaps she'd used Stephan, perhaps she'd used Kurt (and was paying for it) and now perhaps, she was using me. I was either her ticket to a different life or a means of rousing her husband from his marital stupor – it was a subtle game she was playing. No, Anna was not naïve, far from it. Although neither was I and I had my own game to play. But there was still something bothering me.

"What I don't understand though, is why the two of you are still friends? I'd have thought that something like that would have been a barrier between you for ever."

"Life has a funny habit of throwing the oddest people together," Katerina replied. "And I can't deny there was something in her story I found engaging – all that stuff about her parents and her wicked grandmother – and when we first met I suppose I was taken in by her 'little girl lost' act. But once we knew where we stood and she realised I could see right through her, she dropped any attempt at deception and we got on well together. Plus, she's married to Kurt and there's this thing with him and Don. And I still need to keep an eye on her..."

Something clicked in my brain, a quote about keeping your friends close and your enemies even closer.

"So you still don't trust her?"

"Let me answer that by asking you a question."

Our washing-up had come to a halt and Katerina was standing stock-still in the kitchen, a damp plate in one hand and a drying-up cloth in the other. We'd reached the crux of the matter and I sensed I was about to be questioned as to my intentions.

"Go on."

"Are you in love with her?"

"No, Katerina, I'm not."

That, I'd seen coming, if nothing else, and I'd decided on my reply some time in advance. My answer had been the truth, but it was also the lesser of two evils. To say yes was to open myself up to a number of unwanted possibilities. Love, in the eyes of most people, Katerina amongst them, meant marriage and commitment and ultimately staying together. That was not on my agenda. Besides, love wasn't like that, as I knew only too well. On the other hand, to say no was to admit to a degree of callousness and self-interest I might find embarrassing – but I'd rather that than risk misinterpretation.

"Thank God for that."

Katerina's response was reassuring. But there was still another worry as I wondered if she'd shared her concerns.

"Does Don know anything about this?"

"Don?" She raised a sceptical eyebrow. "You must be joking. Don wouldn't know about something like this if it jumped up and bit him on the leg." She'd resumed her drying-up and bent to put a plate away in a cupboard. "No, Don just bumbles along in his own little world, I'm afraid. He's as happy as a sandboy mucking about in his boats but when it comes to this sort of thing, he doesn't have a clue. And I'd rather it stayed that way, quite frankly."

"Well, I certainly won't be saying anything."

"Thank you."

She stopped again, the drying-up cloth dangling from her hand.

"You will be careful, won't you Alan?"

"Me? Of course I will." I was an actuary – it went without saying.

"No, I meant it – seriously. I don't want any upsets."

"No," I said. "There won't be, I promise."

"Good. Now let's get these dishes cleared away."

I dried my hands and started helping her with the plates.

As to my promise, there wasn't much else I could say. I owed her that, if only because I was a guest in her house and didn't want to cause any difficulty. The problem was, some things were beyond my control...

Twelve

That evening, it was decreed we should have another barbecue on the beach. The weather had turned and it had grown hot again. The afternoon had been sultry, the forecast remained good and there was a general feeling that we should all get out of the house and enjoy some fresh air. Indoors, it had begun to feel like a pressure cooker...

There were fresh supplies for the occasion. Katerina and Anna had bought flint steaks at the supermarket. Huge round slabs of pork coated in a spicy paste, they were a favourite of Don's and easy to cook – a few minutes each side and they were done, ideal for a charcoal fire. Together with some baked potatoes and a simple salad, it was all that we would need. Except for alcohol, of course, and now there was plenty, an unopened case of lager, a dozen bottles of wine, and naturally enough, a replenished stock of schnapps. Kurt must have thought his money well-invested.

We trooped down the hill around seven. Everyone had something to carry. It was one of Malaren's unwritten rules that you never went up or down the slope without some kind of cargo – the last thing you needed was to have to go back and fetch the one thing you'd forgotten. The penalty for incurring that extra journey was literally steep – it was a long way down and even longer back up, especially when you'd had a few drinks.

Don and Kurt had been deputed to carry the picnic basket and walked with it slung between them. Katerina had loaded it up to the brim and her extensive collection of cutlery, plates, and glasses clanked ominously at every step. The dubious privilege of carrying the case of lager had fallen to me. It appeared less bulky, but still required two hands and I was further loaded up with the rugs we were to sit on, two on top of the lager and one more over each shoulder. As organisers of our makeshift expedition the girls naturally got away with it, limiting themselves to bringing the food, packed neatly into their beach bags. Laden like beasts of burden, we descended into the dusk. Max came last, bearing nothing but his tennis ball.

It would have been better if someone had been dispatched to get the fire going in advance. But Don and Kurt had been deeply engaged in their latest game of cards and Katerina either hadn't wanted to disturb them or simply hadn't thought of it. I had, but it wasn't my place to interfere and besides, that same streak of wilful malevolence which had once kept me from gardening now prevented me from speaking out. *You can ignore me if you want*, I thought. *You'll pay for it in the end.*

And so the fire had to be started from scratch. Even then I'd have willingly taken it on – the physical challenge of finding some kindling, balling some paper, sparking a flame and providing enough glowing coals to cook by was appealing. There'd been little in the way of achievement in the past ten days and left for an hour on my own, listening to the lap of the waves, I'm sure I could have sorted it out. But now we were all there, this was Don's house and Don's job and as a result, it was an age before the cooking got going and I guess that's when the damage was done. With nothing to eat, all they could do was drink, and before we'd even put a flint steak on the grill, half the case of lager had gone.

Personally, I was hungry and that's what was driving me – but Don was obviously not and appeared in no hurry at all. It made me think they'd already started drinking at the card table (the original consignment of schnapps had yet to be finished) although I knew it wasn't the lager as the case I'd carried down had been full. Anyway, whatever the reason it had slowed him to a crawl and he sauntered over to the woodstore seemingly without a care in the world.

As I'd fully expected, Kurt was of no help whatsoever. I'd spread the rugs out round the old barbecue Don had built and as soon as I'd laid them down, he flung himself onto the one nearest the site of our former fire, stretched himself out and immediately lit a cigarette. It was clear there'd be no assistance coming from that quarter.

Don returned with a bundle of sticks fit for kindling, broke open the case of lager, took one for himself and one for Kurt, then offered one to me. I thanked him but shook my head. I was already thinking of that imaginary line which defined the limits of my sobriety. I was not going to cross it that evening and if I was going to drink at all, I'd enjoy it all the more after something to eat rather than on an empty stomach.

The girls were busily engaged in unpacking the contents of the picnic basket and their beach bags. I'd brought an extra rug on which they could lay it all out – plates, knives, forks, a salad bowl covered in cling film – although the wine and the glasses were left in the basket for fear of them falling over. The baked potatoes were hot and still in their wrappings of silver foil. They, at least, had been cooked in advance. Just as well, I thought, or we'd have nothing to eat before midnight.

Don was having trouble getting the fire started. The kindling looked small enough but he'd put no paper beneath it and he was trying to ignite things directly using the lighter he'd borrowed from Kurt. Even I could have told him that was never going to work. His unusual lack of practicality worried me. It was as if all the skills and fieldcraft he'd taught me during our time together had been forgotten, buried beneath the weight of entertaining Kurt, the stories, the joking, the cards, the alcohol…

I went over to see if I could help.

"Don?"

He turned to face me, a half-empty can of lager in one hand, the useless lighter in the other. I'm not even sure he recognised who I was, and it was that moment more than any other that made me think I'd lost him. His eyes had dimmed to a cold, blank stare and the only expression he could manage was a weak and inane smile.

"Are you alright?" I asked.

"Absolutely fine."

"Good. Why don't I go up to the house and get some paper and a box of matches? It might make things a lot easier."

"Righty-ho. Good plan."

The lighter he clutched was still spouting a pathetically small flame. I retrieved it from his fingers and returned it to Kurt.

"I'm going up to the house," I announced to the company in general. "Anybody want anything while I'm there?"

There was a communal shaking of heads.

Don had not yet taken his eyes off me. For a moment I thought he might add to my list, but clapped a heavy hand on my shoulder instead.

"Thank you, Alan. You're a good man. I don't know what I'd do without you."

"I know," I said, and set off up the hill.

The paper I was seeking was always going to be in the lounge – there was a pile of old magazines on the coffee table or failing that, in the wood-box next to the stove. The matches were kept somewhere in the kitchen and I remembered a drawer I thought I'd seen them in.

I decided to make this my first port of call and I'd just laid hands on them when I heard the porch door swing open and I knew someone else was in the house.

They've come up to use the loo, I thought. *They should have thought of that before.*

I went through to the lounge to collect the paper and there was Anna, scouring the table and chairs on the veranda. Her face wore a pained and troubled expression.

"What's up?" I called from the darkness.

"It's Kurt. He's run out of cigarettes and he's sent me up to fetch some. He said there was a box out here somewhere but I can't find them."

She opened the balcony door to come into the lounge and I

immediately saw that she'd been crying. Her eyes were red and a line of tears had run down her cheek and into the corner of her mouth.

"Hey," I said. "What's this? Come here." I waved her across and she came to me and I folded her up and laid her head on my shoulder. "Come on," I said. "It's nothing to get upset about. It's only a packet of cigarettes. We'll soon find some more." We must have bought two hundred of the damn things that morning at the supermarket.

"I know." She blurted it out between sniffs. "It's not that, it's just that I'm so…"

Unhappy?

I'd become practised at reading between the lines and what little instinct I'd acquired was telling me this was a crucial moment. I sensed it was a prelude to some greater plea and if she was ever going to deliver a 'take me away from all this' speech (and I'd now grown certain that she would), this was as good a time as any. In that sense her timing was immaculate, coming straight on top of our morning together, and with the situation developing down at the beach it was a calculated move. Ironic though that she should choose the very day Katerina had issued her warning.

Well, if that was the case, I didn't want to hear it. This was neither the time nor the place and I'd promised Katerina there wouldn't be any trouble. On top of which, it was beginning to become rather tiresome and on this occasion I declined to fill in the blank she'd so deliberately left empty. I'd had enough tears of my own and the situation was starting to cloy.

I fetched a dry handkerchief from my pocket and discreetly offered it up.

"Here," I said. "Take this. You go on back down." One last sniff and she began dabbing at her cheeks. "I'll find Kurt's cigarettes. If push comes to shove and they're not on the veranda, there's bound to be some in the car."

She nodded and wiped her nose, then turned toward the door. I waited until I was sure that she'd gone then went out onto the balcony.

The cigarettes were exactly where I'd seen her put them, shoved beneath a cushion on one of the easy chairs. I gathered them up, together with the box of matches and the paper, and sat on the veranda for a few minutes wondering what to do.

Down the hill in front of me, Anna's shapely form trailed into the twilight. I had, it was true, lusted after her. But that had not been her only attraction and I was beginning to realise how the look of abject melancholy she so constantly employed chimed with those very same moods of sadness I'd once experienced myself. Here was another danger – that she'd awaken in me thoughts and feelings I believed I'd conquered and drag me down into the pit from which I'd so narrowly escaped. Harbouring a store of such painful memories, I couldn't let that happen but I feared her gift for melodrama far exceeded my capacity to resist.

How much more can I take? I wondered. *At some point, this will have to end. And perhaps that's better sooner rather than later...*

Thirteen

I'd been away for no more than ten minutes but affairs down at the beach had already moved on. The first pair of lager cans had been discarded and a second ripped from the case. Kurt was still sprawled on his rug, waiting for the arrival of his precious cigarettes, but Don had remained standing. Later on, when the fire had been lit and the coals were ready for use, the honour of searing the flint steaks would fall to him as host, and it occurred to me that he'd rather not take the risk of descending to Kurt's level and lie down for fear of not being able to get up again.

The girls had resumed rearranging the crockery and salad. Rather than give the cigarettes directly to Kurt, I passed them discreetly to Anna. She'd stopped crying, although her eyes were still red and she continued to give off her wretched melancholic look.

The fire had clearly not been touched since my departure. Don seemed to show no interest in it and I could see that if we were to get any supper at all that evening it was going to be down to me. I hurriedly screwed up some paper, piled on the kindling and set light to the stack. The tiny flame soon multiplied, building up the colours in turn – blue, red then orange. Don stood by, can in hand, admiring my handiwork.

"That should do it."

"Where do you keep the coals?" I asked.

"Boathouse. Big bag. Under the bench on the left. Put the light on."

"Fine," I said. "I know where to find it."

I noted he didn't offer to come with me.

I fetched the coals and spread a good layer on top of the kindling. Even if all went well, it would be another thirty minutes before we could start cooking. If my meagre experience of barbecuing had taught me nothing else, it was that you were wasting your time putting anything on the grill before the coals were glowing. Thirty minutes at least. Thirty minutes in which there was little else to do except drink more lager...

Watching two men get drunk before dinner is not an edifying sight. In fact it's rather sad. It's also quite rude and discourteous to your host (although in Don's case, he *was* the host – but that's neither here nor there). Getting drunk after dinner is slightly different. There are plenty of excuses – you're celebrating the meal you've just eaten, there's been plenty of good wine and you can take pleasure in a few liqueurs. And if it all gets too much, you can always slide off to bed without creating a great deal of offence. Before dinner, there are no excuses. Your next job is to make a decent attempt at eating the meal the cook has provided – and when you're three sheets to the wind, that's not always easy.

Two more rounds of lager went down in the course of the thirty-minute window, so by the time I announced we were ready to begin cooking, the pile of empty cans had accumulated to eight. The case had originally held twelve and I considered taking one myself in the hopes of stemming the flow, but I realised this was a futile gesture. It was more likely to get *me* into trouble than save Don and Kurt from theirs. I poured myself a glass of red wine instead and took occasional sips.

The fire, thank God, had burnt well and the coals were giving off a fierce heat. I tapped Katerina gently on the shoulder. "I think we can make a start now."

She dipped into one of the bags and fetched out the box of flint steaks. "Here..."

Don stood by the barbecue, swaying gently. At his feet, the fire flickered once or twice but the flames were gone now, their power transferred into the glowing coals. I took the lid off the box and offered it up. He keenly inspected the contents.

"Ah, meat," he said, prodding one of the steaks with a thick forefinger. "Did you hear that, Kurt? We've got some meat at last."

Kurt laughed from the shadows beyond the fire. He remained laid out on his rug, head propped up on one hand, cigarette and can in the other. Kurt wasn't bothered about meat – he was perfectly happy on his diet of lager and tobacco.

Don took a couple of flint steaks from the box and lobbed them onto the grill. They clattered onto the metal and settled down with a sizzle. He reached for a third but simultaneously swayed backwards, his intended toss missing its target and the steak plomped into the sand next to the grill.

"Shit. That one looks like yours, Alan," he said, trying to make a joke of it. "We'll dust the sand off and tart it up a bit – it'll be fine."

Even as he spoke I could taste the grit between my teeth. I shuddered and my stomach turned over. He must have noticed.

"Only joking." He bent awkwardly forward and picked it up from the ground, holding it delicately between thumb and forefinger as if it were somehow infected. "The fish can have that one."

Drawing back his arm, he hurled it forward like a Frisbee so it sailed over the jetty and landed *plosh* in the water.

Kurt laughed again. "Ha, ha, ha! Or a shark!"

"Or a shark..." Don repeated thoughtfully. "That's a good one..."

He returned to the box and this time the two remaining flint steaks found their way safely onto the grill. We were one down and someone, probably the girls, would have to share. I wouldn't have minded sharing one myself – the damn things were so big one of them *could* have fed a shark.

Luckily, there were no more mishaps after that and we soon settled down to eat.

It was now nearing ten and the end of another long day stretched before us. The light was beginning to fade, the sky was obscured by cloud, and with it a chill descended. After we'd finished our steak and potatoes, Katerina and Anna went up to the house to fetch cardigans. They returned with marshmallows and a flask of fresh coffee. We toasted the mallows on wooden skewers over the dying embers of the fire, messy chunks of them melting off uncontrollably and falling onto the coals where they hissed and spat in bubbling pink blobs. The parts we could save were warm and nourishing, as was the coffee, and for a while we could counter the cold.

I'd hoped that the introduction of food might stave off the consumption of alcohol. For a while it looked as if this might succeed, the lager was replaced by coffee and there was a good deal of sobering up. A lull set in as steady digestion took precedence and the atmosphere appeared to settle down with the food. There was a hope it would all end here and that we could soon slope off to our beds and enjoy a good night's sleep, but there was always a brooding nature about the silence as if this were merely the quiet before the storm.

It wasn't long before Kurt felt the call of nature. He needed (as he put it) a 'comfort break'. Where he intended to take it he didn't exactly say, but he raised himself painfully from his rug and staggered off in the direction of the nearest set of bushes. I thought Don might volunteer to accompany him – they seemed permanently joined at the hip and Kurt might need guidance, some bushes being presumably better for the purpose than others. But Don stayed put, either incapable of movement himself or determined not to show weakness in the company of his friend.

Kurt was gone for a good deal longer than seemed natural. And when he did return it was down the hill from the house rather than from the vicinity of the bushes, a bottle of schnapps dangling dangerously from either hand. As he reached the juncture of slope and sand he held them aloft as if in triumph.

"Hey, hey! Look what I've found!"

Don seemed to eye his approach with trepidation and

dragged himself to his feet. There was a sense of 'if you must' about it although his response disguised it well. "Brilliant. Good thinking, that man."

Katerina however, was not so circumspect. Up until now she'd refrained from interfering but at last she relented, getting to her feet to put a restraining hand on her husband's arm. "Don, I really don't think…"

…*that would be a good idea.*

Her admonition was delivered softly and with the best of intentions – but Don roughly shook her off and took the bottle that was offered him. In the shadows behind, Kurt's face wore a clear expression of victory while Katerina was forced to withdraw to her seat on the rug where she sought consolation in the company of her friend.

Don was now free to join up with Kurt and they took themselves off together, retreating some ten yards or so up the hillside. They must have thought that out of sight was out of mind, and if they were going to misbehave themselves it was best done at a distance. Two outlines in the twilight, their voices were clearly audible.

They began with a series of inane comments about the barbecue, and in particular the steak which Don had let drop in the sand and subsequently hurled into the lake. It soon acquired iconic status and was constantly referred to as 'the one that got away'. Then there was a pause, interspersed at regular intervals with a pop as the cork was removed from the neck of a schnapps bottle. Their conversation then resumed, much along the same lines as before, although their words became less and less distinguishable by the minute. And so it went on, another pause, more drinking (or so I guessed) and then more of the talking. I'd clearly misjudged the situation and rather than calling a halt, the ingestion of food and coffee had merely sobered them up to the point where they felt they could take on more alcohol.

A quick count of the pile of empties revealed that all twelve cans of lager were now 'dead'. Somewhere along the line I'd missed the last four – had it been while I was up at the house? Or had I simply miscounted? Perhaps I'd become as insensible as the others and I sought to convince myself otherwise by tearing up the empty cardboard box and feeding the bits to the flames.

After half an hour, Don and Kurt started singing – although it was actually Kurt who began it and Don who was cajoled to join in. Despite their wavering rendition, I recognised it as the chorus from "Helan går!" but if their intention was to recreate the atmosphere of the crayfish party, it all fell rather flat. I should have foreseen what would come next.

"Hey, Alan!" Kurt's voice floated down the hillside.

"What?"

"Give us a song."

"No way."

"Come on, Alan, it's your turn."

"No it isn't – there aren't any turns."

"Yes, there are – and you're next. We want to hear you sing, don't we, Don?"

Don had no option but give a slow nod of the head.

I glanced round at the girls. I was sure they had no desire to hear me sing but if compliance formed the line of least resistance then I might as well have their approval. They shrugged and raised no objection so I launched into two full verses of "Two Men Went to Mow", singing as lustily as I could to forestall any complaints. I didn't want to have to repeat the exercise.

Kurt rather predictably fell about laughing, rolling around on the grass and banging his fist on the ground. Don confined himself to a couple of suppressed snorts and burst into a round of applause – but any satisfaction he may have felt was short-lived as Kurt told him he was next.

Don waved a hand in front of his face. "Definitely not," he protested.

"Yes, yes," insisted Kurt. "Absolutely yes. And you are

English, so we want an English song – don't we, Alan?"

I declined to answer.

"Of course we do," insisted Kurt. "Come on, Don, your turn now. Something English."

Don immediately caved in. Perhaps, like me, he judged it easier to acquiesce than to argue, although I'm not sure there was very much judgement about it. Anyway, there he was, suddenly on his feet, rather unsteady but standing nevertheless. The song that emerged was an old nursery rhyme, and although it was years since I'd heard it, I too could still remember the words:

"Oh, the Grand Old Duke of York
He had ten thousand men.
He marched them up to the top of the hill
And he marched them down again."

And in conjunction with each of the lines, Don took a couple of steps, firstly up the hill and then back down, finishing where he'd started.

Kurt was convulsed with laughter. He doubled up, fell over onto his side and curled up into a ball, seemingly unable to move.

His reaction only served to give Don encouragement and he began belting out the chorus:

"When they were up, they were up
And when they were down, they were down.
And when they were only halfway up
They were neither up nor down."

The steps grew progressively bigger with each line, and for the last two he chose to march on the spot, bringing his knees up to the level of his waist. He also chose to turn in a circle at the same time and this proved to be his downfall, literally, as he overbalanced, fell heavily to the ground and rolled to the bottom of the hill where he lay in a heap on the sand.

I jumped to my feet while the girls anxiously looked round.

For a few vital seconds Don didn't move – but then he gradually sat up and I knew he was going to be alright.

Kurt was already on his way down the hill. He helped Don to his feet and, still laughing, began brushing the sand from Don's clothes.

"When they were up, they were up
And when they were down, they were down.
And when they were only halfway up
They were neither up nor down. Ha, ha, ha!"

Kurt straightened his friend up. Then, with their arms around each other's shoulders, they began to make their way slowly back up the slope, Kurt attempting to persuade Don to continue his song.

"Oh, the Grand Old Duke of York..."

But Don had been shaken by his ordeal and could only mumble a weak accompaniment. They returned to their seats, the singing died down and for the moment the excitement was over.

Common sense dictated I should have gone to bed at this point, and I don't know why I didn't. The barbecue was finished, the tidying-up could wait until morning and matters were following their usual course. Don and Kurt were in cahoots, Katerina and Anna the same and yet again, I was the wallflower.

But something held me back and I stayed on. It must have been a blend of care and curiosity. After the crayfish party I'd lasted out for as long as I could, purely to see what the men would get up to. Tonight, I already knew and I thought I'd seen the worst of it – but the incident with Don had made me wary and I felt I ought to look out for him. Events had taken a turn I didn't like – an easy thing to see when you're sober but far, far harder when you're not.

All remained calm for a while. Further up the hillside, Don and Kurt returned to swapping stories and there was joking and subdued laughter. Over on their rug, the girls continued their conversation, broken from time to time by the raucous call of a seagull. It seemed that we'd all settled down for the evening.

I lay back, closed my eyes and listened for the sounds of the night. The reeds were some way off but I fancied I could still hear them rustling. I must have dozed off as I don't recall the passage of time, although I was conscious enough at one point to hear the word *Shit!* uttered loudly and to start up as an empty bottle of schnapps came bounding down the hill and passed me by on its way to the beach. *Well, at least they've got a spare,* I thought and paid it no attention. It settled in the shallows, rolling back and forth with the surf. I looked to check the fire but it was pretty near dead, just a few flakes of white ash swirling in the breeze.

I'm sure I was asleep when it happened. Later, I was to blame myself for not being more alert – had I been so, I might have been able to stop it. But I was not, and before I knew it, it was over.

I came to at the sound of an argument and sat up to see where it was. All four of my companions were out on the jetty next to the speedboat. Don had the keys in his hand and Katerina had her hand on his arm.

"Don – no," I heard her say, quite firmly.

Kurt was standing by, his hands in his pockets and with his pullover draped over his shoulders in that infuriating way of his, an inane grin on his face.

Half-hidden behind Katerina, Anna waited anxiously for the outcome.

I got up and began walking toward the jetty but it was already too late. Don had tossed the keys to Kurt who'd scrambled down into the well of the boat and was trying to start the engine. Anna stood back, unwilling to physically intervene, but Katerina was still fighting for possession of her husband. In another fit of pique, Don shoved her off, mouthing *Don't you tell me what to do* and joined Kurt in the boat.

I broke into a run, hoping that the engine might falter. But it fired up first time, the familiar *chick-a-boom, boom, boom* turning swiftly to a deep-throated burble. Don cast off the ropes and as I pounded down the boarding, the boat moved off. I arrived in time to see it disappear behind our incomplete extension, and with Kurt at the wheel and its unsecured moorings still trailing out behind, it roared off uncontrollably into the night.

Part Four

Recovery

One

There comes a point in most crime dramas where the main suspects realise they've been rumbled and try to make a break for it. It's usually by car, probably because it's cheaper to film, but occasionally it's by aeroplane or boat. Without a moment's hesitation, the would-be hero invariably goes after them and following an exciting series of stunts, alarms and excursions finally brings the fugitives to justice. Indiana Jones favoured the direct route and would fling himself at a passing truck or swim out to board a submarine. Closer to home, Sven Wonderström initially gave chase by horse, although what means of transport he used in book two was as yet unknown to me. But I was sure he'd find something, they always do.

Well, there were to be no such heroics in my case. I wasn't built for that sort of thing – apart from which, I couldn't swim particularly well and I was already out of breath. I was much fitter now than when I'd first arrived, it's true, but that did not extend to accomplishing feats of Olympic proportions. I came to a halt at the end of the jetty with my hands on my knees and attempted to recover.

"Sorry," I panted, gasping for air. "Couldn't stop them... Fell asleep... Arrived too late..."

But Katerina wasn't listening.

"Alan, you've got to go after them."

"Can't..." I mumbled. "What with?"

"Take the launch."

"No good... Too slow..."

The speedboat had twice the power and would be halfway across the lake before I could even leave the jetty.

"We have to do *something*, Alan. They're both drunk for God's sake. We can't just let them go off like that."

I could see her point – but their ship had literally sailed and at the moment there was no alternative. Like a blip on a radar screen, the speedboat had swiftly become nothing more than a speck on the darkened surface of the lake. Now and then I could hear the high-pitched scream of the engine as the boat leapt out of the water, but that too gradually receded. Soon it would be both out of sight and out of hearing – if not entirely out of mind.

The minute or so which had elapsed since their departure had enabled me to regain my breath. I could now give Katerina a proper reply, although I suspect it was not one she wanted to hear.

"Frankly, there's not much we *can* do. We'll just have to sit and wait it out."

She clenched her teeth with frustration and stood with her hands firmly on her hips, looking out in the direction of the rapidly disappearing boat. She was annoyed, possibly with me for my inability to act, certainly with her husband for his foolish behaviour, and probably with the world in general for its random and uncontrollable ways.

Max had joined us on the jetty. He'd spent most of the evening dozing in front of the fire, but the sudden surge of excitement had woken him and he'd got up to investigate. He took his cue from Katerina and went a couple of yards beyond her, standing with his tail erect and yapping into the night. I'd not heard him bark before, a sign perhaps that he knew something was wrong.

Katerina rather cruelly rounded on him. "Quiet, Max. Keep quiet for goodness' sake, I can't hear myself think."

But he persisted and it was only when she broke her pose and frustratedly snatched him up that he resumed his normal silence. I felt rather sorry for him. He'd really done nothing wrong and yet it was he, rather than I, who was bearing the brunt of Katerina's anger. She turned abruptly on her heel and marched swiftly past, heading back toward the beach with the dog tucked firmly under her arm.

Her sudden exit left me alone with Anna. She'd said nothing since the incident had begun, either while Katerina was pleading with the men on the quay, or afterwards once the boat had gone. Her outward expression seemed to say nothing either and to all intents and purposes she remained implacably emotionless. Her look conveyed neither joy nor sorrow, but it actually spoke volumes. She neither cared whether her husband got drunk and went off in a speedboat, nor whether he stayed ashore. He was going to get drunk anyway, and there was nothing she could do about it. And rather than get upset or angry about it, as Katerina had done, all that this episode of madness could do was further confirm her own state of unhappiness. I was no doubt supposed to fold her in my arms and comfort her once more, but any desires I may have had in that direction had disappeared along with the boat. I restricted myself to attracting her attention with a gentle touch to her elbow.

"We're better off going up to the house. Come on. You'll catch cold out here."

The same thought had potentially occurred to Katerina. With Max rendered silent he'd become a burden to her rather than a concern, and as soon as she reached the beach she sought to dispose of him. Half thrown forward, half leaping from her arms, he plomped onto the sand and stood looking up at her, cocking his head to one side.

She immediately began to clear up the remains of the barbecue, quickly gathering up whatever came to hand and shoving it into the nearest available container. The light had gone; it was hard to see, and in different circumstances it might all have been left until morning but these were difficult times and she was in need of occupation. She'd also imposed on us an angry silence and the clattering of plates, glasses and cutlery served to fill an otherwise embarrassing void.

Anna went to help while I tended to the fire.

A pile of dormant white ash, it looked to be dead but when I kicked the coals apart there was still a remnant of warmth, a dull glow amongst the embers. I snuffed it out with sand shaken from the rugs before folding them into a neat pile.

With just the three of us left we were never going to carry everything up in one go – although I think Katerina would have liked to. It would have given her a sense of achievement to set against her frustration and she loaded herself up with as much as she could carry, if not more, as if she were saying *Look, I'm doing all I can*. It was a pointless gesture, of course.

"There's no need for that," I said. "Leave some of it here. I'll come straight back down and collect whatever we can't manage."

She relinquished a beach bag and a rug, grateful for the help. I volunteered to take the picnic basket (it weighed a ton, packed to the brim with assorted debris) and we set off up the hill in single file. The party was officially over.

I returned to retrieve the bag and the rug and a few other items we hadn't been able to cope with first time round. I also wanted to lay hands on the empty schnapps bottle that had rolled by earlier. If we were to clear the beach and pretend we'd never been there (as I guessed was Katerina's intention) it was an important piece of evidence that needed to be recovered. It was still rolling around in the surf next to the jetty.

I found the other one too, as I walked back up the hill, lying in the hollow where Don and Kurt had held their impromptu drinking session. It was also unsurprisingly empty, and rather than take it indoors I dumped the pair of them straight in the bin at the back of the house. The pile of cans had already disappeared, swept up, I assumed, by Katerina's busy hand.

By the time I got back, most of the tidying-up had been done or was in the process of being completed. Two pairs of hands in the kitchen were more than enough and besides, there was something I felt I should do.

Out on the veranda, Don's pair of binoculars hung from their customary hook. I took them down and scanned the horizon, searching for some sign of life. If I was lucky there'd be a trail of fluorescence left on the water and if so, there was no reason why

I shouldn't see it. Unfortunately, I was prevented from making a full reconnaissance by the irritating presence of the flagpoles. They obscured my line of sight to the east and however far I moved to the left, I struggled to see past them. This was the direction I was sure the truants would have taken. Their return journey, I was equally sure, would be by way of the north and toward the pontoon. The view in that quadrant was fine but as yet there was nothing to be seen.

Katerina soon came to join me.

"Anything?"

"No, not yet. I'll keep looking. As soon as I see something I'll let you know."

"Ok. God, it's cold out here."

She shivered, rubbed the top of her arms then retreated back into the lounge and closed the door behind her. I fetched myself a coat from the hallway, sat down at the table and began my midnight vigil.

Katerina reappeared about half an hour later. I assumed it was for the purpose of a progress report and I immediately shook my head. "Nothing, I'm afraid." Although in fact, she'd come to make an announcement.

"I think I'm going to call the police."

"Isn't it a bit early for that?" I said. "There's still a chance they might show up." I had in mind the idea that Kurt might want to practise a few of his party tricks before returning. Even so, he was taking his time about it.

"Don't try and put me off, Alan, that's what I've decided to do."

"Ok, if you think they can help. Wouldn't we be better off calling the coastguard?"

"Don't be silly – there isn't a coastguard. This is a lake, not the sea, and there isn't a coast."

"Ah…" It was a simple mistake, although perhaps not

deserving of so sharp a rebuke. I told myself it was late and we were tired and under the circumstances it was best to be forgiving. "Sorry, I wasn't thinking clearly."

"That's alright. I'm not sure any of us are at the moment. Anyway, that's what I'm going to do."

I'd have offered to do it myself, but of course any conversation would have had to have been in Swedish, and for me that wasn't possible. The best I could do was lend some moral support, so I followed her out into the hallway.

It proved to be a long and difficult call. Despite what you might read in Swedish novels or see on television, there isn't much crime committed in rural Sweden in the middle of the night and the stations are manned accordingly. The idea that someone like Sven Wonderström is sitting there waiting to leap into action at the first sign of trouble is a myth. Crime fighters of his ilk come at a premium – and anyway, nobody had as yet committed a crime.

But yes, somebody did at least answer the phone, although I had the impression it was a desk clerk whereas Katerina wanted to speak to someone in authority. I couldn't understand all that she was saying, but I did grasp the gist of it and she would occasionally clamp her hand over the mouthpiece and give me an update in English. *They've gone to fetch somebody, a sergeant I think.*

A long wait ensued during which Katerina paced to and fro in the narrow hallway and chewed nervously on a fingernail. Eventually there was a voice at the other end of the line and the pair of them began jabbering away in Swedish. The conversation rebounded back and forth with Katerina becoming progressively more agitated until she finally threw her hand up in a gesture of despair.

"What is it?" I asked.

"They won't do anything."

"Why not?"

"They say that they've nothing to go on. As far as we know, no one's been injured and nothing's been stolen. And until there's a reportable incident, they won't budge. If you ask me, they're too lazy to get off their fat arses and do something when they can sit in the comfort of their police station and warm themselves in front of a fire."

I didn't say so, but human nature being what it is, I could fully understand.

"Did you report them as missing?" I said, in an attempt to be constructive.

"Technically speaking, I can't. They have to be gone twenty-four hours before you can do that."

"Tell them they went off the night before then. That should do it."

"It's too late for that now. And anyway, they won't send a boat out at night – they have to wait until daylight."

And so, it seemed, would we. But at this time of year, daylight was only a couple of hours away...

Katerina hung up in disgust and stood with her arms firmly folded in an attitude of deep personal determination. It seemed that everyone had failed her – and that included me.

"I'm sorry," I said. It wouldn't do much good, but sympathy was all I could offer. "How's Anna taking this by the way?"

"See for yourself." She opened the door to the lounge and invited me to look in.

Anna was stretched out on the settee, her knees drawn up like a child, fast asleep. In the absence of a pillow she'd tucked a cushion beneath her head and there was an angelic look about her, as if she had not a care in whatever world she presently inhabited. Perhaps, with her eyes closed, unconscious, she could find some form of escape...

How I envied her – if only I could do the same! In our current state of crisis, my subconscious mind would naturally revert to Susan, her pain, her suffering, and a funeral I had not so long ago attended. For a while Malaren had distracted me. Its trees, its water, the smell of freshly sawn wood, the promise of work and the companionship of another human being had been enough to paper over the cracks. But all that had been taken from me and I was left with the same empty feeling I'd arrived with. A crime *had* been committed, whatever the police might think. Kurt had stolen my gains and now I was expected to look out for him with the same degree of attention I would have lavished on Don. It was not the first time I'd thought the world an unfair place.

I returned to the balcony to resume my watch, thankful, at least, for the temporary distraction.

Two

It was gone two a.m. when Kurt arrived. I'm embarrassed to admit it but I'd dozed off again (the constant observation of a lake in the middle of the night can be pretty soporific) and it seemed I was destined to miss out on these most fateful moments. I'd completely lost track of time and place, but I was soon reminded of my whereabouts by Katerina's anxious call.

"Alan, come quickly."

As dopey as I was I noted it was me, rather than Anna, that she chose to alert.

I reached the hallway to find the front door half open and Kurt's prostrate form stretched out across the threshold. He'd evidently managed to undo the latch himself and in a desperate attempt to reach home had half stumbled, half fallen, through the gap. He was conscious, but exhausted and barely able to speak.

I pulled the door wide open and stuck my head out to look round the yard, but there was no sign of anyone else. It appeared he'd returned alone.

"Here, help me get him up," I said, motioning to Katerina.

We each took an arm and dragged him to his feet. He was near enough a dead weight, every ounce of energy expended in the effort to get back.

"In there." Katerina inclined her head toward the lounge.

I kicked the door open and we pulled him through.

Anna stirred on the settee. And seeing me and Katerina with the semi-conscious form of her husband suspended between us, she was suddenly wide awake. But instead of coming forward to help she instantly withdrew to the far end of the sofa and sat with her legs tucked up beneath her and a look of fear in her eyes. The aura of peace that had blessed her sleep had gone. Perhaps she'd thought herself rid of him and if so, was now confronted by the disappointment of his return.

Katerina and I dropped Kurt's weary body into the space that

Anna had vacated. He surprisingly chose to sit forward, his elbows resting on his knees and his head hanging down, looking between his feet. He was quite dishevelled; the pullover normally so carefully arranged around his shoulders had gone and he was reduced to just his shirt and shorts. One shoe was missing, and when we eventually wrung his story out of him it was a miracle he'd managed to retain the other. That he'd been in the water, we had no doubt. His clothes were no longer sodden (the three-mile walk from the point where he'd come ashore had helped dry them out) but there was a whiff of wet washing about them which combined with the peat of the lake made for a distinctive aroma. He was in a very sorry condition, but I wasn't going to let that prevent me from conducting a thorough interrogation.

"So," I began. "Where is he? Where's Don?"

Kurt gave a tiny shake of his head and mumbled something unintelligible. Katerina and I exchanged glances. Despite our anxiety for news, it was clear there'd be nothing sensible forthcoming until he was in a fit state to respond.

"We'll have to give him a few minutes to warm up," I said.

Katerina volunteered to find a blanket. "There's some brandy in the cupboard," she added and pointed toward the sideboard.

I nodded, and went to fetch a glass.

The brandy was easy to find as I'd grown familiar with the contents of Don's drinks cabinet. But then, so had Kurt and I wondered whether a further dose of alcohol was wise – or indeed whether it would have any effect at all, given what he'd already taken on board. But the cold of the water, the exercise required to get home and the general shock of it all had served to sober him up and he seemed ready for more. He took the glass and tossed it off in one go, although when I offered him a second he gave another shake of the head. *At last,* I thought, *he's learnt when enough is enough...*

Katerina came through with the blanket and draped it round his shaking shoulders. After a while, when he'd stopped shivering, she laid a hand on his arm and started her own line of questioning. She began in English (which I guess was for my benefit) but he replied in Swedish and she was obliged to translate.

It seemed there'd been an accident. The boat had struck something, a log or a rock, he didn't know which. He'd been thrown clear and had found himself bobbing about in the water. He claimed to have looked round but it was dark and he couldn't see anything. There was no immediate sign of the boat. He could, however, see the shoreline in the opposite direction and had started to swim towards it. (How convenient, I thought – dark where there was danger and responsibility, but light enough to see the way to his own salvation. Uncharitable of me, perhaps, but by now I was tinged with a cynicism I found hard to dismiss.)

He'd no idea how long he'd been in the water (an hour, perhaps, at the most?) but he'd eventually reached the shallows and had hauled himself out onto the rocks. After a short rest, he'd started the long walk home.

I wondered how he'd known where he was and which direction to choose to set off in, but there was enough of the sailor about him to work all that out from the stars and whatever means such people use to navigate. It was a considerable feat of survival, and I had to give him credit for that if nothing else. But there was still something missing from his story, and when Katerina had finished I went back to my original question. Even if she'd pressed him on it already, there'd been no discernible answer.

"So, where is he?" I repeated. "Where's Don?"

Kurt shook his head and mumbled again, this time in English. "I don't know…"

"You don't know? What do you mean, you don't know? You were there, you must have seen him, for Christ's sake. How can you tell me you don't know?"

"I don't know," he insisted. "I didn't see him. It was dark."

"Of course it was dark. It was dark when you left here, you idiot. What did you expect? So how hard did you look?"

"I looked, I tell you. But it was impossible to see anything. There was a cloud."

A feeble excuse. The sky is full of clouds. One floats by every minute.

"So what?" I said. "You could see the shore alright, couldn't you? No cloud there, was there?"

He shook his head once more and shrugged. I desperately wanted him to come clean and say he was sorry, but it seemed that was beyond him. If he could only bring himself to apologise we might be able to make some progress.

I paced up and down the length of the settee, Kurt at one end and Anna (who still retained the look of a frightened rabbit) as far away from him as possible at the other. Katerina stood watchfully to one side.

Eventually I came to rest in front of him and lowered my head down to his level – but he averted his eyes as though he were afraid to look me in the face.

"You left him there, didn't you?" I said, prodding him in the chest. He tried brushing me away but I persisted. "You knew he must have been there somewhere but you were too busy saving your own worthless skin to go and look. D'you know what? You make me sick, people like you. You couldn't give a damn about anyone else, just as long as you're alright. You miserable…"

Piece of shit was how I intended to finish, but I realised I was in the company of ladies. Although that wouldn't have stopped me from punching his lights out and I must have had my fist raised ready to do it because the next thing I knew, Katerina had her hand on my shoulder and was pulling me back.

"Alan… That isn't going to help."

I jerked upright and let my hands drop down by my side. "Right," I said. "I'm off."

"Where are you going?" said Katerina. I think she was

concerned I might be abandoning her.

"You call the police. They should have enough to go on by now. I'm going to get the launch out."

"Let me come with you. You'll need a hand on the boat."

I'd expected as much from Katerina, but in fact it was Anna who was asking. The raft of politics which supported her request was doubtless based on the idea that she was better off anywhere else but in the company of Kurt. I was certain it didn't encompass any thought of Don's well-being.

"No," I said firmly. "You need to stay and look after your husband. If anyone's coming with me it ought to be Katerina." I turned towards her. "How are you on managing a boat, by the way?"

"I'm not the best sailor in the world," she admitted. "Don used to take care of all that. But I know how to hold a torch if it helps."

"That's great," I said. "You'll do for me. Why don't you make that call and get a coat and I'll meet you down on the jetty. It'll take me a few minutes to get everything ready."

Not to mention remembering how the hell to drive a boat... I retrieved my own coat from the balcony and went out into the hallway.

The boat keys were in their usual place, hanging on the hook on the far right-hand end. I knew which ones they were from the big cork bob they were clipped to, and I recalled how Don had told me to make sure I took that so if ever they dropped in the water, the keys would float too. I shoved the ball into my pocket and the keys with it and went out into the yard.

Technically speaking it was still night, but the cloud had gone (if indeed there'd ever been any) and we could enjoy the company of a fairly full moon. With luck, we might not even need a torch.

Max was sitting on the step, his head nestled deep between his paws. My guess was that he'd followed Kurt up to the house when he'd arrived and was waiting for him to reappear. I felt pretty sorry for the old boy. Dogs are exceptionally faithful animals. *It's more than you can say for some of their masters*, I thought, and went on down the hill.

I'd never driven the boat on my own before. In all my lessons with Don he'd always been with me and there'd been comfort in the knowledge that if I ever screwed up he was on hand to put things right. Not that I ever *had* screwed up, of course, but there was always that thought in my mind.

I hadn't actually driven the boat at all for the last couple of weeks, and certainly not since Kurt and Anna had arrived. My boating lessons had gone by the wayside along with the construction of the jetty and there was a danger I was out of touch.

Although that didn't worry me at the moment. Somewhere at the back of my mind, my subconscious was guiding me calmly through the boating process. *Don't stall the engine, don't flood the carb, cast off at the bow, cast off at the stern, don't let the line foul the prop.* My primary concern lay with Don and whether he was still alive and whether I could find him.

On top of all this I was angry, so terribly, terribly, angry. Yes, I was angry with Kurt for his wilful abandonment, but I was angry with Don as well for letting himself be taken in – and I was angry with myself for allowing it to happen. If only I'd acted earlier and stepped in while there was still a chance, it might never have come to this. Instead of which, I'd wasted my time fooling around with Anna.

I was angry with her too. Manipulative in the extreme, she'd led me by the nose and played me at a time when I was at my most vulnerable. She no more loved me than I did her, and I'd been a fool to think so. I suppose you could say it served me right and I deserved what was coming, but there'd been a moment when we needed each other. I didn't regret that – but now it was time to move on.

Her latest ploy in volunteering for the boat had been blatantly transparent. As the next step in her 'take me away from all this' strategy, nothing would have given her more satisfaction at that moment than for the two of us to have sailed off together into the sunset (or, to be more accurate, sunrise). And if we'd never stopped to look for Don on the way, it wouldn't have worried her one little bit. In terms of basic human compassion, it was becoming apparent that she was every bit as bad as her husband.

It seemed I was angry with everyone except Katerina. I could find no fault with her, which was why I'd chosen her as my travelling companion. What I needed was someone steady and reliable, and her commitment to Don was never in doubt. None of us had gone to bed that night but she was the one who'd contrived to stay awake. Now it was down to just the two of us and we were both running on adrenalin.

I'd already got the boat engine going when she walked out onto the jetty to join me, the beam of her small torch swaying back and forth across the planking. There was another, more powerful light in the locker below the steering wheel so I knew we were well-equipped. I helped her clamber aboard.

"So what did the police have to say this time? Were they any more helpful?" I raised my voice above the burble of the motor.

"They're going to send a boat out at dawn."

I looked at my watch. A quarter to three. It was virtually that now…

Katerina cast off bow and stern and came to stand beside me in the wheelhouse. The boat lights had come on and her face was lit from below by the dull glow of the instrument panel. It made her look unnaturally tired, but somehow more determined.

"D'you know where you're going?" she said.

"I think so…" I replied as I eased the throttle forward. We chugged out past the reed bed, then turned to the right and headed for Cormorant Island.

Three

I'd no problem in driving the boat – Don had taught me well. And although she'd professed to have no knowledge of boating, it was comforting to have Katerina on board. There might come a time when we'd need two pairs of hands, plus her moral support was crucial.

I wondered whether she'd prayed or offered something up to her ancient Swedish gods before we left as the conditions they provided were auspiciously in our favour. There was, thankfully, no wind, and the lake was as flat as a pancake. The sky was completely clear (not a cloud in sight, despite Kurt's protesta tions) and a pallid moon glinted on the inky-black surface of the water. To the east, the faint glimmer of a new day had begun to appear from behind the line of trees. Malaren was giving us every chance. If Don was out there, I was sure we'd find him.

I motored slowly so as not to miss some hidden piece of evidence. Katerina looked to the left and out toward the open water while I kept watch to the right where the line of buoys marked the route to the marina. There was a chance they'd taken a southerly route but there was no sign in either direction.

After twenty minutes or so the bare outline of Cormorant Island loomed up out of the darkness on our port side, its dead and broken trees standing stark against the night sky. I turned the wheel and veered towards it, hoping to get a better view of the shoreline. With the moon in the north, the southern side of the island was deep in shadow and it was hard to make anything out. We shone our torches into the gloom but found only rocks and reeds. I was not surprised. If anything had happened here, it was more likely to have been further on at the far end.

We skirted the corner and came out into the light. There was no need for torches here. Away from the shadows at the eastern tip of the island, the surface of the lake was a flat grey sheet beneath the gleaming moon. Dotted here and there, small black lumps protruded from below, blocking the channel. These weren't rocks. I knew this place and they were further to the right. Were they the logs that Kurt had mentioned? Or could these be pieces of wreckage? I wasn't sure which to hope for.

"Here!"

Katerina was pointing at an object floating toward our port bow. She clicked her torch and aimed its beam, although I could see quite clearly without it. And no, it wasn't a log, it was definitely wreckage, the distinct pattern of worked wood formed in the shape of a stern. In the ray of her light, I caught a flash of bright red. *The colour of blood,* I thought.

I veered away to starboard, just in time to see the matching piece of stern bobbing by on my side of the launch. In front of us, the remaining lumps began to take on recognisable shapes and with the aid of Katerina's torch, identifiable colour. There was no doubt about it, this was what was left of the speedboat.

I shall never forget the feeling which the sight of that wreckage induced in me. A sudden cold, clammy sensation, it was beyond heartbreak. I'd experienced something like it once before when I'd stood at Susan's graveside some six months earlier and watched as they threw earth on the lid of her coffin. I'd wanted to tell them to stop and tear the casket open and take her body out and hold it in my arms, but I could not. The thought of facing that again was simply too much to endure. I'd already lost one – I couldn't bear losing another.

But as much as I tried to deny it, the evidence was scattered all around me. It was easy to guess what had happened. As they'd approached the end of the island the boat was carrying too much speed. Kurt would still have been at the wheel (I can't imagine how he'd have let go of it) and instead of pulling back on the throttle to make the turn, he'd left it pushed fully forward. Cornering flat out in a speedboat is fun in open water, but in a confined space it's dangerous. Slow to respond, the boat had careered into the rocks, ripping through the length of its delicate hull and splintering it into pieces. Kurt had been lucky and had been thrown clear. As for Don, we didn't know. All it needed was for his head to smash into a rock...

By now, I'd cut our engine to a crawl – I'd no intention of becoming another victim. Inching forward, we bumped our way through bits of wreckage, each piece a grim reminder of the tragedy that had taken place. Katerina plied them with her torch, searching for clues. Working carefully at the wheel, I tried not to cause damage – any one of them might be a body...

It was Katerina who saw him first. One black lump ahead of us seemed larger than the rest and her light revealed the outline of a pair of shoulders and a head lolled to one side. Beneath them, the wreckage which he clung to floated freely. As luck would have it, one of the buoyancy chambers had remained intact and he'd been flung against it. If not, he surely would have struggled to survive.

"Alan! Over here!" Katerina pointed.

I brought the boat around and came alongside as gently as I could, then cut the throttle and disengaged the engine.

"The anchor!" I called. "Drop the anchor!" The last thing I wanted now was for us to drift away.

Katerina scurried to the stern and I heard a resounding splash.

I'd already let go of the wheel and was leaning over the side, trying to lay hands on something solid. I wanted a hold on his clothing – ideally the scruff of his neck – but the wreckage kept getting in the way. I manoeuvred it round in the water and managed to get a grip on an arm. Katerina was with me now and leaning over too.

"Here," I said. "You hold onto him while I pull him free."

It was easier said than done. Don's hands were clamped to his makeshift life raft like limpets to a rock. It was the devil's own job to persuade him to let go, but while Katerina grasped his arm I managed to prise his fingers loose. I pushed the wreckage away and turned him to face us in the water.

The blood I'd so feared seeing trickled from a gash on his forehead. It had mostly dried and lay in a crusted mass against his eyebrow, making that side of his face seem swollen. I tried not to look too hard, preferring to keep my thoughts positive. At this stage, I wasn't even sure he was alive…

There's a proven technique for getting a man overboard back into a boat. Don't ask me where I got it – perhaps I'd seen it on television, or perhaps Don had shown me himself, but now's not the time to go into that. The idea is that you get a good hold of some clothing, bounce the body three times in the water to gain momentum, then heave them, face forward, over the side. It's not easy, especially when the body in question weighs over sixteen stone and there's an eighteen-inch drop down to the level of the water. It's best done with two of you in the boat to do the heaving. In our case, the team was comprised of me and a woman of limited strength.

But what Katerina lacked in stature, she made up for in heart and there was no way she was going to see us fail now. I explained to her what to do and she took an arm and a hold on the shirt at the top of Don's shoulder. I did the same and we steadied ourselves.

"Right," I said. "On the count of three. Ready? One, two…three!"

And we heaved for all we were worth.

Don shot forwards and up, his chest straddling the gunwale, and for one vital moment I didn't think he'd make it. But as his waist cleared the water I saw he was wearing a belt and I switched my grip to grab hold of it and it was enough to see him home. We fell back into the well of the boat, his body landing between us like a broken doll. I scrambled to my feet, arranged him into the recovery position and searched his face for any sign of life.

I could have wept when he stirred. His impromptu trip over the side had shaken him up and if he wasn't conscious in the water, he was at least conscious now. A shiver ran down his spine, an eye half opened and he lifted a feeble finger of recognition.

"Fetch a blanket!" I cried. "He's breathing!"

Katerina stood close by, her body taut and rigid, too traumatised for tears.

"I didn't bring one," she said.

"Why on earth not?"

"I... I didn't think we'd find him. It was more than I dared hope for."

"Well, there might still be one in the forward locker. Hurry!"

We weren't done yet. But if we didn't keep him warm, it would all be for nothing.

We were in luck and there was a blanket available, the selfsame one we'd used on the pontoon for Katerina. Thankfully, someone had possessed the foresight to return it, but now it seemed quite thin so I contributed my coat and while Katerina covered him up, I went to the stern and raised the anchor. She could tend to him now – my job was to get us home as fast as I could. I took the wheel, engaged the engine and guided us clear of the debris. As soon as I'd rounded the island and got away from those damnable rocks, I could let the throttle rip and speed us back to the house.

Over to the east, the sky had turned pale blue and the tip of an orange sun poked above the horizon. Somewhere near Eskilstuna, the police would be launching their rescue boat. *Too late, my friends, too late! The job's already been done!*

I revved the engine, felt the bow of the boat lift up and a sense of exhilaration as the wind swept into my face. We were on our way home and to safety.

Four

I don't think we'll ever really know how close to death Don had come. It wasn't something we dwelt on at the time – we were just grateful to have found him and that he was alive. But that he'd been in great danger was beyond doubt. Everyone knows that prolonged exposure in water can lead to hypothermia – and hypothermia can cause a man to die. It all depends on how cold the water is and how long you're in it.

And the water doesn't need to be that cold. Anything significantly below the temperature of the body will do, and every stretch of water in northern climes is always that, no matter the time of year. Although right now, at the end of the summer, Malaren was probably at its warmest.

As to time, Don had been in the water for around three hours. Not that long, you might think, especially when there are cases on record of people holding out through the night in much colder temperatures. But there are just as many instances of people dying within minutes of entering the water – there's no guarantee of survival.

His bodyweight must have been an advantage. Don was a big man and it would have taken time for the cold to penetrate. On the other hand, he'd been drinking and the alcohol couldn't have helped.

What, if any, were the signs? He didn't seem to be shivering, although whether that was because he'd passed beyond that stage, we didn't know. He looked very pale – but so did we in that light, and we couldn't tell if any part of him had turned blue. What we *did* know, and what was obvious from the moment we pulled him from the water, was that his flame had burned very low and it would require a lot of care and attention to make sure it didn't blow out altogether.

But if we were unsure as to the extent of his condition, we were equally ignorant as to how to treat it. We'd little medical knowledge between us and we were forced to rely on common sense. Halfway back across the lake I suggested to Katerina that we call an ambulance and get him admitted to hospital, but she wouldn't hear of it.

"No, Alan. He's better off at home."

Her reply ostensibly came from her head, but deep inside I'm sure her heart was saying, *He's mine and I'm not going to give him up now.*

Ironically, the one person who might have known something as to a cure wasn't in a fit state to tell us. Don hadn't moved since we'd got him aboard and he continued to lie motionless in the well of the boat, the only indication of his status being the slight rise and fall of his chest beneath my coat. Another blanket would have been good, but if Katerina had forgotten to bring it, for my part I'd neglected to remember the brandy. That had been left with Kurt and the prospect of another empty bottle awaited us.

Don clearly couldn't stay in the boat and we had to get him up to the house. Our difficulty lay in negotiating the hill. He was sixteen stone, comatose and a dead weight. I was taller but there was no way I could manage him on my own, and although Katerina possessed the strength of mind, she lacked the strength of body. I thought of making a stretcher from some lengths of wood (or wondered whether there was one in the boathouse) but whichever way I looked at it, it was going to want more muscle than we currently had available. That meant calling on Kurt, and I instinctively bucked against it. The very thought of him made me feel ill – but if I wanted to help my friend, I knew I didn't have any choice.

We'd been absent for less than an hour, but it was long enough for things to have changed. The house was cloaked in darkness and when I switched on the light in the lounge, Anna's startled face looked up at me from her makeshift couch on the sofa. Kurt had taken himself off to bed, but she'd stayed put she said, in order to wait up for us. There may have been an element of truth in that, although I'd grown cynical enough to believe it was more down to the fact that she didn't want to share the guesthouse with her husband. Thankfully, the bottle of brandy I'd foolishly left behind stood untouched on the table. Perhaps Kurt was beginning to realise that alcohol was the cause of his problems rather than the solution to them. It would certainly make him easier to rouse.

I made Anna go and fetch him. She protested vehemently at first but I was in no mood to be crossed. While she was gone, I took a slug of the brandy myself. By then I think I needed it as much as Don.

Kurt appeared, bleary-eyed and dishevelled, having hurriedly pulled on some dry clothing. This was no time for a carefully arranged pullover. We walked down to the boat where I'd left Katerina in charge.

So now there were four of us, two men and two women, enough you might think to get the job done – but still it was a struggle. You can have an army of helpers but there are only so many places you can lay hands on a man's body to move it. Once we'd got him out onto the jetty, the only effective method was for Kurt and I each to lift an arm around our shoulders and pull him forward as best we could. I'd abandoned the idea of a stretcher – it would take too long to construct and there was a risk it wouldn't work. Speed was of the essence if we were to prevent Don from losing more heat.

But it was all so damnably slow, and halfway up the hill I felt a shiver pass through him. Was this a sign he was at last recovering consciousness? Or a relapse brought on by the cold morning air? I urged Katerina to fetch the other blanket.

"Go on," I said. "Hurry."

She ran ahead while I redoubled my efforts. Kurt, thank God, responded and eventually so did Don, painfully pulling one foot in front of the other. But he was still very weak and there was little he could do.

We reached the path at the side of the house before Katerina returned, then at last we were on the porch and Max was there come to greet us, tail wagging and running about amongst our ankles. I kicked the front door open and we went through sideways, shuffling our way across the threshold.

Katerina had already opened the door to their room and pulled back the duvet on the bed. Don went straight down onto it like a sack of coal, his feet were swung in (we didn't even stop to take his shoes off), and before you could blink he was all tucked up.

We paused to check his breathing. He'd stopped shaking now, his eyes were closed, and for all the world it looked as though he were peacefully asleep. I couldn't see what else we could do. We went out into the hallway to talk.

"Let's leave him to rest," I said. "Hopefully, he'll get a good night's sleep and we'll check on him in the morning."

It was morning now, of course, but they all knew what I meant.

Katerina nodded. "I'll go and tidy things up in a minute. Frankly, I think we could all do with getting to bed."

She was right. We'd been up all night, we were tired and to push ourselves further was to risk becoming fractious. In the lounge the first shafts of daylight were creeping through the gaps in the curtains and the supply of adrenalin we'd relied on was beginning to run out.

We broke up and went our separate ways. And for the first time since I'd been turfed out of the guesthouse, I was glad of the broom cupboard that was my room, the Black Hole's windowless murk welcoming me with the prospect of extended rest.

I kicked off my shoes, lay down on the bed and pulled up the sheet. All I had to do was close my eyes and I knew I'd drop off, but I forced myself to keep them open for as long as I could. As tired as I was, there was one thing I wanted above sleep – and that was to hear Don snoring. I lay there listening for the slightest sound but there was nothing, save for the odd cry of a gull. Eventually it all went quiet and I guess I must have slipped off.

Prior to Susan's illness I used to sleep like a log. Ninety-nine times out of a hundred my head only had to touch the pillow and I was gone and I rarely woke up before morning. Susan used to say it was a gift, I was lucky and she envied me. Although those weren't quite the terms she used when the children were young and it came to the question of midnight feeds. By contrast, she was a light sleeper and always woke when a baby cried, but she had this notion that the feeding of children was a duty we should share. So when *It's your turn* and the hefty thump of an elbow into my ribs produced no response she would understandably get cross. She soon learnt it was easier to get out of bed and do it herself rather than try and wake me.

That night it was different. And if I'd closed my mind to my kids when they were young, I had an ear open now for Don. I slept fitfully, stirring at the slightest noise and staring into the darkness, hoping for news. Without a window and deprived of daylight I'd no sense of time and relied solely on my instincts. 6 a.m.? 8 a.m.? I didn't know. These were just impressions that surfaced like the lumps of wreckage at Cormorant Island which, together with the image of a drowning man, had haunted whatever rest I'd managed. I must have been dreaming again, although which parts were real and which parts I imagined it was impossible to tell, and I came to fearful of what might really have happened. Eventually I knew I was awake and there was a sound I recognised – a kettle was being filled in the kitchen.

I still had on what I'd been wearing the night before so I got up and went out into the hallway to look for a pair of the fluffy white mules. I opened the door to the kitchen and found Katerina in one of the big bathrobes, making tea. The clock on the wall showed ten-fifteen, so at the most I'd managed five hours – although perhaps not all of them asleep. I failed to stifle a yawn.

"Good morning, Alan."

Katerina was pouring milk into a single cup. His or hers? I wondered. I waited for a clue, but none came. Finally, I had to ask. "And?"

"Don? Oh, he's fine. Still with us, if that's what you mean." She looked up, teapot in hand. "Do you want one, by the way?"

"Please."

She reached into the overhead cupboard and fetched down another cup.

"You see, the reason I ask," I continued, "is because I didn't hear anything last night, and Don often..."

"Snores?"

"Exactly."

"That's when he lies on his back. Last night I managed to keep him on his side. Better for both of us that way."

"I see... Sorry, I didn't mean to be personal."

"That's alright. In fact, you've every right to know. If it hadn't been for you—"

I cut her short. I wasn't sure I wanted to be reminded of our traumatic evening – or whether I wanted to be classed as a hero.

"If it hadn't been for me, I'm sure the police would have found him."

"Hmm... I'm not so sure. You seem to have a lot more faith in our police force than I do. I think you've been reading too many of those detective novels."

"Maybe... And that reminds me. Shouldn't we give them a ring and let them know they can call off their search?"

"I've done that already. I gave them a quick call before I went to bed last night."

If so, then I certainly hadn't heard her. Perhaps I hadn't lain awake after all...

"Anyway, so Don's ok then?"

"I think so. He's still asleep, but he's breathing normally. It might take a day or two, but I'm sure he'll make a full recovery."

We sipped our tea and all I could hear was the slow beat of the clock. Don must still have been lying on his side.

Katerina shortly put down her cup and decisively folded her arms.

"Alan, we need to talk."

"We do? Look, if this is about Anna..." I didn't need another lecture – and besides, I'd already made up my mind on the matter.

"No, it's not about Anna – it's about Kurt."

"Kurt?" This was even more dangerous ground – mention of his name was always going to raise my hackles.

"Yes. You see, we've not been entirely open about things and I feel we owe you an explanation."

"Explanation? Why? What is there to explain?"

"Well, you were right about Kurt in one sense – he's not exactly the best when it comes to running a business. That's why retaining his position at the woodyard was conditional on him taking a partner. Don knew that right from the start but he thought that if he could get his feet under the table it was a risk worth taking. And apart from that, we didn't have an awful lot of choice at the time. Although in fact, things worked out very well and with Don in charge the business prospered, as you know. The problems started when he wanted to get out."

"Really? Surely there must have been some kind of contract."

"Well, yes, there was. And everything looked fine on paper. It wasn't until it was all signed off that we discovered Kurt was deep in debt and wasn't in a position to pay what he'd agreed."

"Call me cynical if you like but why doesn't that surprise me? Wait a minute though – didn't I hear talk of a property portfolio?"

"You may well have done. The assumption was that he'd either sell it or borrow against it to come up with the money. But it turned out it was already mortgaged to the hilt anyway so there was never any chance of Don getting paid."

"So what about all this business with the yacht and so on?"

N.E. David

"That's just a front. We think that's mortgaged too."

"Good God! How do he and Anna get by then?"

"The woodyard continues to tick over – although there's just the one now. The rest were sold to keep things going. Anna's still working of course."

"You mean to say she's effectively supporting him?"

"We think so."

"That's appalling. And let me guess. Whenever Kurt looks like running short, he takes a trip over to Malaren so he can freeload off his old business partner."

"That's about it. And Don doesn't like to turn him away. He says he'd rather keep in with him while there's still a chance of getting paid what he's owed."

"The likelihood of that happening must be pretty low."

"Yes, but you know Don – he doesn't like the thought of giving up."

"Hmm… So how do you feel about all this?"

"It's pretty upsetting, as you can imagine. Although it's not the money that worries me – all I really care about is Don."

Don, my erstwhile friend, who, thanks to his own wilful subjugation had suffered a near-death experience and now lay as weak as a kitten in the room next door…

Katerina retrieved her cup. Her tea had gone cold and she turned to pour it down the sink. "So there you have it. I just thought you should know. I'm really sorry you had to get caught up in all this. You were supposed to come here for a rest and this is probably the last thing you wanted to have to deal with. And I didn't really get the chance to thank you properly for last night."

"You don't need to do that."

"Somebody does. He may not have shown it recently but Don thinks a lot of you, you know."

"Really? I would never have guessed."

"Of course he does. He'd never have invited you here if he didn't."

"Oh? I thought this was all your idea."

"No, it was Don's. We discussed it of course and I agreed, but it all came from him initially. I expect he'll want to talk to you himself as soon as he's fit. He won't mention a word of what I've just told you of course, he's far too proud for that. And besides, he likes to keep things to himself as you've probably discovered. I'm not even sure he's aware I know as much as I do."

There was silence for a moment as the kitchen clock ticked off another minute and advanced to half past ten. Katerina looked up and instantly thought of her duties. "Goodness me, look at the time. I must go and see how His Lordship is doing. If he's awake he's bound to want a cup of tea. And thanks again, Alan, really. I don't know what we'd have done without you."

She bustled past and out into the hallway, then I heard their bedroom door close behind her.

I took my tea and went out onto the veranda. It was another fine morning, a little breezy perhaps, the flags flapping lazily at the heads of their poles, but otherwise quite pleasant. Malaren itself looked a picture, the light-blue brightness of the sky reflected in the waters of the lake. Fifty yards beyond the end of our unfinished jetty, the swimming platform bobbed gently in the swell. How long would it be before that was used again? I wondered.

Everything seemed so peaceful and yet I knew how cruel it could be. Even at its calmest, when its surface was as flat and as smooth as a sheet of glass, it held the deadliest of dangers. I remembered the night, the creamy pallor of the moon and a row of black forbidding lumps protruding from the water. A cold and clammy shudder ran down my spine and rather than dwell on it, I went back to my room to get tidied up and thought about having some breakfast.

After I'd eaten, I decided to take a walk on the headland. A breath of fresh air was in order and I wanted some time to think. The last twenty-four hours (twelve, in fact) had contained some momentous events and a period of reflection was required.

I fervently hoped there'd be no one else about. Katerina had not reappeared, the blinds at the guesthouse were down and there was no imminent sign of life. Outside the front door, Max was dutifully lying in wait for Kurt. My fear was that Anna had got up and gone out early, as was her wont. If so, I'd just have to deal with it. Perhaps this was my chance to have it out with her, although I'd no pressing desire for a meeting as yet. One thing was certain – there'd be no excursion to the boathouse today.

But the coast was literally clear and I had the place to myself. The sun was nearing its highest point and the clearing was flooded with light. Save for a few dead leaves, I found the swing-seat empty and I took my place at the end I'd made my own. It wasn't that long since I'd sat there with Anna after we'd first made love, her head in my lap, and I remembered how she'd asked me if I'd been thinking of Susan. Of course I had! How could I not, just as I was thinking of her now. The reeds were rustling in the breeze and there was a chance that she would speak to me. I'd come to think of the lake as an embodiment of her spirit – there was a calm, transparent beauty that pervaded the place. True, it could be tempestuous, and then there was that dark side. Malaren wasn't perfect, but neither was Susan – it didn't mean I loved her any the less.

Back then, I'd asked for understanding. She'd not replied and I believed that she'd denied me. Now I'd come to confess that my affair with Anna had been a mistake and I wanted Susan to know that I was sorry. I'd never loved Anna, no more than she'd loved me – what good could it possibly have done? Yes, there'd been chemistry between us – more in fact than I could ever have imagined – but I'd a lingering suspicion there'd been an element of spite in it too and that was something I disliked in myself. I was not, at heart, a vindictive person – which made it all the more important for me to explain what I proposed to do next.

I may have recovered Don's body, but I'd yet to recover his soul. That, as far as I could tell, was still in hock to Kurt. Maybe it always had been, maybe he'd never been free, although there was a time when I thought I owned part of it. And perhaps I was being greedy but now I wanted all of it, or at least, as much as I could get my hands on. Of course, a lot of it belonged to Katerina but I didn't think she'd mind if we shared.

I'd been passive for far too long. I'd sat around and watched as things had fallen apart in front of my eyes. I'd calculated risk instead of taking it, and even when I'd taken the plunge with Anna it had been for all the wrong reasons. Yes, we were where we were – but it didn't have to stay that way. If I acted now, there was a chance that things might change.

I said as much to Susan in the hope that she was listening. Somewhere out there on the lake, she was roaming the surface of the water, looking for me. I had a message for her. I loved her, I would always love her, and although she might not see it that way, what I proposed to do was as much for her as it was for me.

I waited for an answer, letting the swing-seat rock to the rhythm of the breeze. At the base of the trees close by, a dunnock sat and reeled its cheerful song.

Then the reeds began to rustle and I heard their vibrant whisper, *Yes, yes, yes...*

Five

After what passed for lunch (late breakfast for some), Don was deemed fit to receive visitors. Katerina had taken charge of his affairs and as well as feeding him bowls of hot soup at regular intervals, had organised a system of appointments. He was still very tired, a bit woozy and could recall little of what had happened the night before – this much I gathered in my allotted half-hour. I'd no need to tell him our story. His wife had already done so and had filled in most of the details – how we'd waited anxiously up at the house, how we'd eventually called the police, Kurt's dramatic arrival and how we'd got the boat out to go and look for him. I provided a brief recap, if only so he'd know I was there, but I'm not sure he was capable of absorbing it all.

He was sitting up in bed, propped against the two pillows his wife had arranged neatly behind him. He said he was feeling weak and it was as though he'd had gastroenteritis and the stuffing had been knocked out of him. *I'm sure it's just a twenty-four hour thing, I'll be as right as rain tomorrow.* But that was what I'd expected him to say – Don wasn't the type to make something out of it. I tried to encourage him to remember the incident itself, but all he could do was shake his head.

"There was nothing," he said. "Even before the smash."

His first memory was of lying face down on the floor of the launch and the sharp tang of boat diesel filling his lungs. "I was drunk, wasn't I?"

"Yes, Don, I'm afraid you were."

There was no point in trying to deny it. The truth was bound to come out at some stage if he didn't know it already.

"Badly?"

"Very badly."

"I'm sorry."

And so you should be, I thought. But you don't say that to someone in his condition – although had it been Kurt, I doubt I'd have been so forgiving.

"Don't even think about it, Don. There's nothing to be sorry for."

Don picked at a piece of cotton that had looped up from the duvet in front of him. "Well actually, I think there is. You see, there's something I should've told you."

"You mean about you and Kurt."

"Yes, how did you know?" Don looked up from the duvet he was in the process of steadily dismantling.

"There's no need to put yourself to the trouble," I assured him. "Katerina's already told me all about it – or at least, enough for me to get the general gist of things."

"I see..." He looked away now, the cotton in his hand having finally come free. "I've never really liked him, you know."

"Kurt?"

"Yes."

"You could have fooled me. The way the two of you were going on, I thought you were bosom pals."

"Good God, no – although I can see how you might get that impression. No, the fact of the matter is I can't stand the sight of him, never could. Frankly, I think he's a complete shit and I can't wait to get shot of him. It didn't matter too much when we were working together. Business is business, we rubbed along and you do what you have to do. But then, when we split up, he wanted to make it personal. And I didn't have any choice. Needs must when the devil drives and all that."

"Because of the money?"

"Yes and no. It's not the money itself – although I wouldn't have given up on that anyway, I've got a lawyer in Stockholm working on it now even as we speak. No, it's the principle – plus the fact that it represents Katerina's inheritance. That was what bailed us out in the first place and I didn't want to let her down and see it all go to waste."

"Let me tell you something," I said.

"Go on."

"I don't think Katerina gives two hoots about her inheritance. Oh, I know it came from her parents and there must be a great deal of emotion attached to it, but I think she's far more concerned about you."

"You do?"

"Absolutely." I remembered how she'd pushed herself to stay awake while I'd fallen asleep and how she'd insisted on coming out in the boat with me. "If you'd seen the look of determination on her face when we were trying to haul you out of the water…"

Don looked away again but this time the duvet remained intact.

"D'you know what? I've been a bloody fool, Alan, and I might as well admit it."

I wasn't going to contradict him. Earlier on I'd have been generous and given him the benefit of the doubt – but there comes a point when you have to move on and perhaps this was it for him as well as me.

"God knows what'll happen now…"

I wondered whether I should tell him, but I could see he was getting tired and besides, he'd find out soon enough anyway. In the meanwhile, a wry smile had crept across his face, crinkling his weather-beaten cheeks.

"Good job I taught you how to drive that boat though, eh?"

"Yeah, good job you did. We'd have been well and truly stuck otherwise."

The smile turned into a chuckle. "Good times, those, Alan, good times."

"Yes, Don, they were."

"One day we'll get round to finishing off that bloody jetty."

"I hope so, Don, I hope so. Whenever you're ready. But first you need to get some rest."

"Yeah, rest…"

He smiled again, but this time his eyes began to close as if there were a weight he couldn't resist pressing on the lids and he mouthed the word *Tomorrow*... Then his head lolled to one side, he'd slipped off and I knew there was no point in continuing. Suddenly, my half-hour was up and we were done. What little conversation we'd managed to construct had been short but informative and it seemed we'd covered a lot of ground. And far from dissuading me from what I was about to do, it had served as a form of encouragement.

It wasn't until later that afternoon that I was able to get into the guesthouse. And I don't mean break in by the way, that wasn't necessary as the place was never locked. Even if it had been, I could easily have found the key – it was one of the bunch hanging next to the coat rack in the hallway. Although I suppose what I was doing amounted to much the same thing – I was trespassing, it was probably illegal and I had every intention of stealing something.

I'd waited until the occupants were well out of the way. Around half past three Kurt and Anna were ushered into Don's presence and allowed to sit by his bedside. Their half-hour of conversation gave me the opportunity I needed and I slipped away to do my nefarious deed.

It was hard to imagine what Kurt and Don could find to say to each other. Anna, of course, would say next to nothing, even if her husband weren't there. She and Don had nothing in common, her interest lay solely with Katerina and in the company of Kurt her silence was almost guaranteed. He'd doubtless be trying to justify himself. There'd be a repeat of the story he'd told us the night before. *There was a cloud. It was dark. I couldn't see a thing.* He'd had twelve hours to work on it, so unless it had radically changed there'd been time to embellish it a little. *It was cold. I was confused. I couldn't see you. I was worried.* And Don, oblivious to the facts, was in no position to contradict him.

I still had to wait out the hour or so until three-thirty. I passed it with tea and a few pages of Sven Wonderström's latest adventure. Then, as soon as Kurt and Anna left for their appointment, I put the book down and made my way across the yard.

It was a while since I'd been in the guesthouse – a fortnight at least, according to my calculations, although recent events had caused me to lose count. It instantly brought back memories – the smell of it for a start, that heady mix of warm wood and human habitation that pervades a Swedish house in summer. Now there was a hint of Anna in it too, and a scent I recognised from the boathouse.

The blind over the sloping window in the ceiling had been pulled down (permanently, I imagined – Kurt was not the type to welcome morning), but the room was full of afternoon light which streamed in through the slats above the small chest of drawers. It revealed an unmade bed, the covers thrown back from rumpled sheets, and a crowded, untidy mess. On the left, a pair of shorts had been cast aside, landing on top of Kurt's brown loafers. On the right, the lid of an open suitcase rested against the wall while its contents spilled out onto the floor. The top of the chest of drawers was barely visible beneath a mountain of clutter – a camera, a watch, a wallet, several pairs of sunglasses and a pile of what appeared to be used handkerchiefs.

None of this, I noticed, bore any relation to Anna and I was obliged to search the room carefully to find evidence of her presence. Hidden behind Kurt's pile of handkerchiefs stood a solitary bottle of perfume and a can of hairspray, and in the corner opposite the bottom of the bed, another suitcase, shut this time, which I assumed had to be hers. Next to it, laid out on the floor, were a pair of cushions and a rug which bore the imprint of a human form. A blanket had been carefully folded up and left nearby. That Kurt and his wife weren't sleeping together came as no surprise – but that they did so in separate beds and in this strange and bohemian fashion was a revelation. It was an arrangement more suited to Max than anyone else.

I thought to pull the door closed behind me, although frankly, I didn't care if I were caught. In fact, it might have been easier if I had been and we could have had it out there and then, but I was concerned that if it were Katerina who happened across the yard rather than our visitors, I'd have more explaining to do than I was prepared for.

I began by searching through the chest of drawers but for all the mess on the floor and elsewhere, they themselves were empty. The answer, I thought, must lie in Anna's suitcase. I unzipped it and lifted the lid. A compact, some lipstick and a mirror were laid out neatly on top of her clothing. Burrowing into it, I found what I was looking for and discreetly loaded my pocket. Then I replaced everything as carefully as I could, zipped the lid back up and retraced my steps to the door.

Max was waiting outside, having padded across from his resting place in the outhouse. He wagged his stumpy tail and cocked a curious head – but I'd no intention of letting him in on what I'd been doing.

"Shush, not a word," I said, raising my finger to my lips. Thank God he couldn't talk.

Six

If there were a manual on the subject of revenge, I'm sure it would start with that old dictum about it being best served cold. Apart from which, we all know that action taken in the heat of the moment is often regretted. Well, even if I *was* plotting revenge (which, by the way, I dispute – it was merely a means to an end), I'd no intention of waiting until things had cooled down. My mind was made up, I knew I was right and I needed to strike while the iron was hot.

Susan used to say I didn't have any emotions. *You know what, Alan Harrison? Sometimes I don't believe there's an emotional bone in your body.* Ok, so I wasn't always effusive about birthdays or anniversaries or Christmas, but that doesn't mean to say I didn't care. I'm an actuary for goodness' sake and we're not supposed to be emotional, we're supposed to be cool and calculating and objective, and I guess that's how I usually appeared.

In Kurt's case I intended it should stay that way. The logic behind my actions was irrefutably simple – I'd had an affair with his wife and I'd begun by calculating the risk that he'd find out. Now, there was a risk that he wouldn't, and I needed to make sure he got the message. As to timing, I'd simply reached the end of my tether. Frankly, I was bored with it all – his rudeness, his indifference toward me, his indifference toward his wife, (even toward Katerina), anyone in fact except Don. And his treatment of *him* had been abysmal. I wanted Kurt to know that the rest of us existed and for him to acknowledge the fact.

As for Anna, I guess I'd got tired of her too. In the beginning I'd been taken in by the childlike persona she tried to portray, just as Katerina had been, and for a while I'd gone along with it. But then I'd been put wise to her scheming, I'd seen how she'd tried to manipulate me and from that moment on I'd known that our relationship was never going to be long term. Now was as good a time to end it as any.

I decided to wait no longer than dinner. It meant there would just be the four of us. Don was still in bed, although reports were filtering through that he was improving rapidly after his day's rest and would be ready to join us in the morning. But this was essentially my problem rather than his, and I didn't really want him involved.

The evening began quietly enough and there was a subdued atmosphere round our little wooden table. We'd nothing to celebrate other than Don's survival and that was best done discreetly. It seemed pointless to try for anything more in his absence and this was a far cry from the high spirits and unqualified excitement of the crayfish party.

Don't for the life of me ask what we had to eat – probably stew or something of the sort; I can't say I took that much notice. What I can remember is that there was no alcohol. The head of the household was absent and without him as host, Katerina declined to offer it. In keeping with our sober mood, a jug of iced water appeared on the table together with four glasses and we were obliged to content ourselves with that. Rather ironically, I wouldn't have minded a glass of wine for once as it might have helped stiffen my resolve.

The first course was cleared away and Katerina retreated to the kitchen, presumably to prepare our dessert. If there'd been any form of conversation I wasn't really aware of it, but it wasn't as though I was waiting for one particular moment. Kurt may well have been speaking but I was always going to cut across him anyway, in the same way he'd have cut across me.

I retrieved the contents of my pocket and held them up in front of Anna.

"These are yours I believe?"

Anna blanched, her face slowly draining of colour.

I turned to Kurt. "You may not recognise them – it's probably been a long time since you've seen them, or anything like them in fact. However, you might like to know that your wife left them in

the boathouse the last time she and I were down there together."
I omitted the words *making love* as it seemed just a little too
obvious.

In Shakespeare's *Othello* the villainous Iago betrays
Desdemona with the aid of her spotted handkerchief. But we
were four hundred years on and in this day and age a handkerchief was never going to cut it so I'd borrowed a pair of Anna's
underwear – a nice frilly pink pair with a little bow at the front.
I'd recognised them immediately as I'd remembered personally
removing them a week or so before. Whether Kurt recognised
them or not, I haven't a clue, but Anna certainly did. Her colour
quickly returned and her cheeks, hitherto white, burned a
virulent red. Those deep blue eyes whose gaze I'd previously
fallen into now flashed with a mixture of shame and fear and
hatred. Hatred for me, I hasten to add, as instead of bursting into
tears as I'd expected she might, she snatched her panties from my
hand and hissed at me like a wildcat. She spat out a word, in
Estonian or Swedish, I don't know which, but roughly translated
I could easily guess as to its meaning.

Bastard.

It had taken a while, but her true character was at last showing
through.

Kurt sat straight-faced and silent. For one unlooked-for and
disappointing moment I thought that he'd not fallen in – but
when you're confronted with a pair of your wife's underwear in
the hands of another man, you have to be pretty stupid not to put
two and two together and make four. At last I'd got his attention
– as indeed had his wife. I was no Iago – and he was no Othello –
but the effect was pretty much the same. He stood up slowly
from the table and stared at me and then at Anna and began to
speak to her in a quiet and measured tone. This time it was
definitely in Swedish and to guess from the strength and
intonation of their voices, I'd say the gist of their conversation
went pretty much as follows.

And is this true? Have you been having an affair with this man? So what if I have? I don't suppose it means anything to you. You slut.

Don't you call me that, I'm not a slut.

So what are you then if you're not a slut?

I'm your wife. Not that you'd know anything about that as you've not taken the slightest bit of notice of me since we arrived.

I haven't?

At this point I detected an inflection in Kurt's voice which told me that Anna might be starting to turn things around.

No, you haven't. You've been too busy carousing with the old man with the beard in there (she pointed toward the bedroom where Don lay sleeping) *to see beyond the end of your nose. This man* (now she was pointing at me) *has at least had the decency to pay me some kind of attention.*

Kurt turned to look at me and for the first time since we'd met, he was forced to acknowledge my presence.

I'm sorry to say that the only response I could muster was what must have looked like a moronic grin. Meanwhile, beneath the table, my hand gripped into a fist as I prepared for the inevitable show of violence.

"You find this amusing?" Kurt asked, changing into English.

"Not in the least," I said. "In fact I think it's rather sad when a man can't take proper care of his wife and has to rely on someone else to do it for him – especially when she's as attractive as yours."

It wasn't my specific intention to rub salt into Kurt's already gaping wound – or to insult his manhood – but my words stung him into a predictable response. "Perhaps we should go outside where I will teach you the lesson you deserve."

The clichéd nature of his challenge made me want to laugh. "And perhaps not," I said. "Oh, I'd love to take you on, believe me." My weeks of body-building exercise had induced a feeling of confidence I could trust and I fancied my chances against his unrelenting diet of cigarettes and schnapps. "But I have no intention of exchanging blows with you over the possession of this woman. She's yours and you're welcome to her. In fact, I can't think of two people more ideally suited. Besides which, you couldn't punch a hole in a wet paper bag. And if there're any lessons to be learnt, I think I've taught you yours already."

In general, bullies despise weakness and I'm convinced it was my show of strength that caused Kurt to back off. He turned his attention to Anna instead and they resumed their foreign conversation.

You will come with me. We will go somewhere private where we can discuss this.

Willingly. But first you must let go of my arm as you're hurting me.

Kurt had grasped hold of her elbow and was squeezing her skin in the pincer of thumb and forefinger as she tried to wriggle free.

Yes, but not half as much as I will hurt you if you don't come with me now.

He bundled her round the end of the table, scraping one of the chairs across the floor. I might have wanted rid of her but I wasn't prepared to see Anna become the target of Kurt's anger – she might be culpable but physical punishment was more than she deserved.

"Not while I'm around," I said, quietly standing up. "You can save that sort of thing for another time. If you want to have a pop at me, that's fine, but let's leave the women out of it."

Thus encouraged, Anna roughly shook Kurt off and began making her way toward the door. She stopped in front of me, and in a move I can only imagine was designed for Kurt's personal benefit, she deliberately spat on my shirt. I responded with the same moronic smile I'd given Kurt. If that was the price I had to pay…

Then they were both in the hallway and the front door closed behind them.

Katerina came through from the kitchen. She carried a tray which supported a pot of yoghurt, an array of fruit and four bowls. She immediately noticed that some of her guests had vanished and set it down on the table.

"So, what's been going on here?" she asked in all innocence.

"Kurt and Anna have taken a time-out."

"Whatever for?"

I gave her a brief resume of the story to date, being careful to leave out the more contentious parts. She still looked utterly dismayed.

"That was a terrible thing to do, Alan. Was it really necessary?"

"Yes," I said. "In my book it was. I may even have done Anna a favour."

"How so? I can't see it."

"Well, they've gone off to the guesthouse to resolve their domestic differences. My guess is they'll either make up or break up. One way or the other, they need to sort it out."

Katerina unfastened the tapes on her apron and began pulling the halter over her head. "I'm going over there…"

I put a gentle restraining hand on her arm and guided her down onto a chair. "I'd let them get on with it if I were you."

"But we can't just—"

"Oh yes we can – and in fact I think we should. And anyway, if I know anything at all about Anna, it'll be make up, trust me. She won't want to risk losing another man, that's for sure." It was this irresistible piece of logic that made the tension flow out of Katerina's body. She'd known Anna for longer than I had and could surely see the sense in it.

"You may be right…"

"You can bet on it," I said. "You'll see. Now…" I took two of the bowls from the tray and set them down in front of us. "Tell me what's for pudding."

I wasn't to see either Kurt or Anna again for the rest of that evening. Wherever they'd taken themselves off to for their private tête-à-tête (I'd assumed it was the guesthouse) they'd clearly decided to stay put. The longer their absence, the better, I thought. My surprise intervention had lit a touchpaper beneath their relationship and there was the potential for a massive explosion. As time went by, chances were that the fuse would peter out. Perhaps it was better that way.

Katerina and I kept ourselves at a safe and respectful distance. After our fruit and yoghurt, I helped her clear up in the kitchen, quietly washing plates while we waited for the bang. But none came, and we eventually retired to the lounge where we resorted to reading our books.

I was well into the third of the Sven Wonderström murder-mystery series and really enjoying it. The action was set in a theatre and on the night of the dress rehearsal, the curtain had gone up to reveal a body lying on the stage. No great surprise, you might think, as the play was a murder-mystery itself – except that the murder wasn't supposed to take place until the end of Act Two and the body was actually a dead one.

But, as we well know, 'the show must go on', and lo and behold, our daring detective, Sven Wonderström, is drafted in to help. Alongside his many other accomplishments it seems he's also a gifted actor, and he steps up to take on the part of the deceased. And just as I'd correctly forecast the outcome of the football saga (3-1 down at half-time in the final match of the season, Sven scores a second-half hat-trick, simultaneously winning his team the league and nailing the villains) I could guess what would happen at the theatre. In front of a packed audience, the on-stage denouement would turn into a real one with Sven dramatically unmasking the perpetrator, while the gun waved around to great effect in the final scene would be loaded with live ammunition instead of the customary blanks. Predictable, but hugely entertaining.

I may not have seen our guests again that evening, but I was certainly to hear them. Two hours of reading and I was just about ready for bed – I'd been up half the night, remember, and it was beginning to catch up with me. Katerina had already taken her leave. Don had been stirring and she'd marked her place and gone to him and hadn't returned. I waited for a few minutes, but when she failed to reappear I decided to follow in her footsteps. Turning out the light in the lounge, I headed for the spare room.

But first I thought to take a turn outside and get a breath of fresh air. Other than my trip to the headland in the morning and my illicit visit to the guesthouse that afternoon, I'd spent the rest of the day indoors. And ever since coming to Sweden, I'd grown used to life outdoors and I felt the call of the country.

I wandered into the yard, hoping to find Max, but he was nowhere to be seen. The time was not yet ten o'clock; it was still quite light although dusk was beginning to settle. Set against the twilight, a dull glow shone out from behind the blinds in the guesthouse. Had the bedside lamp been left on? I wondered. I stopped walking so my feet were silent on the gravel.

I half expected to hear the sounds of an ongoing argument and voices raised in anger, but I was wrong. Anna's moan was audible even from twenty yards away. I'd heard it before in the boathouse. Then, it had worried me in case we should be discovered. But it hadn't concerned Anna, and it didn't concern her now as she was intent on pleasing her husband – and to judge by the tone of his response, she was succeeding. The thought of such conjugal bliss gave rise to an expression of my own and I let out a long and hearty laugh.

What she'd said to him beforehand must have been devilishly enticing. I could read her like a book, and just as I'd come to foresee Sven Wonderström's every move, so I could anticipate hers. *How I've missed you, Kurt. You've no idea what I've been through without you.* Cunning little bitch! How perilously close had I come to being ensnared?

There'd been no love in our union. I hoped that there'd be some in theirs, but somehow I doubted it – we were all too damaged to love. What they *did* have though, was desire, and that was better than nothing. Now he'd been rudely awakened, Kurt would want to assert himself while Anna was content to be possessed – if she could not at all be loved, then at least she could be wanted.

As for me, I thought myself well out of it. Each in their separate ways, they thoroughly deserved one another. I did not want to stand in their path – my true needs had long since lain elsewhere. I yawned, fiddled with the key in my pocket, turned back toward the house and let them get on with it in peace.

Seven

I've probably told you all there is to know about my sleeping habits – how I used to drop off as soon as my head touched the pillow, how I'd sleep like a log and the trouble Susan would have in waking me, and how I'd be bright-eyed and bushy-tailed first thing in the morning, ready to go to work. I famously slept through an earthquake once (you can look it up if you like, 5.2 on the Richter scale). Susan told me afterwards that she'd felt the tremor and had got up and gone out into the street where the neighbours had all gathered to talk about it. When she came back to bed I was still fast asleep and knew nothing about it until I watched it on the news the following day. That's how narcoleptic I can get.

Things have changed, of course, since Susan died and I don't feel as secure without her. I don't always go off straight away either for thinking about her, and then there's those weird and recurrent dreams that make my rest more fitful. On top of that there's the age thing of course, and having to get up at least once in the night, but I suppose that was always going to happen. Although when it does I can usually go straight back to sleep.

And so, that night, when I found myself wide awake and needing to visit the loo, I thought nothing of it and it never occurred to me that I might have been disturbed for a purpose. I hadn't a clue as to the time (it was pitch black in the spare room, remember) and I'd no desire to turn on the light and look for my watch. And even if there *had* been a noise, then I certainly wasn't aware of it. Chances are, I wouldn't have heard it anyway since Don had returned to his snoring.

To visit the bathroom indoors risked waking him, and rather than do that I resigned myself to trekking across the yard and using the outhouse privy. I'd done it often enough when I was formally resident in the guesthouse. I borrowed a coat from the hallway and as the mules weren't up to taking on the gravel, I pulled on a pair of trainers.

There was at least daylight outside. The season had moved on but the nights were still short, although the idea of any midnight sun had long since faded. My best guess told me it was between 4 and 5 a.m. – I'd still been up at this hour the day before, so I'd had practice at gauging the time. The sun had yet to rise above the trees to the east, but there was enough of it to make the bellies of the clouds turn pink. To the west, a blanket of gunmetal grey signalled a change in the weather.

The light was still on in the guesthouse. Surely they couldn't still be at it? Well, bully for them if they were, I thought. Could that have been the noise that I'd heard? Probably not, as the voices were now more subdued and engaged in the course of normal conversation. I suppressed my desire to laugh again. Not having spoken for weeks, they clearly had much to catch up on.

I unlatched the privy and set about making myself comfortable. With a bit of luck I could look forward to a couple more hours of sleep.

I'd just about finished when a door opened somewhere behind me. I hurriedly zipped up and turned to peer through one of the gaps in the woodwork.

Kurt emerged from the guesthouse, fully dressed and trailing a suitcase behind him. Framed by the doorway, a dull yellow glow illuminated the entrance to their room. Somewhere within, a figure passed in front of the light and cast a long shadow out onto the narrow porch. Then the light went out and Anna followed in his footsteps, trailing a suitcase of her own. She stopped to pull the door to behind her.

Short of actually carrying their cases, they could not avoid scrunching the gravel as they traversed the yard and headed for their car. I inwardly begged them to be quiet, although my greatest fear was that they would suddenly decide they needed the loo before they left and would find me hidden in the closet like some bumbling amateurish spy. I dropped the latch hoping that it could not now be opened from outside and resumed my clandestine surveillance.

I was in luck – they had no such intentions and were focused on getting away. Kurt raised the door to the back of the estate and hurriedly loaded the cases while Anna was sent in front to open the gate. Thankfully, the car started both reliably and gently (well done Volvo!) and eased forward with a low-pitched rumble. Then I heard the gate click shut behind them; Anna scrambled into the passenger seat and pulled the door to and the car moved off into the forest. They were gone.

I breathed a sigh of relief and opened the toilet door.

I didn't feel like going back to bed – leastways, not in the spare room. Unless I was dog-tired, the Black Hole had never been very welcoming, and besides, other accommodation had recently become available. So whether it was that and my desire to immediately regain possession, or whether it was purely out of curiosity, I turned to the right instead of the left and walked across to the guesthouse.

Anna had left a key, but I didn't need to use it as the door hadn't been locked. I turned the bedside light back on and took a look around.

The place was much as it had been when I'd moved out, i.e. clean and neat and tidy. The floor had been cleared of its debris, as had the chest of drawers, and the covers on the bed had been pulled up and the pillows neatly arranged. *A woman's hand,* I thought. It was actually a chalet-maid's dream with not a trace of its former occupants, except perhaps a vague hint of the scent I'd found there before and the lingering presence of Anna. Maybe it would be the same in the boathouse…

I sat down on the edge of the bed and ran my hand across the top of the chest of drawers. No dust; no chance of it given what had been piled onto that narrow space. All I'd ever kept there was a watch and a wallet.

High above, the blind which had continually troubled me had

been left pulled down to cover the ceiling window. Later, when the sun was fully up I would want its brightness to flood into the room, but for the moment I was happy enough in the half-light.

I suddenly felt sleepy, my shoulders slumped as the tension went out of me and so I swung my legs up onto the covers and set my head down on a pillow. I didn't even bother to reach over and turn out the light.

I must have slept for at least two hours, maybe three, who knows – time didn't seem to matter anymore. I woke refreshed and unsurprised at where I was; the sun had risen above the level of the trees and so I guessed it must have gone seven. I turned out the bedside lamp and went outside.

Max was waiting on the patch of grass next to the gravel. His scarred and ancient tennis ball lay between his paws and he was playing at seated lion. His head remained cocked to one side although today he was asking a different question, not *What are you up to?* but rather *Will you come and play?*

"Come on then," I said, and I picked up the ball and we walked toward the house together.

I was in the mood for fresh air and exercise and I thought we'd take a stroll along the beach, but first I needed to change my clothing. The trainers I had on were fine but the coat concealed nothing but a T-shirt and my own set of underwear, and Lord knows, we'd seen enough of that sort of thing to last us a lifetime. I left Max outside while I went back to the Black Hole and retrieved a pair of shorts.

My mobile phone was nestled in one of the pockets. It must have been there for days and I'd not given it a thought. Max was at my heels and as he and I walked down the hill, I turned it on. A stream of messages came flooding through from Philippa. I could imagine what she'd been saying and somehow I knew I was in trouble. I clicked on the latest and opened it up.

Worried about you now. Why don't you answer? Phil x

I lobbed the tennis ball far into the bushes. Max ambled off and while he was away, I composed a quick reply.

Sorry. Haven't been well. Ok now. Lul Dadx.

Yes, I know, it was a lie, but it was a white lie and there were times we needed those – she was far too young to know the truth.

We reached the bottom of the hill, I looked up and saw that the boathouse doors were open. Don was standing outside, a pencil pushed up the side of his baseball cap and fondling a piece of wood. Beyond the headland, out toward the lake, the breeze had got up and I could hear the reeds were rustling. Then he began to whistle a ragged version of "Two Men Went to Mow" and I knew it was going to be alright again.

Biography

N.E. David is the pen name of York author Nick David. Nick began writing at the age of 21 but like so many things in life, it did not work out first time round. After a rewarding career in industry and then personal finance, he took it up again and had initial success with a series of short novellas. His debut novel, *Birds of the Nile*, was published by Roundfire in 2013 and quickly became their top-selling title in adult fiction. His second novel, *The Burden*, soon followed.

Nick writes character-based contemporary fiction where he focuses on stories of human interest and drama. He maintains he has no personal or political message to convey but his initial objective is to entertain the reader and he hopes this is reflected in his writing.

Besides being a regular contributor to literary events in the North East Region, Nick is a founder member of York Authors and formerly co-presented "Book Talk" on BBC Radio York. He has recently been appointed to the committee of York Literature Festival and is enjoying contributing to the literary life of the city.

Other Works

Carol's Christmas
Feria
A Day at the Races
Birds of the Nile
The Burden

For more information visit the author's website at
www.nedavid.com.
You can also follow N.E.David on Twitter @NEDavidAuthor.

Roundfire

FICTION

Put simply, we publish great stories. Whether it's literary or popular, a gentle tale or a pulsating thriller, the connecting theme in all Roundfire fiction titles is that once you pick them up you won't want to put them down.
If you have enjoyed this book, why not tell other readers by posting a review on your preferred book site. Recent bestsellers from Roundfire are:

The Bookseller's Sonnets
Andi Rosenthal
The Bookseller's Sonnets intertwines three love stories with a tale of religious identity and mystery spanning five hundred years and three countries.
Paperback: 978-1-84694-342-3 ebook: 978-184694-626-4

Birds of the Nile
An Egyptian Adventure
N.E. David
Ex-diplomat Michael Blake wanted a quiet birding trip up the Nile – he wasn't expecting a revolution.
Paperback: 978-1-78279-158-4 ebook: 978-1-78279-157-7

Blood Profit$
The Lithium Conspiracy
J. Victor Tomaszek, James N. Patrick, Sr
The blood of the many for the profits of the few... Blood Profit$
will take you into the cigar-smoke-filled room where American
policy and laws are really made.
Paperback: 978-1-78279-483-7 ebook: 978-1-78279-277-2

The Burden
A Family Saga
N.E. David
Frank will do anything to keep his mother and father apart. But
he's carrying baggage - and it might just weigh him down...
Paperback: 978-1-78279-936-8 ebook: 978-1-78279-937-5

The Cause
Roderick Vincent
The second American Revolution will be a fire lit from an
internal spark.
Paperback: 978-1-78279-763-0 ebook: 978-1-78279-762-3

Readers of ebooks can buy or view any of these bestsellers by
clicking on the live link in the title. Most titles are published
in paperback and as an ebook. Paperbacks are available in
traditional bookshops. Both print and ebook formats are
available online.

Find more titles and sign up to our readers' newsletter at
http://www.johnhuntpublishing.com/fiction.
Follow us on Facebook at https://www.facebook.com/JHPfiction
and Twitter at https://twitter.com/JHPFiction.